CHEKHOV
The Early Stories
1883–88

Chosen and translated by
Patrick Miles and Harvey Pitcher

First published in Great Britain by
John Murray (Publishers) Ltd 1982
Published in Abacus by
Sphere Books Ltd 1984
30–32 Gray's Inn Road, London WC1X 8JL

Reproduced, printed and bound in Great Britain by
Hazell Watson & Viney Limited,
Member of the BPCC Group,
Aylesbury, Bucks

Contents

Introduction

I write under the most atrocious conditions. My non-literary work lies before me flaying my conscience unmercifully, the offspring of a visiting kinsman is screaming in the next room, in another room Father is reading aloud *The Sealed Angel* to Mother . . . Someone has just wound up the musical box and it's playing La Belle Hélène . . . I'd like to clear off to the country, but it's already one in the morning. . . Can you conceive of more atrocious surroundings for a literary man? My bed's taken up by the visiting relation, who keeps coming over to me and engaging me in medical conversation. 'My daughter must have colic, that's why she's screaming . . .' I have the great misfortune to be a medic, so every man-jack feels duty bound to 'talk medicine' with me. And when they've had enough of talking medicine, they start on literature . . .

Letter from Chekhov to Leykin, August 1883

By contrast, *The Huntsman* (1885) was written in the peace of the countryside . . . scribbled out by its author as he lay on the floor of a bathing-house, and posted off to the editor just as it was.

Yet it was in those hectic early years, when literature was still competing with medicine, that Chekhov the writer was at his most prolific – with so many members of the family to support financially, he had to be. Of all his published fiction, 528 items were written between 1880 and March 1888, and only 60 in the period 1888–1904. This is a striking imbalance, even given that many of the earlier works are short ephemera. And these 528 items do not include his weekly column of Moscow gossip, his reporting, theatre notices and other occasional journalism.

He was as versatile as he was productive. He wrote captions to cartoons; literary parodies; comic calendars, diaries, questionnaires, aphorisms and advertisements; innumerable sketches; and even a detective novel. In his endless search for story material, he made use of his own experiences and raided the lives of friends and relatives. He could be frivolous or serious, now topical, now seasonable, hilarious as a parodist, and ingenious with comic twists. Thus *A Dreadful Night* (1884) is probably autobiographical in inspiration, it is seasonable (a Christmas tale published on December 27th), has a twist ending, and must be the send-up to end all send-ups of the traditional Christmas horror story!

The largest single group among Chekhov's early work, though, consists of stories of knockabout romance. Here we meet a small army of foolish young men, silly young girls, matchmakers, mothers, and mothers-in-law. The heroes and heroines of this world are either striving desperately to find a wife or husband, or striving desperately to be unfaithful to one. Such well-worn themes could be relied upon to raise an easy laugh when all other inspiration failed. A brilliant last flowering of the genre was *Notes from the Journal of a Quick-Tempered Man* (1887), with its huge cast of 'variegated young ladies' and Machiavellian mothers, all in hot pursuit of the only two, not very eligible, bachelors in the summer datcha colony. By that time, however, Chekhov had already written the first of his distinctive serious love stories; although non-love story might be a better description of *Verochka* (1887).

Another very large group, particularly prominent in 1883 and 1884, produced several of the best known of Chekhov's earliest works. The gigantic Tsarist bureaucracy had long been a target for satire. Chekhov extracts his own brand of absurdist humour from its rituals and conventions, its red tape, bribery and corruption ('You seem to have left something behind in my hand,' says the official in one sketch to a petitioner when his chief appears at an awkward moment), and the arrogance or servility displayed by people towards those below or above them in the bureaucratic hierarchy. Not that Chekhov is sentimentally disposed towards the servile underdog. Few tears, it seems from his laconic account, need be shed for the hero of *The Death of a Civil Servant* (1883), little sympathy felt for the thin man in *Fat and Thin* (1883). These tales are inspired with a youthful exasperation and disgust at the absence of the most basic notions of self-respect; or, as in the case of the landowner's behaviour in *The Daughter of Albion* (1883), of respect for others.

Chekhov was successful as a young writer-journalist because he catered for the market. His stories appealed to young men of roughly his own age and social status who could easily identify themselves with heroes on the look-out for a good match or forced to lick the boots of their departmental chief. From the cheerfully low-brow Moscow *Alarm Clock* and *The Dragonfly* (which had published his first contribution in March 1880, when he was just twenty), he graduated to the St Petersburg *Splinters*, widely regarded as Russia's leading comic sheet. 'I have always maintained a serious tone even in matters of humour,' wrote its editor, Leykin. Chekhov was introduced to him in October 1882, and it was Leykin who, by imposing strict limits on the length of contributions, taught the prolix young Chekhov a lesson that he never forgot: how to be succinct. Whilst still working for *Splinters*, he also began to write for the respectable *Petersburg Gazette* and in February 1886 made his début in the major newspaper *New Times*. Its editor, Suvorin, had been told about this promising new writer by the veteran author Grigorovich, who himself had first become aware of Chekhov from reading *The Huntsman* in the *Petersburg Gazette* of July 18th, 1885.

In *The Huntsman* several qualities that will mark Chekhov out as a short story writer achieve their first successful artistic expression. A place, an atmosphere, are evoked powerfully, but by the slenderest, poetic means; and this natural setting interacts subtly with the characters themselves. Whilst ostensibly doing no more than describe the meeting and conversation of two people on a hot summer's day (the story was first subtitled 'A Scene'), Chekhov succeeds both in throwing into relief how each sees the world, and in making palpable the whole texture of their lives – past, present, and even future. As a result, the unresolved ending, the unsentimental way in which he shows the impossibility of any rapprochement between them, satisfies by its emotional and psychological authority.

In March 1886 Grigorovich wrote directly to Chekhov. He was generous in praise of his talent, 'which places you far beyond the modern generation of writers', but urged him strongly to respect that talent by writing with more care and at greater leisure. He also suggested he should attempt a major longer work. In his reply, Chekhov sought to excuse himself. No one had ever taken his writing seriously, he wrote, he was immersed in medicine, and he had never spent more than twenty-four hours on a single story. Nevertheless, he adds that while writing stories in this 'mechanical' way he had been very careful not to waste on them 'images and scenes which are precious to me and which for some reason I carefully saved up and put aside'.

Grigorovich's advice was heeded, but did not take effect all at once. Chekhov could still not afford to stop writing to a deadline for several publications simultaneously, he still had comic writing in his blood, and he still had much to contribute to the life of the very short story (reading which, as Chekhov put it, 'feels rather like swallowing a glass of vodka'). In 1887 he wrote almost as prolifically as in 1886.

In fact, some of his best comic stories belong to this period, and even in 1887 he was still writing occasionally for *The Alarm Clock*.

That he had been 'saving up' his best material, however, seems to have been true. From the very start, even in his most prolific and hasty work, Chekhov saw himself as a professional writer. He was constantly experimenting with genres, forms and narrator's masks. On several occasions he tried to persuade Leykin to accept non-humorous work from him for *Splinters*. He read the masters of Russian prose exhaustively and critically. Even in these early years he is known to have kept notebooks in which he collected scraps of living speech and potential literary material. Whenever a previous work of his was to be republished, he laboured meticulously over revising and retouching it to his current standards. Thus when given the opportunity to write longer and more serious stories for Suvorin, he was able to raise the quality of his writing, and widen the range of his themes, apparently without effort.

The quieter psychological note already heard in *The Huntsman* now comes to the fore. People matter more than situations. From the start he had shown a keen eye for the quirkiness of human behaviour, whether its harmless foibles, as in *Rapture* (1883) or *The Complaints Book* (1884), or its more harmful and ominous perversions (*Sergeant Prishibeyev*, 1885); but in such stories behaviour is inevitably seen from the outside only. What the young Chekhov now shows, however, is a marvellous ability to *enter into* the lives of characters, completely to 'inform', as Keats said of the poet, the lives of men, women, children, animals, and even plants and landscapes, and make the reader experience the world from their point of view. Fascinatingly, the eye may still be momentarily that of a humorist, but more and more it is that of an observer in whom imaginative empathy with his subjects is coupled with a strong scientific sense of what is physically and psychologically plausible. In *Oysters* (1884) and *Typhus* (1886) he makes direct use of his medical knowledge to describe abnormal physical states, but these are not mere 'clinical studies': they are transformed by Chekhov's vital, imaginative involvement. With the same blend of imagination and authenticity he enters into the lives of children, whether growing up normally, as in *Kids* and *Grisha* (both 1886), or in the intolerable conditions depicted in *Vanka* (1886) or *Let Me Sleep* (1888). And because he inhabits his characters so fully, moral judgment of them is suspended.

It is in several of the most ambitious stories of 1886 and 1887 that the lyrical qualities of *The Huntsman* are perpetuated. Atmosphere and the spirit of place are evoked particularly hauntingly in *Easter Night* (1886), and in *Verochka*, *The Reed-Pipe* and *The Kiss* (1887). Themes begin to emerge that are personal to Chekhov. There is the concern with unfulfilled lives, as in *The Witch* (1886), with its claustrophobic sense of thwarted emotional and sexual potency. In *Dreams* (1886) there is the pathetic discrepancy between what men dream of and aspire to, and what life allows them to achieve. In *The Reed-Pipe* (1887) a theme is touched on that we recognise later in Dr Astrov's maps in *Uncle Vanya* – the degeneration of the natural environment. Then there is the mysterious way in which life 'feels' so different at different times. Which is the 'truer' experience: the exultation of the believers on Easter Night or the grey dawn that follows, the exultation that Ryabovich feels after he receives the accidental kiss, or the sense of futility so powerfully conveyed in the story's closing passages?

* * *

Chekhov's early stories have long held a secure place in the hearts of Russian readers. His *Motley Tales* of May 1886 ran through fourteen editions in as many years, and today any three-volume Russian selection of his works is bound to devote at least one volume to the pre-1888 period. 'Antosha Chekhonte', the pseudonym by which the young Chekhov has come to be known, is a far more familiar and accessible figure to most Russians than Anton Chekhov the playwright. These well-read and well-loved early works have led an irrepressible life of their own, untouched by the earnest censure of Chekhov's Populist contemporaries, who accused him of wasting his talent and being unprincipled because they could not find an ideological message in his writing; or by the equally earnest praise of more recent critics who have no difficulty at all in seeing him as the scourge of Russia's pre-Revolutionary régime. The Chekhov who wrote *The Complaints Book, Romance for Double-Bass, The Orator* and *Notes from the Journal of a Quick-Tempered Man* remains an 'unprincipled' comic artist; the Chekhov who wrote *Fat and Thin, The Chameleon* and *Sergeant Prishibeyev* is a deeply subversive writer for all seasons and societies.

Translations of Chekhov into English have been numerous but, as

Ronald Hingley points out, 'in general, highly unsystematic and unscholarly'. With the completion in 1980 of the nine-volume *Oxford Chekhov*, Hingley has himself solved the major part of this problem: Vols. 1–3 contain all the drama, and Vols. 4–9 all the fiction from 1888–1904. Among translations of the 528 stories of the earlier period, however, a state of unsystematic and unscholarly chaos still prevails. Chekhov's most prolific translator into English, Constance Garnett, translated 147 of them, and did so, on the whole, very competently, although she was never at ease with dialogue, especially the racier peasant variety. It was she who was largely responsible for introducing Chekhov to English readers, and whose translations were read by, and in some ways influenced, such writers as Arnold Bennett, James Joyce, Katherine Mansfield and Virginia Woolf. Where she performed something of a disservice to Chekhov and his English readership, however, was in failing to present the stories in any kind of chronological order, with the result that no picture could emerge of how Chekhov evolved as a writer, or of the distinctive qualities of his early fiction. In any case, Garnett's thirteen volumes, published between 1916 and 1922, have long been out of print, as are the two-volume *Select Tales* (containing eighteen early stories), last re-issued in 1967 and 1968 respectively.

Thus the basic aim of the present volume is to offer a larger and more representative selection of Chekhov's early stories than has ever been available in English in one volume before. Our selection ends where *The Oxford Chekhov* begins. The last story, *Let Me Sleep*, was written in January 1888 to earn Chekhov some quick cash while he was busy on *The Steppe*, the hundred-page narrative published in March which marked his début in the serious literary periodicals.

Implicit in this aim, though, is a belief in the stories themselves. We hope to persuade the English reader that these works would still be worth reading today even if Chekhov had not gone on to write *A Lady with a Dog* or *Three Sisters*. The young Chekhov, we believe, deserves better than to be represented by one or two items at the start of the Chekhov anthologies: he deserves a volume to himself.

It also seemed important to enable the English reader to see Chekhov's early work in the process of developing. The stories are therefore grouped by year, but have been slightly rearranged within each year to achieve a better balance.

Finally, we wanted to give due prominence to the purely comic side of Chekhov's early writing. This passed most of his first English admirers by completely and has been little better appreciated since; regrettably, for that sense of fun and sublime ridiculousness was something that Chekhov never lost. Whether one regards *The Cherry Orchard*, for instance, as tragedy, comedy, history or pastoral, no critic should attempt to comment on that play who is not thoroughly steeped in the comic writing of Antosha Chekhonte.

The thirty-five stories included here still represent only a fraction of the total output. How were they chosen?

Chekhov himself passed judgment on his early writing when he selected the stories for his *Collected Works* in 1899. Of the 528 items, he included 186. All fifty or so stories published between 1880 and 1882 were excluded, and all but twenty of the hundred-odd stories of 1883. These proportions are steadily reversed until fifty of the sixty-four stories of 1887 are included.

We have respected Chekhov's exclusions, with one exception: *An Incident at Law* (1883) has been resurrected. Our distribution of stories over different years is also roughly commensurate with his. If we include relatively few stories from 1887, this is because the average length of Chekhov's stories has increased considerably by then. It would have been impossible, for example, to exclude *The Kiss*, widely regarded as Chekhov's finest work before *The Steppe*, even though it consumes the space of about four earlier items. In general our policy was to look for what seemed best in a particular vein, thereby avoiding duplication. *The Huntsman*, for example, was chosen in preference to the almost equally powerful, but rather similar, *Agafya*. Some hard decisions had to be taken in the choice of longer stories, but it seemed to us far more important not to sacrifice the shorter stories of 1883–1885 than to find room for one more long story from 1886 or 1887 – even though, as we learned from bitter experience, the shorter the story the more difficult to translate!

It would be inappropriate to dwell too long on the problems of translation. Certain aspects of the young Chekhov's style, however, do deserve mention here. One of his subtlest methods of taking the reader into a character is to blend fragments of that character's indirect speech – from whole sentences to the merest inflexions of voice – freely into his own narration (particularly clear examples occur in *Kids* and *Let Me Sleep*). This may give rise to repetitions, which we have been careful to respect. Then there is the way a narrative may modulate through a range of tenses that would be unusual in English fiction, as in *The Little Joke* and *Vanka*. Here, too, we have tended to follow Chekhov, even at the risk of sounding strange, since we regard the young Chekhov as nothing if not an innovator in style and technique. Finally, there is his use of three dots. Sometimes this is very personal: the dots are carefully deployed by Chekhov as *points de suspension*. Often, however, as with his use of exclamation marks, the three dots are simply dictated by the conventions of Russian punctuation. We have considered each instance on its merits, and occasionally this has led to our cutting these forms in translation completely, or replacing them with others.

The collaboration of the translators has been very much more than a simple division of labour. After one of the translators had produced a first draft, this was sent off to Cambridge or Cromer and subjected to unsparing criticism by the other, who returned it disfigured by amendments and suggestions for improvement. These were incorporated or rejected by the original translator. The translators then met, and the revised draft was subjected to the further test of being read aloud, revealing new defects, especially in the rendering of dialogue. In many cases discussion rumbled on for weeks and months after that.

To translate Chekhov sometimes requires familiarity with highly specialised areas of knowledge. We express heartfelt thanks to all those friends, relations and experts who advised us in these areas, and especially to Nikolay and Gill Andreyev (Cambridge), Nikolay Bokov (Paris), and M.P. Gromov and L.D. Opulskaya (Moscow) for their authoritative assistance with numerous points of Russian language and manners. Our gratitude to Richard Davies (Leeds), and everyone else who so patiently listened to, read, and re-read our drafts, cannot be overstated. Needless to say, the responsibility for the text and any errors it may contain remains our own, and we shall welcome correspondence concerning both.

Patrick Miles

July 1981 *Harvey Pitcher*

Rapture 1883

Midnight.

Wild-eyed and dishevelled, Mitya Kuldarov burst into his parents' flat and dashed into every room. His parents were about to go to bed. His sister was in bed already and had just got on to the last page of her novel. His schoolboy brothers were asleep.

'Where've you come from?' his parents exclaimed in astonishment. 'Is something wrong?'

'Oh, I don't know how to tell you! I'm staggered, absolutely staggered! It's . . . it's quite incredible!'

Mitya burst out laughing and collapsed into an armchair, overcome with happiness.

'It's incredible! You'll never believe it! Take a look at this!'

His sister jumped out of bed and came over to him, wrapping a blanket round her. The schoolboys woke up.

'Is something wrong? You look awful!'

'I'm so happy, Mum, that's why! Now everyone in Russia knows about me! Everyone! Till now only you knew of the existence of clerical officer of the fourteenth grade, Dmitry Kuldarov, but now everyone in Russia knows! O Lord, Mum!'

Mitya jumped up, ran round every room and sat down again.

'But tell us what's happened, for goodness' sake!'

'Oh, you live here like savages, you don't read the papers, you've no idea what's going on, and the papers are full of such remarkable things! As soon as anything happens, they make it all public, it's down there in black and white! O Lord, I'm so happy! Only famous people get their names in the paper, then all of a sudden – they go and print a story about me!'

'What?! Where?'

Dad turned pale. Mum looked up at the icon and crossed herself. The schoolboys jumped out of bed and ran over to their elder brother, wearing nothing but their short little nightshirts.

'They have! About *me*! Now I'm known all over Russia! You'd better keep this copy, Mum, and we can take it out now and then and read it. Look!'

Mitya pulled the newspaper out of his pocket and handed it to his father, jabbing his finger at a passage ringed with blue pencil.

'Read it out!'

Father put on his glasses.

'Go on, read it!'

Mum looked up at the icon and crossed herself. Dad cleared his throat and began:

'On December 29th at 11 p.m. clerical officer of the fourteenth grade, Dmitry Kuldarov –'

'See? See? Go on, Dad!'

' . . . clerical officer of the fourteenth grade, Dmitry Kuldarov, emerging from the public ale-house situated on the ground floor of Kozikhin's Buildings in Little Bronnaya Street and being in a state of intoxication –'

'It was me and Semyon Petrovich . . . They've got all the details! Go on! Now listen, listen to this bit!'

'. . . and being in a state of intoxication, slipped and fell in front of a cab-horse belonging to Ivan Knoutoff, peasant, from the village of Bumpkino in Pnoff district, which was standing at that spot. The frightened horse, stepping across Kuldarov, dragged over him the sledge in which was seated Ivan Lukov, merchant of the Second Guild in Moscow, bolted down the street and was arrested in its flight by some yard-porters. Kuldarov, being at first in a state of unconsciousness, was taken to the police-station and examined by a doctor. The blow which he had received on the back of the head –'

'I did it on the shaft, Dad. Go on, read the rest!'

'. . . which he had received on the back of the head, was classified as superficial. A police report was drawn up concerning the incident. Medical assistance was rendered to the victim –'

'They dabbed the back of my head with cold water. Finished? So what do you say to that, eh?! It'll be all over Russia by now! Give it here!'

Mitya grabbed the newspaper, folded it and stuffed it into his pocket.

'Must run and show the Makarovs . . . Then on to the Ivanitskys, Nataliya Ivanovna and Anisim Vasilich . . . Can't stop! 'Bye!'

Mitya put on his official cap with the cockade and radiant, triumphant, ran out into the street.

The Death of a Civil Servant

One fine evening, a no less fine office factotum, Ivan Dmitrich Kreepikov, was sitting in the second row of the stalls and watching *The Chimes of Normandy* through opera glasses. He watched, and felt on top of the world. But suddenly . . . You often come across this 'But suddenly . . .' in short stories. And authors are right: life is so full of surprises! But suddenly, then, his face puckered, his eyes rolled upwards, his breathing ceased – he lowered his opera glasses, bent forward, and . . . atchoo!!! Sneezed, in other words. Now sneezing isn't prohibited to any one or in any place. Peasants sneeze, chiefs of police sneeze, and sometimes even Number 3's in the Civil Service. Everyone sneezes. Kreepikov did not feel embarrassed at all, he simply wiped his nose with his handkerchief and, being a polite kind of person, looked about him to see if he had disturbed anyone by sneezing. But then he did have cause for embarrassment. He saw that the little old gentleman sitting in front of him, in the first row, was carefully wiping his pate and the back of his neck with his glove, and muttering something. And in the elderly gentleman Kreepikov recognised General Shpritsalov, a Number 2 in the Ministry of Communications.

'I spattered him!' thought Kreepikov. 'He's not my chief, it's true, but even so, it's awkward. I'll have to apologise.'

So he gave a cough, bent respectfully forward, and whispered in the General's ear:

'Please excuse me, Your Excellency, for spattering you . . . it was quite unintentional . . .'

'That's all right, that's all right . . .'

'Please, please forgive me. I–I didn't mean to!'

'Oh do sit down, please, I can't hear the opera!'

Disconcerted by this, Kreepikov gave a stupid grin, sat down, and began to watch the stage again. He watched, but no longer did he feel on top of the world. He began to feel pangs of worry. In the interval he went over to Shpritsalov, sidled along with him, and, conquering his timidity, stammered:

'I spattered you, Your Excellency . . . Please forgive me . . . I – it wasn't that –'

'Oh for goodness' sake . . . I'd already forgotten, so why keep on about it!' said the General, and twitched his lower lip impatiently.

'Hm, he says he's forgotten,' thought Kreepikov, eyeing the General mistrustfully, 'but looks as nasty as you make 'em. He won't even talk about it. I'll have to explain that I didn't want – that sneezing's a law of nature . . . Otherwise he may think I meant to *spit* at him. And if he doesn't now, he may later! . . .'

When he got home, Kreepikov told his wife about his breach of good manners. His wife, he felt, treated the incident much too lightly: at first she had quite a fright, but as soon as she learned that Shpritsalov was 'someone else's' chief, she calmed down again.

'Even so, you go along and apologise,' she said. 'Otherwise he'll think you don't know how to behave in public!'

'That's right! I did apologise to him, but he acted sort of strangely . . . I couldn't get a word of sense out of him. There wasn't time to discuss it, either.'

Next day, Kreepikov put on his new uniform, had his hair trimmed, and went to Shpritsalov to explain . . . As he entered the General's audience-room, he saw a throng of people there, and in their midst the General himself, who had just begun hearing petitions. After dealing with several petitioners, the General looked up in Kreepikov's direction.

'Yesterday at the Arcadia Theatre, Your Excellency, if you recall,' the little clerk began his speech, 'I sneezed, sir, and – inadvertently spattered . . . Forg–'

'Drivel, sir! . . . You're wasting my time. Next!' said the General, turning to another petitioner.

'He won't even talk about it!' thought Kreepikov, going pale. 'He must be angry, then . . . No, I can't leave it at that . . . I must explain to him . . .'

When the General had finished interviewing the last petitioner and was on his way back to the inner recesses of the department, Kreepikov strode after him and mumbled:

'Your Excellency! If I make so bold as to bother Your Excellency, it is only from a sense of – of deep repentance, so to speak! . . . I'm not doing it on purpose, sir, you must believe me!'

The General pulled an agonised face and brushed him aside.

'Are you trying to be funny, sir?' he said, and vanished behind a door.

'Funny?' thought Kreepikov. 'Of course I'm not trying to be

funny! Calls himself a general and can't understand! Well, if he's going to be so snooty about it, I'm not going to apologise any more! To hell with him! I don't mind writing him a letter, but I'm not coming all the way over here again. Oh no!'

Such were Kreepikov's thoughts as he made his way home. He did not write to the General, though. He thought and thought, but just could not think what to say. So next morning he had to go to explain in person.

'Yesterday I came and disturbed Your Excellency,' he started stammering, when the General raised his eyes questioningly at him, 'not to try and be funny, as you so kindly put it. I came to apologise for sneezing and spattering you, sir – it never occurred to me to try and be funny. How could I dare to laugh?! If we all went about laughing at people, there'd be no respect for persons, er, left in the world –'

'Clear out!!' bellowed the General suddenly, turning purple and trembling with rage.

'Wha-what?' Kreepikov asked in a whisper, swooning with terror.

'Clear out!!' the General repeated, stamping his feet.

Something snapped in Kreepikov's stomach. Without seeing anything, without hearing anything, he staggered backwards to the door, reached the street, and wandered off . . . He entered his home mechanically, without taking off his uniform lay down on the sofa, and . . . died.

An Incident at Law

The case occurred at a recent session of the N. district court.

In the dock was Sidor Felonovsky, resident of N., a fellow of about thirty, with restless gipsy features and shifty little eyes. He was accused of burglary, fraud and obtaining a false passport, and coupled with the latter was a further charge of impersonation. The case was being brought by the deputy prosecutor. The name of his tribe is Legion. He's totally devoid of any special features or qualities that might make him popular or bring him huge fees: he's just average. He has a nasal voice, doesn't sound his k's properly, and is forever blowing his nose.

Whereas defending was a fantastically celebrated and popular advocate, known throughout the land, whose wonderful speeches are always being quoted, whose name is uttered in tones of awe . . .

The role that he plays at the end of cheap novels, where the hero is completely vindicated and the public bursts into applause, is not inconsiderable. In such novels he is given a surname derived from thunder, lightning and other equally awe-inspiring forces of nature.

When the deputy prosecutor had succeeded in proving that Felonovsky was guilty and deserved no mercy, when he had finished defining and persuading and said: 'The case for the prosecution rests' – then defence counsel rose to his feet. Everyone pricked up their ears. Dead silence reigned. Counsel began his speech . . . and in the public gallery their nerves ran riot! Sticking out his swarthy neck and cocking his head to one side, with eyes a-flashing and hand upraised, he poured his mellifluous magic into their expectant ears. His words plucked at their nerves as though he were playing the balalaika . . . Scarcely had he uttered a couple of sentences than there was a loud sigh and a woman had to be carried out ashen-faced. Only three minutes elapsed before the judge was obliged to reach over for his bell and ring three times for order. The red-nosed clerk of the court swivelled round on his chair and began to glare menacingly at the animated faces of the public. Eyes dilated, cheeks drained of colour, everyone craned forward in an agony of suspense to hear what he would say next . . . And need I describe what was happening to the ladies' hearts?!

'Gentlemen of the jury, you and I are human beings! Let us therefore judge as human beings!' said defence counsel *inter alia*. 'Before appearing in front of you today, this human being had to endure the agony of six months on remand. For six months his wife has been deprived of the husband she cherishes so fondly, for six months his children's eyes have been wet with tears at the thought that their dear father was no longer beside them. Oh, if only you could see those children! They are starving because there is no one to feed them. They are crying because they are so deeply unhappy . . . Yes, look at them, look at them! See how they stretch their tiny arms towards you, imploring you to give them back their father! They are not here in person, but can you not picture them? (*Pause*.) Six months on remand . . . Six . . . They put him in with thieves and murderers . . . a man like this! (*Pause*.) One need only imagine the moral torment of that imprisonment, far from his wife and children, to . . . But need I say more?!'

Sobs were heard in the gallery . . . A girl with a large brooch on her bosom had burst into tears. Then the little old lady next to her began snivelling.

Defence counsel went on and on . . . He tended to ignore the facts, concentrating more on the psychological aspect.

'Shall I tell you what it means to know this man's soul? It means knowing a unique and individual world, a world full of varied impulses. I have made a study of that world, and I tell you frankly that as I did so, I felt I was studying Man for the first time . . . I understood what Man is . . . And every impulse of my client's soul convinces me that in him I have the honour of observing a perfect human being . . .'

The clerk of the court stopped staring so menacingly and fished around in his pocket for a handkerchief. Two more women were carried out. The judge forgot all about the bell and put on his glasses, so that no one would notice the large tear welling up in his right eye. Handkerchiefs appeared on every side. The deputy prosecutor, that rock, that iceberg, that most insensitive of organisms, shifted about in his chair, turned red, and started gazing at the floor . . . Tears were glistening behind his glasses.

'Why on earth did I go ahead with the case?' he thought to himself. 'How am I ever going to live down a fiasco like this!'

'Just look at his eyes!' defence counsel continued (his chin was trembling, his voice was trembling, and his eyes showed how much his soul was suffering). 'Can those meek, tender eyes look upon a crime without flinching? No, I tell you, those are the eyes of a man who weeps! There are sensitive nerves concealed behind those Asiatic cheekbones! And the heart that beats within that coarse, misshapen breast – that heart is as honest as the day is long! Members of the jury, can you dare as human beings to say that this man is guilty?'

At this point the accused himself could bear it no longer. Now it was his turn to start crying. He blinked, burst into tears and began fidgeting restlessly . . .

'All right!' he blurted out, interrupting defence counsel. 'All right! I *am* guilty! It was me done the burglary and the fraud. Miserable wretch that I am! I took the money from the trunk and got my sister-in-law to hide the fur coat. I confess! Guilty on all counts!'

Accused then made a detailed confession and was convicted.

Fat and Thin

Two friends bumped into each other at the Nikolayevsky railway station: one was fat, the other thin. The fat man had just dined in the station restaurant and his lips were still coated with grease and gleamed like ripe cherries. He smelt of sherry and *fleurs d'oranger*. The thin man had just got out of a carriage and was loaded down with suitcases, bundles and band-boxes. He smelt of boiled ham and coffee-grounds. Peeping out from behind his back was a lean woman with a long chin – his wife, and a lanky schoolboy with a drooping eyelid – his son.

'Porfiry!' exclaimed the fat man, on seeing the thin. 'Is it you? My dear chap! I haven't seen you for ages!'

'Good Lord!' cried the thin in astonishment. 'It's Misha! My old schoolmate! Fancy meeting you here!'

The two friends kissed and hugged three times and stood gazing at each other with tears in their eyes. It was a pleasant shock for both of them.

'My dear old chap!' began Thin after they had finished kissing. 'Who would have guessed! Well what a surprise! Let's have a good look at you! Yes, as smart and handsome as ever! You always were a bit of a dandy, a bit of a lad, eh? Well I never! And how are you? Rich? Married? I'm married, as you see . . . This is my wife Luise, née Wanzenbach . . . er, of the Lutheran persuasion . . . And this is my son Nathaniel – he's in the third form. Misha was my childhood companion, Nat! We were at grammar-school together!'

Nathaniel thought for a moment, then removed his cap.

'Yes, we were at grammar-school together!' Thin continued. 'Remember how we used to tease you and call you "Herostratos", because you once burned a hole in your school text-book with a cigarette? And they called me "Ephialtes", because I was always sneaking on people. Ho-ho . . . What lads we were! Don't be shy, Nat! Come a bit closer . . . And this is my wife, née Wanzenbach . . . er, Lutheran.'

Nathaniel thought for a moment, then took refuge behind his father's back.

'Well, how are you doing, old chap?' asked Fat, looking at his friend quite enraptured. 'In the Service, are you? On your way up?'

'Yes, old boy, I've had my Grade 8 two years now – and I've got my St Stanislas. The pay's bad, but, well, so what! The wife gives music lessons and I make wooden cigarette-cases on the side – good ones, too! I sell them at a rouble a time, and if you buy ten or more then I give a discount. We manage. First, you know, I worked in one of the Ministry's departments, now I've been transferred here as head of a sub-office . . . So I'll be working here. And what about yourself? You must be a 5 now, eh?'

'No, try a bit higher, old chap,' said Fat. 'Actually I'm a Number 3 . . . I've got my two stars.'

Thin suddenly went pale, turned to stone; but then his whole face twisted itself into an enormous grin, and sparks seemed to shoot from his eyes and face. He himself shrank, bent double, grew even thinner . . . And all his cases, bundles and band-boxes shrank and shrivelled, too . . . His wife's long chin grew even longer, Nathaniel sprang to attention and did up all the buttons on his uniform . . .

'Your Excellency, I – This is indeed an honour! The companion, so to speak, of my childhood, and all of a sudden become such an important personage! Hee-hee-hee . . .'

'Come now, Porfiry!' frowned Fat. 'Why this change of tone? You and I have known each other since we were children – rank has no place between us!'

'But sir . . . How can you –' giggled Thin, shrinking even smaller. 'The gracious attention of Your Excellency is as – as manna from on high to . . . This, Your Excellency, is my son Nathaniel . . . and this is my wife Luise, Lutheran so to speak . . .'

Fat was about to object, but such awe, such unction and such abject servility were written on Thin's face that the Number 3's stomach heaved. He took a step back and offered Thin his hand.

Thin took his middle three fingers, bent double over them, and giggled 'Hee-hee-hee' like a Chinaman. His wife beamed. Nathaniel clicked his heels and dropped his cap. It was a pleasant shock for all three of them.

The Daughter of Albion

A handsome barouche with rubber tyres, a fat coachman and velvet-upholstered seats drew up in front of Gryabov's manor-house. Out jumped the local Marshal of Nobility, Fyodor Andreich Ottsov. He was met in the anteroom by a sleepy-looking footman.

'Family at home?' asked the Marshal.

'No, sir. Mistress has took the children visiting, sir, and Master's out fishing with Mamselle the governess. Went out first thing, sir.'

Ottsov stood and pondered, then set off for the river to look for Gryabov. He came upon him a couple of versts from the house. On looking down from the steep river bank and catching sight of him, Ottsov burst out laughing . . . A big fat man with a very big head, Gryabov was sitting cross-legged on the sand in Turkish fashion. He was fishing. His hat was perched on the back of his head and his tie had slid over to one side. Next to him stood a tall thin Englishwoman with bulging eyes like a lobster's and a large bird-nose that looked more like a hook than a nose. She was wearing a white muslin dress, through which her yellow, scraggy shoulders showed quite clearly.

On her gold belt hung a little gold watch. She too was fishing. They were both as silent as the grave and as still as the river in which their floats were suspended.

'Strong was his wish, but sad his lot!' said Ottsov, laughing. 'Good day, Ivan Kuzmich!'

'Oh . . . it's you, is it?' asked Gryabov, without taking his eyes off the water. 'You've arrived then?'

'As you see . . . Still sold on this nonsense, are you? Not tired of it yet?'

'Been here since morning, damn it . . . They don't seem to be biting today. I haven't caught a thing, nor's this scarecrow here either. Sit sit sit, and not so much as a nibble! It's been torture, I can tell you.'

'Well, chuck it in then. Let's go and have a glass of vodka!'

'No, hang on . . . We may still catch something. They bite better towards dusk . . . You know, I've been sitting here since first thing this morning – I'm bored stiff! God knows what put this fishing bug into me. I know it's a stupid waste of time but still I go on with it! I sit here chained to this bank like a convict and stare at the water as if I was daft. I ought to be out haymaking and here I am fishing. Yesterday the Bishop was taking the service at Khaponyevo, but I didn't go, I sat here all day with this . . . this trout . . . this old hag . . .'

'Are you crazy?' Ottsov asked in embarrassment, glancing sideways at the Englishwoman. 'Swearing in front of a lady . . . calling her names . . .'

'To hell with her! She doesn't understand a word of Russian anyway. You can pay her compliments or call her names for all she cares. And look at that nose! Her nose alone is enough to freeze your blood. We fish here for days on end and she doesn't say a word. Just stands there like a stuffed dummy, staring at the water with those goggle eyes.'

The Englishwoman yawned, changed the worm on her line and cast out again.

'You know, it's a very funny thing,' Gryabov continued. 'This fool of a woman has lived over here for ten years and you'd think she'd be able to say *something* in Russian. Any tinpot aristocrat of ours can go over there and start jabbering away in their lingo in no time, but not them – oh no! Just look at her nose! Take a really good look at that nose!'

'Oh come now, this is embarrassing . . . Stop going on at the woman . . .'

'She's not a woman, she's a spinster. I expect she spends all day dreaming of a fiancé, the witch. And there's a kind of rotten smell about her . . . I tell you, old man, I hate her guts! I can't look at her without getting worked up! When she turns those huge eyes on me, I get this jarring sensation all over, as if I'd knocked my funny-bone. She's another one who likes fishing. And look at the way she goes about it: as if it were some holy rite! Turning up her nose at everything, damn her . . . Here am I, she says to herself, a member of the human race, so that makes me superior to the rest of creation. And do you know what her name is? Wilka Charlesovna Tvice! Ugh, I can't even say it properly!'

Hearing her name, the Englishwoman slowly brought her nose round in Gryabov's direction and measured him with a look of contempt. Then, raising her glance from Gryabov to Ottsov, she poured contempt over him too. And all of this was done in silence, solemnly and slowly.

'You see?' said Gryabov, roaring with laughter. 'That's what she thinks of us! Old hag! I only keep the codfish because of the children. But for them, I wouldn't let her within a hundred versts of the estate . . . Just like a hawk's beak, that nose . . . And what about her waist? The witch reminds me of a tent-peg – you know, take hold of her and bang her into the ground. Hang on, I think I've got a bite . . .'

Gryabov jumped up and lifted his rod. The line went taut . . . He gave a tug but could not pull the hook out.

'It's snagged!' he said, frowning. 'Caught behind a stone, I expect . . . Blast!'

Gryabov looked worried. Sighing, scuttling from side to side and muttering oaths, he tugged and tugged at the line – but to no effect. Gryabov paled.

'Blow it! I'll have to get into the water.'

'Oh, give it up!'

'Can't do that . . . They bite so well towards dusk . . . What a ruddy mess! I'll simply have to get into the water. Nothing else for it! And I'd do anything not to have to undress! It means I'll have to get rid of the Englishwoman . . . I can't undress in front of her. She is a lady, after all!'

Gryabov threw off his hat and tie.

'Miss . . . er . . . Miss Tvice!' he said, turning to the Englishwoman. '*Je vous prie* . . . Now how can I put it? How can I put it so you'll understand? Listen . . . over there! Go over there! Got it?'

Miss Tvice poured a look of contempt over Gryabov and emitted a nasal sound.

'Oh, you don't understand? Clear off, I'm telling you! I've got to undress, you old hag! Go on! Over there!'

Tugging at the governess's sleeve, Gryabov pointed to the bushes and crouched down – meaning, of course, go behind the bushes and keep out of sight . . . Twitching her eyebrows energetically, the Englishwoman delivered herself of a long sentence in English. The landowners burst out laughing.

'That's the first time I've heard her voice. It's a voice all right! What am I going to do with her? She just doesn't understand.'

'Forget it! Let's go and have some vodka.'

'Can't do that, this is when they should start biting . . . At dusk . . . Well, what do you propose I do? It's no good! I'll have to undress in front of her . . .'

Gryabov removed his jacket and waistcoat, and sat down on the sand to take off his boots.

'Look, Ivan Kuzmich,' said the Marshal, spluttering with laughter. 'Now you're actually insulting her, my friend, you're making a mockery of her.'

'No one asked her not to understand, did they? Let this be a lesson to these foreigners!'

Gryabov took off his boots and trousers, removed his underwear, and stood there in a state of nature. Ottsov doubled up, his face scarlet from a mixture of laughter and embarrassment. The Englishwoman twitched her eyebrows and blinked . . . Then a haughty, contemptuous smile passed over her yellow face.

'Must cool down first,' said Gryabov, slapping his thighs. 'Do tell me, Fyodor Andreich, why is it I get this rash on my chest every summer?'

'Oh hurry up and get in the water, you great brute, or cover yourself with something!'

'She might at least show some embarrassment, the hussy!' said Gryabov, getting into the water and crossing himself. 'Brrr . . . this water's cold . . . Look at those eyebrows of hers twitching! She's not going away . . . She's above the crowd! Ha, ha, ha! She doesn't even regard us as human beings!'

When he was up to his knees in the water, he drew himself up to his full enormous height, winked and said:

'Bit different from England, eh?!'

Miss Tvice coolly changed her worm, gave a yawn and cast her line. Ottsov turned aside. Gryabov detached the hook, immersed himself and came puffing out of the water. Two minutes later he was sitting on the sand again, fishing.

Oysters 1884

It does not require a great feat of memory for me to recall in all its detail that rainy autumn evening when I was standing with my father on one of Moscow's crowded streets and began to feel a strange illness gradually take hold of me . . .

There is no pain at all, but my legs are giving way beneath me, words stick in my throat, and my head is lolling helplessly to one side. I am evidently on the point of falling down unconscious.

Had I been admitted to hospital at that moment, the doctors would have had to write on my card *Fames* – an illness that does not appear in any of the medical textbooks.

Beside me on the pavement stands my dear father in a threadbare summer coat and a little tricot cap with a piece of white wadding sticking out. He is wearing large heavy galoshes. A vain man, he is afraid of people noticing that he is wearing the galoshes over bare feet, and so has pulled an old pair of boot-tops tight round his shins.

This poor, foolish old clown, for whom my love grows stronger as his rather dandified summer coat gets more and more dirty and tattered, arrived in the city five months ago to seek an appointment in the clerical line. These five long months he has been wandering round the city asking for a job, and today for the first time he has brought himself to go out onto the streets and beg . . .

Opposite us is a large three-storey building with a blue sign that says 'Eating-House'. My head is tilted back feebly to one side, so I cannot help looking up at its lighted windows. Human figures flit across them and I can make out the right-hand corner of a mechanical organ, two oleographs, some hanging lamps . . . Peering through one of the windows, I discern a shining white spot. Because it does not move and has straight edges, this spot stands out sharply from the general background of dark brown. Straining my eyes, I see that it is a white placard on the wall. Something is written on it – but what, I can't make out . . .

For half an hour I stare and stare at the placard. Its gleaming whiteness lures my eyes and seems to hypnotise my brain. I try to read it, but my efforts are futile.

Finally the strange illness comes into its own.

The noise of the passing carriages begins to sound like thunder, in the stench of the street I detect thousands of different smells, while the lights of the eating-house and the street-lamps fill my eyes with blinding flashes of lightning. All my senses are at fever pitch and abnormally receptive. I begin to see things that I couldn't see before.

'Oy-sters' – I make out on the placard.

What a strange word! I've lived on this earth for eight years and three months exactly, but not once have I heard that word before. What does it mean? Can it be the surname of the landlord? But boards with surnames are hung on doors, not walls!

'Papa, what does "oysters" mean?' I ask in a hoarse voice, straining to turn my head in his direction.

My father doesn't hear. He is scrutinising the movements of the crowds and following each person who goes past . . . I can tell from his eyes that he wants to speak to them, but the fatal word hangs on his trembling lips like a heavy weight, and simply will not detach itself. He even took a step after one passer-by and touched his sleeve, but when the man turned round he said 'Sorry', became flustered, and retreated again in confusion.

'Papa,' I repeat, 'what does "oysters" mean?'

'It's a kind of animal . . . It lives in the sea . . .'

In a trice I have pictured this mysterious sea creature to myself. It must be a cross between a fish and a crayfish. Since it is from the sea, it can obviously be used to make very tasty broth with fragrant pepper and a bay leaf floating in it; thick, sourish soup with bits of backbone; crayfish sauce; fish in aspic with horse-radish . . . I vividly imagine this animal being brought straight from the market, quickly cleaned, and popped in the pot – all so quickly, quickly, because everyone's so hungry, terribly hungry! And from the kitchen wafts the smell of fried fish and crayfish soup.

I can feel this smell tickling my palate and nostrils, and gradually taking possession of my whole body. Everything smells of it – the eating-house, Father, the white placard, my sleeves – and the smell is so strong that I begin chewing. I chew and I swallow, as though I actually had a piece of the sea creature in my mouth.

My legs buckle under me from this pleasurable sensation, and so as not to fall I grab my father's sleeve and press up against his wet summer coat. My father is trembling and clutching himself: it's so cold . . .

'Papa,' I ask, 'can you eat oysters in Lent?'

'You eat them alive,' says Father. 'They live in shells like tortoises . . . but in two halves.'

The delicious smell instantly ceases to tickle my body, the illusion vanishes . . . I see it all now!

'Horrible,' I whisper, 'horrible!'

So that's what 'oysters' means! I imagine an animal like a frog. This frog sits inside a shell, looking out with large, gleaming eyes and champing with its disgusting jaws. I see this animal being brought in its shell from the market, with its claws, its gleaming eyes and slimy skin . . . The children all hide, but the cook, screwing up her face in disgust, takes hold of the animal by one claw, puts it on a plate, and carries it into the dining-room. The grown-ups take hold of it and they eat it – eat it alive, eyes, teeth, feet and all! And it squeaks loudly and tries to bite them on the lip . . .

I screw up my face, but . . . but why is it my teeth have begun chewing? The creature is vile, disgusting, terrifying, but I am eating it all the same, bolting it down so as not to discover what its real taste and smell are. One animal is finished and already I can see the gleaming eyes of a second and a third . . . I eat them too . . . And I end up eating the serviette, the plate, Father's galoshes, the white placard . . . I eat everything in sight, because I know that only eating will cure my illness. The oysters shoot horrible glances at me, they are disgusting, I tremble at the thought of them, but I must eat, I must eat!

'Give me some oysters! Some oysters!' I suddenly find myself shouting, and stretch out my arms.

At the same time I hear Father's hollow, strangled voice saying: 'Help us, gentlemen! I'm ashamed to be asking, but God knows, I'm at the end of my tether!'

'Give me some oysters!' I shout, tugging at Father's coat-tails.

'Do you mean to say you eat oysters? A little boy like you?'

someone laughs beside me.

Two gentlemen in top-hats are standing in front of us, looking into my face and laughing.

'Do you eat oysters, lad? Do you really? Most remarkable. And how do you eat them?'

I remember a strong hand dragging me into the brightly-lit eating-house. Within a minute a crowd gathers round and watches me with curiosity and amusement. I am sitting at a table and eating something slimy, salty, smelling of damp and mould. I eat greedily, without chewing, without looking and without trying to discover what I am eating. I'm sure that if I open my eyes, I shall see those gleaming eyes, those claws and sharp teeth . . .

Suddenly I begin chewing something hard. There is a crunching sound.

'Ha, ha! He's eating the shells!' roars the crowd. 'You don't eat those, you little chump!'

After that I remember a terrible thirst. I am lying on my bed and can't get to sleep from indigestion and a strange taste in my burning mouth. My father is pacing up and down, gesticulating to himself.

'I seem to have caught a chill,' he is mumbling. 'I've got this feeling in my head . . . Like there was someone in it . . . Or maybe it's because I haven't . . . well, because I haven't eaten today. I'm an odd one, I really am, a bit of a fool . . . I saw those gentlemen paying ten roubles for oysters, so why didn't I go up and ask them for a few roubles . . . on loan? They'd have given me them.'

Towards morning I fall asleep and dream of a frog with claws, sitting inside a shell and rolling its eyes. At midday I wake up feeling thirsty and look round for my father: he's still pacing up and down gesticulating . . .

A Dreadful Night

Ivan Petrovich Spektroff's face grew pale and his voice quavered as he turned down the lamp and began his story:

'It was Christmas Eve 1883. The earth lay shrouded in impenetrable darkness. I was returning home from the house of a friend (who has since died), where we had all been sitting up late attending a seance. For some reason the streets through which I was passing were unlit, and I had almost to grope my way along. I was living in Moscow, near the Church of St Mary-in-the-Tombstones, in a house belonging to the civil servant Kadavroff – in other words, in one of the remotest parts of the Arbat district. My thoughts as I walked along were gloomy and depressing . . .

"The end of your life is at hand . . . Repent . . ."

Such had been the words addressed to me at the seance by Spinoza, whose spirit we had succeeded in calling up. I asked for confirmation, and the saucer not only repeated the words, but added: "This very night." I am not a believer in spiritualism, but the thought of death, or even the merest allusion to it, is enough to plunge me into despondency. Death is inevitable, my friends, it is commonplace, but nevertheless the thought of death is repugnant to human nature . . . Now, as cold, unfathomable darkness hemmed me in and raindrops whirled madly before my eyes, as the wind groaned plaintively above my head and I could neither see a single living soul nor hear a single human sound around me, my heart filled with a vague, inexplicable dread. I, a man free from superstition, hurried through the streets afraid to look around or glance to either side. I felt sure that if I did look round, I would see an apparition of death close behind me.'

Spektroff gulped for breath, drank some water and continued:

'This feeling of dread, which despite its vagueness you will all recognise, did not leave me even when I climbed to the third floor of Kadavroff's house, unlocked the door and entered my room. It was dark in my humble abode. The wind was moaning in the stove and tapping on the damper, almost as though it were begging to be let into the warm.

If Spinoza was telling the truth, I reflected with a smile, then I am to die this night to the accompaniment of these moans. What a gruesome thought!

I lit a match . . . A violent gust of wind raced across the roof. The quiet moaning turned to a ferocious roar. Somewhere down below a half-loose shutter started banging, and the damper began whining plaintively for help . . .

Pity the poor devils, I thought, without a roof over their heads on a night like this.

The moment was to prove inopportune, however, for reflections of that kind. When the sulphur of my match flared up with a blue flame and I looked round the room, an unexpected, a terrifying spectacle met my eyes . . . Oh, why didn't that gust of wind blow out my match? Then perhaps I should have seen nothing and my hair would not have stood on end. I gave a wild cry, took a step backwards towards the door, and filled with terror, amazement and despair, closed my eyes . . .

In the centre of the room stood a coffin.

The blue flame did not last long, but I had time to make out the coffin's main features . . . I saw its richly shimmering pink brocade, I saw the gold-embroidered cross on its lid. There are certain things, my friends, which imprint themselves on one's memory, even when one has glimpsed them but for a single moment. So it was with that coffin. I saw it but for a second, yet I recall it in the most minute detail. It was a coffin made for a person of medium height, and judging by the pink colour, for a young girl. The expensive silk brocade, the feet, the bronze handles – all these suggested that the deceased came from a wealthy family.

I rushed headlong from my room, not stopping to think or consider but experiencing only unutterable fear, and flew downstairs. The staircase and corridors were in darkness, I kept tripping over my coat-tails, and how I avoided tumbling head-over-heels down the stairs and breaking my neck, I shall never know. Finding myself in the street, I leant up against a wet lamp-post and tried to recover my composure. My heart was thumping horribly and I had a tight feeling across the chest . . .'

One of the listeners turned up the lamp and moved her chair closer to the narrator, who continued:

'I would not have been so taken aback if I had discovered in my room a fire, a thief or a mad dog . . . I would not have been so taken aback if the ceiling had come down, the floor had collapsed or the walls had caved in . . . All that is natural and comprehensible. But how could a coffin have turned up in my room? Where had it come from? How had an expensive coffin, evidently made for a young girl of noble birth, found its way into the miserable room of a minor civil servant? Was the coffin empty or was it – occupied? And who was this *she*, this rich young aristocrat who had quitted life so prematurely and paid me this dread, disturbing visit? It was a tantalising mystery!

If it's not a case of the supernatural, the thought flashed through my mind, then there's foul play involved.

I became lost in conjecture. My door had been locked while I was out, and only my very close friends knew where I kept the key. But the coffin certainly hadn't been left by friends. Then it was also conceivable that the undertakers had delivered the coffin to me in error. They might have muddled up the names, mistaken the floor number or the door, and taken the coffin to the wrong place. But who ever heard of Moscow undertakers leaving a room without being paid, or at least waiting for a tip?

The spirits foretold my death, I thought. Perhaps they've already set about providing me with a coffin, too?

I am not a believer in spiritualism, my friends, nor was I then, but such a coincidence is enough to plunge even a philosopher into a mood of mysticism.

But all this is absurd, I decided, and I'm being as cowardly as a schoolboy. It was an optical illusion – no more than that! On my way home I was in such a gloomy state of mind that it's hardly surprising my overwrought nerves thought they saw a coffin . . . Of course, an optical illusion! What else could it be?

The rain was lashing my face, and the wind kept tugging angrily at my hat and coat-tails . . . I was wet through and chilled to the bone. I would have to find shelter – but where? To go back home would mean running the risk of seeing the coffin again, and that was a spectacle beyond my powers of endurance. Not seeing a single living soul or hearing a single human sound around me, left alone in the company of a coffin which perhaps contained a dead body, I might easily lose my reason. But to remain on the street in the cold and pouring rain was equally impossible.

I decided to go and spend the night with my friend Lugubrovitch (who, as you know, was later to shoot himself). He lived in a block of furnished rooms belonging to the merchant Skeletoff – the ones on the corner of Deadman's Passage.'

Spektroff wiped away the beads of cold perspiration that had gathered on his pallid brow, and with a deep sigh continued:

'I did not find my friend at home. After knocking on his door and deciding he must be out, I felt for his key on the lintel, unlocked the door and went in. I flung my wet coat on the floor, and feeling my way to the sofa, sat down to recuperate. It was very dark . . . The wind droned mournfully in the ventilator. Behind the stove a cricket chirped over and over again its monotonous song. The Kremlin bells had begun to ring for Christmas morning communion. Hastily I struck a match. But its light did not dispel my gloomy mood; on the contrary. A dreadful, unutterable terror seized me again . . . I cried out, staggered backwards, and rushed blindly from the apartment . . .

In my friend's room I had seen the same as in my own – a coffin!

My friend's coffin was almost twice as large as mine, and its subfusc upholstery gave it a peculiarly gloomy appearance. How had it got there? That it was an optical illusion now seemed quite certain – there couldn't be a coffin in every room! I was obviously suffering from a nervous disorder, from hallucinations. Wherever I now went, I would see before me the dreadful dwelling-place of death. In other words I was going mad, I was suffering from a kind of "coffinomania", and the cause of my derangement was not hard to find: I had only to recall the spiritualist seance and the words of Spinoza . . .

I'm going mad! I thought to myself with terror, clutching my head. Oh my God! What am I to do?!

My head was splitting and my knees shaking . . . The rain was pouring down in buckets, the wind was piercing right through me, and I had neither coat nor hat. To go back to the apartment for them was impossible, beyond my powers of endurance . . . Fear gripped me firmly in her cold embrace. My hair was standing on end and cold perspiration streamed down my face, even though I believed that the coffin was only an hallucination.'

'What was I to do?' Spektroff continued. 'I was going mad and in danger of catching a violent cold. Fortunately I remembered that not far from Deadman's Passage lived my good friend Kryptin, a recently qualified doctor, who had also been at the seance with me that night. I hurried round to his place. This was before he married his merchant heiress, and he was still living on the fourth floor of a house belonging to state counsellor Nekropolsky.

At Kryptin's my nerves were fated to undergo yet another ordeal. As I was climbing to the fourth floor, I heard above me a terrible din of running footsteps and slamming doors.

"Help!" I heard a soul-piercing cry. "Help! Porter!"

And a moment later a dark figure in a coat and battered top-hat came hurtling down the stairs towards me . . .

"Kryptin!" I exclaimed, recognising my friend. "Is that you, Kryptin? Whatever's wrong?"

Kryptin pulled up short and clutched my hand convulsively. He was pale, breathing heavily and trembling. His eyes were rolling wildly and his chest was heaving . . .

"Is that you, Spektroff?" he asked in a sepulchral voice. "Is that really you? You're as white as a ghost . . . Are you quite sure you're not a hallucination? . . . My God . . . you scare me stiff . . ."

"But what about you? You look ghastly!"

"Phew, let me get my breath back, old chap . . . It's wonderful to see you, if it really is you and not an optical illusion. That damned seance . . . Would you believe it, my nerves were so overwrought that when I got back to my room just now I thought I saw – a coffin!"

I could not believe my ears and asked for confirmation.

"A coffin, a real coffin!" said the doctor, sitting down exhausted on one of the stairs. "I'm no coward, but the devil himself would get a fright if he came home after a seance and bumped into a coffin in the dark!"

Stumbling and stammering, I told the doctor about the coffins I had seen . . .

For a moment we gazed at each other, our eyes popping and our mouths gaping in astonishment. Then, to make sure we were not seeing hallucinations, we began pinching each other.

"We both feel pain," said the doctor, "which means that we're not asleep and seeing each other in a dream. And that means the coffins – mine and your two – are not optical illusions but really do exist. So what's our next move, old man?"

After standing for a solid hour on the cold staircase and losing ourselves in conjecture and surmise, we were chilled to the bone and made up our minds to cast aside cowardly fear and wake up the floor-porter, in order to return with him to the doctor's room. This we did. On entering the apartment, we lit a candle and there indeed we saw a coffin, covered in white silk brocade, with a gold fringe and tassels. The porter crossed himself reverently.

"Now we can find out," said the doctor, pale-faced and trembling all over, "whether this coffin is empty, or – or – inhabited!"

After an understandably long period of indecision, the doctor bent over, and gritting his teeth in dread and anticipation, wrenched off the lid of the coffin. We looked inside and . . .

The coffin was empty.

There was no dead body, but we did find a letter which read as follows:

"My dear Kryptin! As you know, my father-in-law's business has been going from bad to worse. He's up to his neck in debt. Tomorrow or the day after they're coming to make an inventory of all his stock, which will deal the death blow to his family and mine, and to our honour, which is dearer to me than anything. At our family conference yesterday we decided to hide everything precious and valuable. As my father-in-law's stock consists entirely of coffins (he is, as you know, a master coffin-maker, the best in town), we decided to hide away all the best coffins. I appeal to you as a friend to help me save our fortune and our honour! In the hope that you will assist us in preserving our stock, I am sending you one coffin, old chap, with the request that you keep it until it is required. Without the help of our friends and acquaintances we shall certainly perish. I hope this is not too much to ask, especially as the coffin will not be with you for more than a week. I have sent a coffin each to all those I consider our true friends and am relying on their nobility and generosity.

Affectionately yours, Ivan Nekstovkin."

For three months afterwards I was under a specialist in nervous disorders, whilst our friend, the coffin-maker's son-in-law, not only saved his honour and his stock, but set up a funeral parlour and deals in memorials and tombstones. His business is none too healthy, and now, when I come home each evening, I am always afraid I'm going to see a white marble memorial or a catafalque by my bedside.'

Minds in Ferment

(From the Annals of a Town)

The earth was like an inferno. The afternoon sun beat down with such a vengeance that even the thermometer hanging in the excise office lost its head, shot up to 112·5, and hovered there in a dither . . . Sweat poured off the town's inhabitants as though they were hard-ridden horses, and dried where it was: they hadn't the energy to wipe it off.

Across the broad market square, where all the surrounding buildings were tightly shuttered, walked two such inhabitants: chief cashier Skrabbitch and town solicitor Optimov (veteran local correspondent of *Son of the Fatherland*, to boot). They walked in silence on account of the heat. Optimov felt the urge to castigate the council for all the dust and litter lying about the market place, but knowing the peaceful disposition and moderate views of his companion, he refrained.

When they reached the middle of the square, Skrabbitch suddenly stopped and stared up at the sky.

'What are you looking at, Yevpl Serapionych?'

'That flock of starlings there. I wonder where they'll settle? Clouds and clouds of them! Say you were to take a pot-shot at them from here, say you were to go and pick them up afterwards . . . and say . . . They've settled in the Dean's orchard!'

'No, you're wrong, Yevpl Serapionych, they're in Deacon Pandemonoff's. If you were to take a pot-shot at them from here, you wouldn't hit anything. The pellets are too small, once they'd got that far their strength would have gone. Anyway, what do you want to kill them for? The bird's a menace to fruit, I grant you, but it's one of God's creatures, don't forget, a work of the Lord. A starling, for example, can sing . . . And wherefore does he sing, you may ask? To give praise, that's why. "Let everything that hath breath praise the Lord!" No, you're right, I do believe they've settled in the Dean's orchard.'

Whilst they were conversing thus, three old women, wandering pilgrims carrying scrips and wearing big bast shoes, walked silently by. Puzzled by the way in which Skrabbitch and Optimov were staring at the Dean's house, they slowed down, drew to one side, stopped, took another look at the two friends, and proceeded to gaze at the Father's house in their turn.

'You were quite right, they have settled in the Dean's orchard,' Optimov went on. 'His cherries have just ripened, so they've flown in for a peck.'

At this moment, Father Kantiklin himself came out of his garden gate with Yevstigney, his server. Seeing so much attention directed towards his house and wondering what everyone was staring at, he stopped, and he and his server also began looking up in the air, to find out.

'I expect the good Father's taking an office,' said Skrabbitch. 'The Lord be his succour!'

Some workers from Purov's factory who were just returning from a swim in the river now hove into view in the space between the two friends and Father Kantiklin. Seeing the latter with his gaze fixed on the firmament above, and the pilgrims standing stockstill and also staring on high, they stopped and stared in the same direction. A little boy leading a blind beggar, and a peasant who had come out to tip a barrelful of rotten herrings onto the square, did likewise.

'Looks as though something's up,' said Skrabbitch. 'Do you reckon it's a fire? No, it can't be, there's no smoke. Hey, Kuzma!' he shouted at the peasant. 'What's going on over there?'

The peasant said something in reply, but Skrabbitch and Optimov did not catch it. Sleepy shopkeepers began to appear in all the doorways. Some plasterers working on the front of merchant Fertikulin's corn-chandler's left their ladders and joined the factory-workers. A fireman, who had been describing circles at the top of the watch-tower in his bare feet, came to a halt, and after a few moments' observation, descended. The fire-tower was now deserted. This looked suspicious.

'Perhaps there's a fire somewhere? Hey, stop shoving will you! Pig face!'

'What's all this about a fire, then? What fire? Come on, gentlemen, move along, will you! I'm asking you politely!'

'Must be a fire indoors!'

'Politely, he says, and then starts barging about. Stop swinging your arms around! You may be head constable, but no one's given you a perfect right to make free with your fists!'

'Ow, you've trodden on my corn! May you choke, damn you!'

'Choke? Who's choking? Lads, someone's been crushed!'

'Why's this crowd here? What's all this in aid of?'

'Someone's been crushed, yeronner!'

'Where? D-is-perse! I'm asking you all politely – you too, blockhead!'

'You can shove the peasants, but don't you dare touch a gentleman! Keep your hands off!'

'Call yourselves people? You could talk nicely to this lot till you were blue in the face! Sidorov, go and fetch Akim Danilych! At the double! It'll be worse for you now, gentlemen! Once Akim Danilych comes you'll be for it! What, you here too, Parfen?! A blind holy man here too! He's as blind as a bat, but he has to go along and resist the law just like other people! Smirnov, take Parfen's name!'

'Yessir! Am I to put down Purov's men as well, sir? Him over there with the swollen cheek – he's one of Purov's!'

'No, don't put Purov's men down yet . . . It's Purov's saint's-day party tomorrow!'

The starlings rose in a dark cloud above Father Kantiklin's orchard, but Skrabbitch and Optimov did not even notice them; they were too busy gazing into the air and trying to work out why such a big crowd had gathered and what it was staring at. Then Akim Danilych came round the corner. Still chewing something and wiping his lips, he gave a sudden bellow and dived into the crowd.

'Firemen, stand by! Crrrowd, d-is-perse! Mr Optimov, disperse yourself please or it'll be the worse for you. Instead of writing all these criticisms of decent people for the papers, you should try behaving a bit more substantially yourself! The papers never improved anyone!'

'I'll thank you to leave the public press out of it!' flared up Optimov. 'I am a professional writer, and I will not allow you to cast aspersions on the press – even if I do consider it my duty as a citizen to respect you as a father and benefactor!'

'Firemen, turn on the hose!'

'There's no water, yeronner!'

'Stop answering back! Go and get some! At-the-double!'

'Nothing to go on, your honour. The major's taken the brigade horses to drive his auntie to the station!'

'Disperse, will you! Move back, damn the lot of you . . . You deaf? Right, take the blighter's name for him!'

'I've lost my pencil, yeronner . . .'

The crowd was growing bigger and bigger . . . Goodness knows what proportions it would have reached, had not someone in Sleezkin's tavern chosen this moment to try out the new mechanical organ that had recently arrived from Moscow. Hearing the most popular tune of the day, the crowd gave an 'Aah!' and piled into the tavern. Thus nobody ever did discover why the crowd had gathered, and Optimov and Skrabbitch had long forgotten all about the starlings who were the real cause of the incident. An hour later, the town was absolutely still and quiet again, and only a single solitary human being could be seen – the fireman walking round and round the top of his watch-tower . . .

That evening, Akim Danilych sat in Fertikulin's grocery shop sipping fizzy lemonade laced with brandy, and wrote: 'In addition to my official communication, I venture, Your Excellency, to append some supplementary remarks of my own. My Father and Benefactor! Verily it could only have been through the prayers of your most virtuous spouse residing in her salubrious datcha close by our town that we were saved from disaster! I cannot begin to describe all that I have been through this day. The efficiency displayed by Krushensky and Major Portépéeyeff of the fire brigade beggars all description. I glory in these worthy servants of our fatherland! As for myself, I did all that a frail man can whose sole desire is the well-being of his neighbour, and now that I am sitting in the bosom of my family, I offer up thanks with tears in my eyes to Him Who spared us bloodshed. In the absence of evidence, the guilty parties are at the moment under lock and key, but I propose to release them in a week or so. It was their ignorance that led them astray!'

The Complaints Book

It lies, this book, in a special little desk inside the railway station. To get at it you have to 'Apply to the Station Policeman for Key' – but it's all nonsense about the key, since the desk is always unlocked. Open the book and you will read:

'Dear Sir! Just testing the pen?!'

Below this is a funny face with a long nose and horns. Underneath it says:

'I'm a picture, you're a blot, you're a pig, I'm not. I am your ugly mug.'

'Approaching this station and admiring the seenery, my hat blue off. I. Harmonkin.'

'I know not who it was that writ, but him that reads it is a twit.'

'Fobbemoff, Head of Small Claims Office, was here.'

'I wish to register a complaint against Ticket-Collector Krumpkin for rudeness with respect to my wife. My wife wasn't kicking up a row but on the contrary was trying to keep it all as quiet as possible. Also against Constable Kuffkin for Grabbing me by the shoulder. My place of residence is the estate of Andrey Ivanovich Snoopin who knows my mode of behaviour. Paragonsky, estate clerk.'

'Nikandroff's a Socialist!'

'Whilst the impression of this disgraceful incident is still fresh – (crossed out). Passing through this station I was shocked to the depths of my being by the following – (crossed out). I witnessed with my own eyes the following disgraceful occurrence, vividly illustrating the state of affairs pertaining on our railways – (everything else crossed out, except for the signature –) Ivan Svot, Upper Sixth Form, Kursk Grammar School.'

'While awaiting the departure of the train I studied the station-master's physiognomy and was not at all pleased by what I saw. Am passing this information along the line. An undespairing nine-to-fiver.'

'I know who wrote that. It was M.D.'

'Gentlemen! Teltsovsky's a card-sharp!'

'The station policeman's wife took a trip over the river with Kostka the barman yesterday. Good luck to them! Chin up, constable!'

'Passing through this station and requiring sustenance in the form of something to eat I was unable to obtain any lenten fare. Deacon Cheruboff.'

'Stuff in what they've got, mate!' . . .

'Will anyone finding a leather cigar-case kindly hand it in to Andrey Yegorych at the ticket office.'

'Right, if you're sacking me because you say I get drunk, I'm telling everyone you're a load of dirty rogues and swindlers. Kozmodemyansky, telegraph-operator.'

'Rejoice in good deeds.'

'Katinka, I love you madly!'

'Please refrain from making irrelevant entries in this complaints book. B.A.Ivanoff (pp. Station-master).'

'B.F.Ivanoff, more like.'

The Chameleon

Across the market square comes Police Inspector Moronoff. He is wearing a new greatcoat and carrying a small package. Behind him strides a ginger-headed constable bearing a sieve filled to the brim with confiscated gooseberries. There is silence all around . . . Not a soul in the square . . . The wide-open doors of the shops and taverns look out dolefully on the world, like hungry jaws; even their beggars have vanished.

'Bite me, would you, you little devil?' Moronoff suddenly hears. 'Catch him, lads, catch him! Biting's against the law now! Grab him! Ouch!'

A dog squeals. Moronoff looks round – and sees a dog run out of merchant Spatchkin's woodyard, hopping along on three legs and glancing backwards. A man in a starched calico shirt and unbuttoned waistcoat comes chasing out after it. He runs behind, bends down right over it, and tumbles to the ground catching the dog by the hind legs. There is another squeal and a shout: 'Hold him, lads!' Sleepy countenances thrust themselves out of the shop windows and soon a crowd has sprung up from nowhere by the woodyard.

'Looks like trouble, your honour!' says the constable.

Moronoff executes a half-turn to his left and marches towards the throng. He sees that the aforementioned man in the unbuttoned shirt is standing at the yard gates and with his right hand raised high in the air is showing the crowd a bloodstained finger. His half-sozzled face seems to be saying 'You'll pay for this, you scoundrel!' and his very finger has the air of a victory banner. Moronoff recognises the man as Grunkin the goldsmith. On the ground in the midst of the crowd, its front legs splayed out and its whole body trembling, sits the actual cause of the commotion: a white borzoi puppy with a pointed muzzle and a yellow patch on its back. The expression in its watering eyes is one of terror and despair.

'What's all this about?' asks Moronoff, cutting through the crowd. 'Why are you lot here? What's your finger – ? Who shouted just now?'

'I was walking along, your honour, minding me own business . . .' Grunkin begins, giving a slight cough, 'on my way to see Mitry Mitrich about some firewood – when all of a sudden, for no reason, this little tyke goes for my finger . . . Beg pardon, sir, but I'm a man what's working . . . My work's delicate work. I want compensation for this – after all, I may not be able to lift this finger for a week now . . . There's nothing in the law even that says we have to put up with that from beasts, is there your honour? If we all went round biting, we might as well be dead . . .'

'Hm! All right . . .' says Moronoff sternly, clearing his throat and knitting his brows. 'Right . . . Who owns this dog? I shall not let this matter rest. I'll teach you to let dogs run loose! It's time we took a closer look at these people who won't obey regulations! A good fat fine'll teach the blighter what I think of dogs and suchlike vagrant cattle! I'll take him down a peg! Dildin,' says the inspector, turning to the constable, 'find out who owns this dog, and take a statement! And the dog must be put down. Forthwith! It's probably mad anyway . . . Come on then, who's the owner?'

'Looks like General Tartaroff's!' says a voice from the crowd.

'General Tartaroff's? Hm . . . Dildin, remove my coat for me, will you? . . . Phew it's hot! We must be in for rain . . . What I don't understand, though, is this: how did it manage to bite you?' says

Moronoff, turning to Grunkin. 'How could it reach up to your finger? A little dog like that, and a hulking great bloke like you! I expect what happened was, you skinned your finger on a nail, then had the bright idea of making some money out of it. I know you lot! You devils don't fool me!'

'He shoved a fag in its mug for a lark, your honour, but she weren't having any and went for him . . . He's always stirring up trouble, your honour!'

'Don't lie, Boss-Eye! You couldn't see, so why tell lies? His honour here's a clever gent, he knows who's lying and who's telling the gospel truth . . . And if he thinks I'm lying, then let the justice decide. He's got it all written down there in the law . . . We're all equal now . . . I've got a brother myself who's in the po-lice . . . you may like to know –'

'Stop arguing!'

'No, it's not the General's . . .' the constable observes profoundly. 'The General ain't got any like this. His are more setters . . .'

'Are you sure of that?'

'Quite sure, your honour –'

'Well of course I know that, too. The General has dogs that are worth something, thoroughbreds, but this is goodness knows what! It's got no coat, it's nothing to look at – just a load of rubbish . . . Do you seriously think he'd keep a dog like that?! Use your brains. You know what'd happen if a dog like that turned up in Petersburg or Moscow? They wouldn't bother looking in the law books, they'd dispatch him – double quick! You've got a grievance, Grunkin, and you mustn't let the matter rest . . . Teach 'em a lesson! It's high time . . .'

'Could be the General's, though . . .' muses the constable aloud. 'It ain't written on its snout . . . I did see one like that in his yard the other day.'

'Course it's the General's!' says a voice from the crowd.

'Hm . . . Help me on with my coat, Dildin old chap . . . There's a bit of a breeze got up . . . It's quite chilly . . . Right, take this dog to the General's and ask them there. Say I found it and am sending it back. And tell them not to let it out on the street in future. It may be worth a lot, and if every swine is going to poke cigarettes up its nose, it won't be for much longer. A dog's a delicate creature . . . And you put your hand down, you oaf! Stop showing your stupid finger off! It was all your own fault!'

'Here comes the General's cook, let's ask him . . . Hey, Prokhor! Come over here a moment, will you? Take a look at this dog . . . One of yours, is it?'

'You must be joking! We've never had none like that!'

'Right, we can stop making enquiries,' says Moronoff. 'It's a stray! We can cut the chat . . . If everyone says it's a stray, it is a stray . . . So that's that, it must be put down.'

'No, it's not one of ours,' Prokhor continues. 'It belongs to the General's brother what come down the other day. Our General don't go much on borzois. His brother does, though –'

'You mean to say his Excellency's brother's arrived? Vladimir Ivanych?' asks Moronoff, his face breaking into an ecstatic smile. 'Well blow me down! And I didn't know! Come for a little stay, has he?'

'He's on a visit . . .'

'Well I never . . . So he felt like seeing his dear old brother again . . . And fancy me not knowing! So it's his little dog, is it? Jolly good . . . Take him away with you, then . . . He's a good little doggie . . . Pretty quick off the mark, too . . . Took a bite out of this bloke's finger – ha, ha, ha! No need to shiver, little chap! "Grr-rrr" . . . He's angry, the rascal . . . the little scamp . . .'

Prokhor calls the dog over and it follows him out of the woodyard . . . The crowd roars with laughter at Grunkin.

'I'll deal with you later!' Moronoff threatens him, and wrapping his greatcoat tightly round him, resumes his progress across the market square.

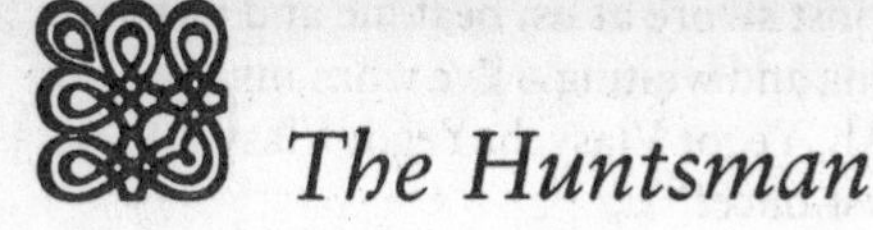

The Huntsman 1885

It is midday, hot and close. Not a puff of cloud in the sky . . . The sun-parched grass looks at you sullenly, despairingly: even a downpour won't turn it green now . . . The forest stands there silent and still, as if gazing somewhere with the tops of its trees, or waiting for something.

Along the edge of the scrub ambles a tall, narrow-shouldered man of about forty with a lazy, rolling gait and wearing a red shirt, patched trousers that were his master's cast-offs, and big boots. He is ambling along the road. To his right is the green of the scrub, to his left a golden sea of ripe rye stretching to the very horizon . . . He is red in the face and sweating. Perched jauntily on his handsome, flaxen head is a small white cap with a stiff jockey peak to it – evidently a present from some young gentleman in a fit of generosity. He has a shooting-bag over his shoulder, with a rumpled black grouse hanging out of it. The man is holding a cocked twelve-bore in his hands and keeping a weather eye on his lean old dog, who has run ahead and is sniffing round the bushes. All is completely quiet, not a sound in the air . . . Every living thing has hidden away from the heat.

'Yegor Vlasych!' the sportsman suddenly hears a soft voice say.

He starts, looks round, and frowns. Right beside him, as though she had just sprung out of the ground, stands a pale-faced peasant woman of about thirty, with a sickle in her hand. She tries to look into his face, and smiles at him bashfully.

'Oh, it's you, Pelageya!' says the sportsman, stopping and slowly uncocking his gun. 'Hm! . . . What brings you to these parts?'

'The girls from our village are working here, so I've come over with them . . . As a labourer, Yegor Vlasych.'

'Uhuh . . .' grunts Yegor Vlasych, and slowly continues on his way.

Pelageya follows him. They walk about twenty paces in silence.

'It's a long time since I saw you last, Yegor Vlasych . . .' says Pelageya, looking fondly at the rippling motion of his shoulders. 'Not since you came into our hut for a drink of water at Eastertide – that was the last time we saw you . . . Yes, you came inside for a minute at Easter, and Lord knows the state you were in – under the influence, you were . . . You just swore at us, beat me and went off again . . . And I've been waiting and waiting – I've worn my eyes out looking for you to come . . . Ah, Yegor Vlasych, Yegor Vlasych! You could have called in once, just once!'

'To do what?'

'Not to do anything, of course, but . . . it is your household, after all . . . Just to see how everything is . . . You are the head . . . Oh, you've shot a little grouse. Ye-gor Vlasych! Why not sit down and have a rest –'

As she says all this, Pelageya keeps laughing like a simpleton and looking up at Yegor's face . . . Her own face positively breathes happiness . . .

'All right, I'll sit down for a bit . . .' Yegor says nonchalantly, choosing a spot between two fir-trees growing side by side. 'What are you standing up for? You sit down too!'

Pelageya sits a little way off in the sun and, ashamed to show how happy she is, keeps covering her smiling mouth with her hand. A couple of minutes pass in silence.

'You could have called in just once,' Pelageya says quietly.

'What for?' sighs Yegor, taking off his cap and mopping his ruddy brow with his sleeve. 'What's the point? Calling in for an hour or two's just a bother, it just gets you worked up, and as for living in the village all the time – my soul couldn't take it . . . You know yourself I've been mollycoddled . . . I need a bed to sleep in, good tea to drink, fine conversations . . . I need everything to be just right . . . and all you've got there in the village is poverty and grime . . . I couldn't stick it for a day. Supposing they even made a decree, saying I had to live with thee come what may, I'd either burn the hut down, or I'd lay hands on myself. I've loved the easy life since I was a kid, you won't change me.'

'And where are you living nowadays?'

'At the master's, Dmitry Ivanych's, as one of his shooters. I provide game for his table, but really . . . he just likes having me around.'

'It's not a proper way of life, that, Yegor Vlasych . . . For other people that's their leisure, but it's as though you've made it your trade . . . like a real job . . .'

'You're stupid, you don't understand anything,' says Yegor, gazing dreamily at the sky. 'Never in all your born days have you understood what kind of a man I am, nor will you . . . You think I'm crazy, I've ruined my life, but to those as knows, I'm the top shot in the whole district. The gents know that all right, and they've even written about me in a magazine. There's not a man can compare with me when it comes to hunting . . . And I don't despise your village jobs because I'm spoilt or proud. You know I never done anything else since I was small than shooting and keeping a dog, don't you? If they took my gun away, I'd use my line, if they took my line away, I'd catch things with my hands. I did a bit of horse-dealing, too, I went the round of the fairs when I had money, and you know yourself that once a peasant's joined the huntsmen and horse-dealers, it's goodbye to the plough. Once that free spirit's got into a man, there's no winkling it out. Just like when a gent goes off with the players, or one of them other arts, he can't work in an office or be a squire again. You're a woman, you don't understand, but you got to.'

'I do understand, Yegor Vlasych . . .'

'You can't do, if you're going to cry about it . . .'

'I – I'm not crying . . .' says Pelageya, turning away. 'It's a sin, Yegor Vlasych! You could at least have some pity and spend a day with me. It's twelve years now since I married you, and . . . and there's never once been *love* between us! . . . I'm not crying . . .'

'Love . . .' mumbles Yegor, scratching the back of his hand. 'There can't be any love. We're man and wife in name only, we're not really, are we? To you I'm a wild man, and to me you're just a simple girl who doesn't understand anything. Call that a match? I'm free, I'm mollycoddled, I come and go as I please, and you're a working-girl, you trudge around in bast shoes all day, you live in dirt, your back's always bent. The way I see myself, when it comes to hunting I'm number one, but when you look at me you just feel pity . . . What kind of a match is that?'

'But we were married in church, Yegor Vlasych!' Pelageya sobs loudly.

'Not freely we weren't . . . You haven't forgotten, have you? You can thank the Count, Sergey Pavlych, for that – and yourself. Because he was so jealous I could shoot better'n him, the Count got me drunk on wine for a month, and when a man's drunk you can make him change his religion, never mind get married. He went and married me off drunk to you, to get his own back . . . A huntsman to a cowherd! You could see I was drunk, so why did you marry me? You're not a serf, you could have gone against his will! 'Course, it's a great thing for a cowherd, marrying a huntsman, but why didn't you stop and think first? Now it's nothing but tears and tribulation. The

Count has his laugh, and you're left crying . . . banging your head against a wall . . .'

They fall silent. Three mallard fly in above the scrub. Yegor looks up and stares after them until they turn into three barely visible points, and come down far beyond the forest.

'What do you do for money?' he asks, turning back to Pelageya.

'Nowadays I work in the fields, but in winter I take in a little baby from the orphanage and feed him with a bottle. I get a rouble and a half a month for it.'

'Uhuh . . .'

Once more there is silence. Over in the cut rye, someone begins softly singing, but breaks off almost immediately. It's too hot to sing . . .

'I hear you've put up a new hut for Akulina,' says Pelageya.

Yegor does not reply.

'So she must be to your liking.'

'That's how it is, such is life!' says the sportsman, stretching. 'Have patience, orphan. I must be going, though, I've been chatting too long . . . I've got to be in Boltovo by nightfall . . .'

Yegor rises, stretches again, and slings his gun over his shoulder. Pelageya stands up.

'So when will you be coming to the village?' she asks quietly.

'No point. I'll never come sober, and a drunk's not much use to you. I get mad when I'm drunk . . . Goodbye, then!'

'Goodbye, Yegor Vlasych . . .'

Yegor sticks his cap on the back of his head, calls his dog over with a tweet of the lips, and continues on his way. Pelageya stays where she is and watches him go . . . She can see his shoulder-blades rippling, the rakish set of his cap, his lazy, casual walk, and her eyes fill with sadness and a deep tenderness . . . Her gaze runs all over the slim, tall figure of her husband and caresses and strokes him . . . He stops, as if feeling this gaze, and looks round . . . He says nothing, but from his face and hunched-up shoulders, Pelageya can tell that he wants to say something to her. She goes up timidly to him and looks at him with pleading eyes.

'Here!' he says, turning aside.

He hands her a very worn rouble note and moves quickly away.

'Goodbye, Yegor Vlasych!' she says, mechanically taking the rouble.

He walks off down the road, which is as long and straight as a taut thong . . . Pale and still, she stands there like a statue, and her eyes devour every stride he takes. But now the red of his shirt merges with the dark of his trousers, his strides become invisible, his dog cannot be distinguished from his boots. Only his little cap can be seen, then . . . Suddenly Yegor turns off sharply to the right into the scrub and his cap disappears among the green.

'Goodbye, Yegor Vlasych!' whispers Pelageya, and rises on tiptoe to try and catch a last glimpse of his little white cap.

The Malefactor

Before the examining magistrate stands a short, extremely skinny little peasant wearing a shirt made of ticking and baggy trousers covered in patches. His face, which is overgrown with hair and pitted with pock-marks, and his eyes, which are barely visible beneath their heavy, beetling brows, wear a grim, sullen expression. He has a whole shock of tangled hair that has not seen a comb for ages, and this lends him an even greater, spider-like grimness. He is barefoot.

'Denis Grigoryev!' the magistrate begins. 'Stand closer and answer my questions. On July 7th of this year Ivan Semyonov Akinfov, the railway watchman, was making his morning inspection of the track, when he came across you at verst 141 unscrewing one of the nuts with which the rails are secured to the sleepers. This nut, to be precise! . . . And he detained you with the said nut in your possession. Is that correct?'

'Wossat?'

'Did all this happen as Akinfov has stated?'

'Course it did.'

'Right. So why were you unscrewing the nut?'

'Wossat?'

'Stop saying "Wossat?" to everything, and answer my question: why were you unscrewing this nut?'

'Wouldn't have been unscrewing it if I hadn't needed it, would I?' croaks Denis, squinting at the ceiling.

'And why did you need it?'

'What, that nut? We make sinkers out of them nuts . . .'

'Who do you mean – "we"?'

'Us folks . . . Us Klimovo peasants, I mean.'

'Listen here, my friend, stop pretending you're an idiot and talk some sense. I don't want any lies about sinkers, do you hear?'

'Lies? I never told a lie in my life . . .' mutters Denis, blinking. 'We got to have sinkers, haven't we, your honour? If you put a live-bait or a worm on, he won't sink without a weight, will he? Hah, "lies" . . .' Denis sniggers. 'Ain't no use in a live-bait that floats on the top! Your perch, your pike and your burbot always go for a bait on the bottom. Only a spockerel takes one that's floating on top, and not always then . . . There aren't no spockerel in our rivers . . . He likes the open more, does that one.'

'Why are you telling me about spockerels?'

'Wossat? You asked me, that's why! The gents round here fish that way, too. Even a little nipper wouldn't try catching fish without a sinker. 'Course, those as don't understand anything about it, they might. Fools are a law unto 'mselves . . .'

'So you are saying you unscrewed this nut in order to make a sinker out of it?'

'What else for? Not for playing fivestones with!'

'But you could have used some lead for a sinker, a piece of shot . . . or a nail . . .'

'You don't find lead on the railway, you got to buy it, and a nail's no good. You won't find anything better than a nut . . . It's heavy, and it's got a hole through it.'

'Stop pretending you're daft, as though you were born yesterday or fell off the moon! Don't you understand, you blockhead, what unscrewing these nuts leads to? If the watchman hadn't been keeping a look-out, a train could have been derailed, people could have been killed! You would have killed people!'

'Lord forbid, your honour! What would I want to kill people for? Do you take us for heathens or some kind of robbers? Glory be, sir, in all our born days we've never so much as thought of doing such things, let alone killed anyone . . . Holy Mother of Heaven save us, have mercy on us . . . What a thing to say!'

'Why do you think train crashes happen, then? Unscrew two or three of these nuts, and you've got a crash!'

Denis sniggers, and peers at the magistrate sceptically.

'Hah! All these years our village's been unscrewing these nuts and the Lord's preserved us, and here you go talking about crashes – me killing people . . . Now if I'd taken a rail out, say, or put a log across that there track, then I grant you that'd brought the train off, but a little nut? Hah!'

'But don't you understand, it's the nuts and bolts that hold the rails to the sleepers!'

'We do understand . . . We don't screw them all off . . . we leave some . . . We're not stupid – we know what we're doing . . .'

Denis yawns and makes the sign of the cross over his mouth.

'A train came off the rails here last year,' says the magistrate. 'Now we know why . . .'

'Beg pardon?'

'I said, now we know why the train came off the rails last year . . . I understand now!'

'That's what you're educated for, to understand, to be our protectors . . . The Lord knew what he was doing, when he gave you understanding . . . You've worked out for us the whys and wherefores, but that watchman, he's just another peasant, he has no understanding, he just grabs you by the collar and hauls you off . . . First work things out, then you can haul us off! It's as they say, if a man's a peasant, he thinks like a peasant . . . You can put down as well, your honour, that he hit me twice on the jaw and in the chest.'

'When your hut was searched, they found a second nut . . . Where did you unscrew that one, and when?'

'You mean the nut that was lying under the little red chest?'

'I don't know where it was lying, but they found it in your hut. When did you unscrew that one?'

'I didn't; Ignashka, One-Eye Semyon's son, gave it me. The one under the little red chest, that is. The one in the sledge out in the yard me and Mitrofan unscrewed.'

'Which Mitrofan is that?'

'Mitrofan Petrov . . . Ain't you heard of him? He makes fishing nets round here and sells them to the gents. He needs a lot of these here nuts. Reckon there must be ten to every net . . .'

'Now listen . . . Article 1081 of the Penal Code says that any damage wilfully caused to the railway, when such damage might endanger the traffic proceeding on it and the accused knew that such damage would bring about an accident – do you understand, *knew*, and you couldn't help but know what unscrewing these nuts would lead to – then the sentence is exile with hard labour.'

'Well, you know best, of course . . . We're benighted folks . . . you don't expect us to understand, do you?'

'You understand perfectly! You're lying, you're putting all this on!'

'Why should I lie? You can ask in the village, if you don't believe me . . . Without a sinker you'll only catch bleak, and they're worse 'n gudgeon – you'll not catch gudgeon without a sinker, either.'

'Now you're going to tell me about those spockerels again!' smiles the magistrate.

'Spockerel don't live in our parts . . . If you float your line on the water with a butterfly on it, you might catch a chub, but seldom even then.'

'All right, now be quiet . . .'

There is silence. Denis shifts from foot to foot, stares at the green baize table-top, and blinks strenuously, as if he's looking into the sun rather than at a piece of cloth. The magistrate is writing quickly.

'Can I go?' asks Denis after a while.

'No. I have to take you into custody and commit you to gaol.'

Denis stops blinking and, raising his thick brows, looks at the official in disbelief.

'How do you mean, gaol? I ain't got time, your honour, I've got to go the fair, I've got to pick up three roubles off Yegor for some lard –'

'Quiet, you're disturbing me.'

'Gaol . . . If there was due cause I'd go, but . . . I been leading a good life . . . What do I have to go for, eh? I haven't stole anything, I haven't been fighting . . . And if it's the arrears you're worried about, your honour, then don't you believe that elder of ours . . . You ask the zemstvo gentleman what deals with us . . . He's no Christian, that elder of ours –'

'Be quiet!'

'I am being quiet . . .' mutters Denis. 'And I'll swear on oath that elder fiddled our assessment . . . There are three of us brothers: Kuzma Grigoryev, Yegor Grigoryev, and me, Denis Grigoryev . . .'

'You're distracting me . . . Hey, Semyon!' shouts the magistrate. 'Take him away!'

'There are three of us brothers,' Denis mutters, as two brawny soldiers grab hold of him and lead him from the courtroom. 'One brother doesn't have to answer for another . . . Kuzma won't pay, so you, Denis, have to answer for him . . . Call that justice! The general our old master's dead, God rest his soul, or he'd show you, you "judges" . . . A judge must know what he's doing, not hand it out any old how . . . He can hand out a flogging if he knows he's got to, if a man's really done wrong . . .'

A Man of Ideas

Midday. Not a sound, not a movement in the sultry air . . . The whole of nature resembles some huge estate, abandoned by God and men alike. Beneath the overhanging foliage of an old lime tree which stands near his quarters, prison superintendent Yashkin and his guest Pimfoff, the local headmaster, are sitting at a small three-legged table. They are both without jackets; their waistcoats are unbuttoned; their red, perspiring faces are immobile, rendered expressionless by the paralysing heat . . . Pimfoff's face has slumped into a state of complete apathy, his eyes are all bleary and his lower lip is hanging down loosely. Some signs of activity can still be detected, however, in Yashkin's eyes and forehead; he seems to be thinking about something . . . They gaze at each other in silence, expressing their torment by puffing and blowing and clapping in the air at flies. A carafe of vodka, some stringy boiled beef and an empty sardine tin encrusted with grey salt are standing on the table. Already they're on the fourth glass . . .

'Dammit,' Yashkin exclaims suddenly and so unexpectedly that a dog dozing by the table gives a start and runs off with its tail between its legs. 'Dammit! I don't care what you say, Filipp Maksimych, there are far too many punctuation marks in Russian!'

'How do you make that out, old man?' Pimfoff asks timidly, extracting the wing of a fly from his glass. 'There may be a large number, but each has its rightful place and purpose.'

'Oh, come off it now! Don't kid me your punctuation marks serve any purpose. It's just a lot of showing-off . . . A chap puts a dozen commas in one line and thinks he's a genius. Take old Kastratoff, the deputy prosecutor – he puts a comma after every word. What on earth for? Dear Sir, comma, while visiting the prison on such-and-such a date, comma, I observed, comma, that the prisoners, comma . . . ugh, it gives you spots before the eyes! And it's just the same in books . . . Colons, semi-colons, ordinary commas, inverted commas – it's enough to make you sick. And some smart alec isn't satisfied with one full stop, he has to go and stick in a whole row of them . . . Why, I ask you, why?'

'It's what the experts demand,' sighs Pimfoff.

'Experts? Charlatans, more likely. They only do it to show off, to pull the wool over people's eyes. Or take spelling, for example. If I spell "mediaeval" with "e" in the middle instead of "ae", does it really make a blind bit of difference?'

'Now you're going too far, Ilya Martynych,' says Pimfoff, offended. 'How can you possibly spell "mediaeval" with "e" in the middle? This is getting beyond a joke.'

Pimfoff drains his glass, blinks with a hurt expression and starts looking in the other direction.

'Yes, I've even been thrashed over that diphthong!' Yashkin continues. 'The teacher called me up to the blackboard one day and dictated: "Our beloved teacher is an outstanding paedagogue." I went and wrote "paedagogue" with just "e" at the beginning. Wrong, bend over! A week later he calls me out again and dictates: "Our beloved teacher is an outstanding paedagogue." This time I wrote "ae". Bend over again! "But sir," I said, "that's not fair. It was you told us 'ae' was correct!" "I was mistaken last week," he says, "yesterday I was reading an article by a member of the Academy which proves that 'paedagogue' is derived from the Greek *paidos* and should be spelt 'ai'. I am in agreement with the Academy of Sciences and it is therefore my bounden duty to give you a thrashing." Which he did. It's the same with my son Vasya. He's always coming home with a thick ear because of that diphthong. If I were Minister of Education, I'd soon stop you people having us on with your diphthongs.'

'I bid you good day,' sighs Pimfoff, blinking rapidly and putting on his jacket. 'When you start attacking education, that really is too much . . .'

'Oh, come, come, come . . . now you're offended,' says Yashkin, placing a restraining hand on Pimfoff's sleeve. 'You know I only say these things for something to talk about . . . Come on, sit down . . . Let's have another!'

The offended Pimfoff sits down, drains his glass and looks in the other direction. Silence descends. Martha, the cook, walks past the table carrying a bucketful of slops. A loud splash is heard, immediately followed by a dog's yelp. Pimfoff's lifeless face softens up even more; any moment now it will melt away completely in the heat and start running down his waistcoat. Furrows gather on Yashkin's brow. He gazes fixedly at the stringy beef and thinks . . . An old soldier comes up to the table, squints morosely at the carafe of vodka and seeing that it is empty, brings a fresh supply . . . They knock back another glass.

'Yes, dammit!' Yashkin says suddenly.

Pimfoff gives a start and looks up fearfully at Yashkin, anticipating new heresies.

'Yes, dammit!' Yashkin says again, gazing thoughtfully at the carafe. 'There are far too many sciences, that's what I reckon!'

'How do you make that out, old man?' Pimfoff asks quietly. 'Which sciences do you reckon are superfluous?'

'All of 'em . . . The more subjects a man knows, the more he starts thinking a lot of himself and becoming conceited . . . I'd scrap the whole lot of 'em, all the so-called learned sciences . . . Oh, come, come . . . now you're offended! You're so touchy, I daren't say a single word. Sit down, have another!'

Martha comes up to the table, and bustling about angrily with her plump elbows, places a pot of thick nettle soup in front of the two friends. Loud slurping and champing noises ensue. Three dogs and a cat appear from nowhere. They stand in front of the table and gaze imploringly at the chewing mouths. The soup is followed by a bowl of semolina pudding, which Martha bangs down on the table so viciously that all the spoons and crusts of bread jump off. Before turning to the pudding the friends knock back another glass in silence.

'Everything's superfluous in this world!' Yashkin remarks suddenly.

Pimfoff drops his spoon on to his lap, gazes fearfully at Yashkin and is about to protest, but his tongue has become weak from so much vodka and is all caught up in the semolina pudding . . . Instead of his usual 'How do you make that out, old man?', the only thing he can manage is a kind of bleat.

'Everything's superfluous,' Yashkin continues. 'The learned sciences, human beings . . . prisons, those flies . . . this pudding . . . And you're superfluous too . . . You may be a decent fellow and believe in God, but you're superfluous too . . .'

'Good day to you, old man!' Pimfoff mumbles, struggling to put on his jacket but completely failing to find the sleeves.

'Here we've been, stuffing and gorging ourselves, and what on earth for? No, it's all superfluous . . . We eat and don't know ourselves why we're eating . . . Oh, come, come . . . now you're offended! You know I only say these things for something to talk about. And where can you go now? Come on, sit down and have a chat . . . Let's have another!'

Silence descends, broken only occasionally by the clinking together of glasses and by drunken burps. The sun is already beginning to sink in the west and the shadow of the lime tree grows longer and longer. Martha comes out and spreads a rug by the table, snorting fiercely and jabbing her arms about. The friends knock back a final glass in silence, settle themselves on the rug and turning their backs to each other, begin to drop off . . .

'Thank the Lord he didn't get round to the creation of the world or the hierarchy today,' thinks Pimfoff. 'That's enough to make anyone's hair stand on end . . .'

Sergeant Prishibeyev

'Staff-Sergeant Prishibeyev! You are accused of using insulting language and behaviour on the 3rd of September of this year towards Police Officer Zappsky, District Elder Berkin, Police Constable Yefimov, Official Witnesses Ivanov and Gavrilov, and six other peasants; whereof the first three aforenamed were insulted by you in the performance of their duties. Do you plead guilty?'

Prishibeyev, a shrivelled little sergeant with a crabbed face, squares his shoulders and answers in a stifled, croaky voice, clipping his words as though on the parade ground:

'Your Honour Mr Justice of the Peace – sir! What it says in the law is: every statement can be mutually contested. I'm not guilty – it's them lot. This all came about because of a dead corpse, God rest his soul. I was walking along on the 3rd – quiet and respectable like – with my wife Anfisa, when suddenly I spy this mob of varied persons standing on the river-bank. "What perfect right has that mob got to be assembled there?" I ask myself. "What do they think they're up to? Where's it written down that common folk can go around in droves?" So I shout, "Hey, you lot – disperse!" I started shoving them, to get them to go indoors, I ordered the constable to lay into them, and –'

'Just one moment. You're not a police officer or elder: is it your business to be breaking up crowds?'

'No, it ain't! It ain't!' voices cry from different corners of the courtroom. 'He's the bane of our lives, yeronner! Fifteen years we've put up with him! Ever since he gave up work and came back here the village ain't been worth living in. He's driving us mad!'

'It's quite true, yeronner,' says the elder who is one of the witnesses. 'The whole village complains of him. He's impossible to live with. Whether we're taking the icons round the village, or there's a wedding, or some do on, say, he's out there shouting at us, kicking up a row and calling for order. He goes about pulling the kids' ears, he spies on our womenfolk to see they're not up to something, like he was their own father-in-law . . . The other day he went round the huts ordering everyone to stop singing and put all their lights out. "There's no law permitting you to sing songs," he says.'

'All right, you'll have time to give evidence later,' says the magistrate. 'At the moment let's hear what else Prishibeyev has to say. Go on, Prishibeyev.'

'Yessir!' croaks the sergeant. 'You were pleased to observe, your Honour, that it's not my business to be breaking up crowds . . . Very good, sir . . . But what if there's a disturbance? We can't allow them to run riot, can we? Where's it written down that the lower orders can do what they like? I can't let them get away with that, sir. And if I don't tell them to break up, and give them what for, who will? No one round here knows what proper discipline is, you might say I'm the only one, your Honour, as knows how to deal with the lower orders, and, your Honour, I know what I'm talking about. I'm not a peasant, I'm a non-commissioned officer, a Q.M.S. retired, I served in Warsaw as a staff-sergeant, sir, after I got an honourable discharge I worked in the fire-brigade, sir, then I had to give up the fire-brigade by virtue of health and worked for the next two years as janitor in an independent classical school for young gentlemen . . . So I know all about discipline, sir. But a peasant's just a simple fellow, he doesn't know any better, so he must do what I tell him – 'cause it's for his own good. Take this business, for example. I break up the crowd and there lying in the sand on the river-bank is the drownded corpse of a dead man. On what possible grounds can he be lying there, I ask myself. Do you call that law and order? Why's the officer just standing there? "Hey, officer," I say, "why aren't you informing your superiors? Maybe this drownded corpse drowned himself, or maybe it smacks of Siberia – maybe it's a case of criminal homicide . . ." But officer Zappsky doesn't give a damn, he just goes on smoking his cigarette. "Who's this bloke giving orders?" he says. "Is he one of yours? Where'd he spring from? Does he think we don't know what to do without his advice?" he says. "Well you can't do, can you, dimwit," says I, "if you're just standing there and don't give a damn." "I informed the inspector yesterday," he says. "Why the inspector?" I ask him. "According to which article of the code? In cases like this, of people being drowned or strangulated and suchlike and so forth, what can the inspector do? It's a capital offence," I says, "a case for the courts . . . You'd better send a dispatch to his Honour the examining magistrate and the justices straightaway," I says. "And first of all," I says, "you must draw up a document and send it to his Honour the Justice of the Peace." But the officer, he just listens to me and laughs. And the peasants the same. They were all laughing, your Honour. I'll testify to that on oath. That one there laughed – and this one – and Zappsky, he laughed too. "What are you all grinning at?" I says. Then the officer says: "Such matters," he says, "are nothing to do with the J.P." Well, the blood rushed to my head when I heard him say that. That is what you said, isn't it, officer?' the sergeant asks, turning to Zappsky.

'That's what I said.'

'Everyone heard you say them words, for all the common people to hear. "Such matters are nothing to do with the J.P." – everyone heard you say them words . . . Well, the blood rushed to my head, your Honour, I went quite weak at the knees. "Repeat to me," says I, "repeat, you . . . so-and-so, what you just said!" He comes out with them same words again . . . I goes up to him. "How dare you say such things," says I, "about his Honour the Justice of the Peace? A police officer and you're against authority – eh? Do you know," I says, "that if he likes, his Honour the Justice of the Peace can have you sent to the provincial gendarmerie for saying them words and proving unreliable? Do you realise," says I, "where his Honour the Justice of the Peace can pack you off to for political words like that?" Then the elder butts in: "The J.P.," he says, "can't deal with anything outside his powers. He only handles minor cases." That's what he said, everyone heard him . . . "How dare you," says I, "belittle authority? Don't you come that game with me, son," I says, "or you'll find yourself in hot water." When I was in Warsaw, or when I was janitor at the independent classical school for young gentlemen, soon as I heard any words as shouldn't be said I'd look out on the street for a gendarme and shout, "Step in here a minute, will you, soldier?" – and report it all to him. But who can you tell things to out here in the country? . . . It made me wild. It really got me, to think of the common people of today indulging in licence and insubordination like that, so I let fly and – not hard of course, just lightly like, just proper, so's he wouldn't dare say such things about your Honour again . . . The officer sided with the elder. So I gave the officer one, too . . . And that's how it started . . . I got worked up, your Honour. But you can't get anywhere without a few clouts, can you? If you don't clout a stupid man, it's a sin on your own head. Especially if there's good reason for it – if he's been causing a disturbance . . .'

'But there are other people appointed to keep public order! That's what the officer, the elder and the constable are there for –'

'Ah, but the officer can't keep an eye on everybody, and he don't understand what I do . . .'

'Well understand now that it's none of your business!'

'Not my business, sir? How do you make that out? That's queer . . . People behave improperly and it's none of my business? What am I supposed to do – cheer them on? They've just been complaining to you that I won't let them sing songs . . . And what good is there in songs, I'd like to know? Instead of getting on with something useful, they sing songs . . . Then they've got a new craze for sitting up late with a light burning. They ought to be in bed asleep, but all you hear is laughing and talking. I've got it all written down!'

'You've got what written down?'

'Who sits up burning a light.'

Prishibeyev takes a greasy slip of paper from his pocket, puts his spectacles on, and reads:

'Peasants what sit up burning a light: Ivan Prokhorov, Savva Mikiforov, Pyotr Petrov. The soldier's widow Shustrova is living in illicit union with Semyon Kislov. Ignat Sverchok dabbles in black magic, and his wife Navra is a witch, she goes around at night milking other people's cows.'

'That's enough!' says the magistrate and turns to examining the witnesses.

Sergeant Prishibeyev pushes his glasses onto his forehead and stares in amazement at the J.P. – who is evidently not on his side. His eyes gleam and start out of his head, and his nose turns bright red. He looks from the J.P. to the witnesses and simply cannot understand why the magistrate should be so het up and why from every corner of the courtroom comes a mixture of angry murmurs and suppressed laughter. The sentence is equally incomprehensible to him: one month in custody!

'For what?!' he asks, throwing up his arms in disbelief. 'By what law?'

And he realises that the world is a changed place, a place impossible to live in. Dark, gloomy thoughts possess him. But when he comes out of the courtroom he sees some peasants huddled together talking about something and by force of a habit which he can no longer control, he squares his shoulders and bawls in a hoarse, irate voice:

'You lot – break it up! Move along! Diss-perse!'

The Misfortune

Grigory Petrov, a turner with the reputation of being the best craftsman and the most useless peasant in the whole of Galchino district, is taking his old woman to the zemstvo hospital. He has nearly thirty versts to cover and the road is so atrocious that even the government mail would be unable to get through, let alone a layabout like Grigory the turner. A biting cold wind buffets straight into him. Wherever he looks, great clouds of snowflakes are whirling round in the air, so that it's difficult to make out whether the snow is coming down from the sky or up off the earth. Forest, fields and telegraph-poles are all indistinguishable through the thick fog of snow, and whenever a particularly strong gust of wind swoops down on Grigory even the yoke above the shafts disappears from sight. The decrepit, feeble little nag can barely drag herself along. All her energy has been used in picking her hooves up out of the deep snow and jerking her head forward. The turner is in a hurry. He keeps fidgeting about on his seat and every so often lashes at the horse's back with his whip.

'Don't you cry, Matryona . . .' he mumbles. 'Just have a bit of patience. We'll get you to the hospital, God willing, and in a trice you'll – it'll be all right . . . Old Pavel Ivanych'll give you some of them drops, or have you bled, or maybe his worship'll decide to rub you down with some of that spirit stuff . . . that'll draw it out of your side for you. Pavel Ivanych'll do his best . . . Of course, he'll holler and stamp his feet, but he'll do his best all right . . . He's a fine gent, real obliging, may the Lord preserve him . . . As soon as we get there, he'll come rushing out of his 'partments and raise hell at me, he will. "What's the meaning of this? What do you think you're up to?" he'll shout at me. "Why didn't you come at the right time? Do you take me for a dog or something, making me run round after you blighters all day? Why didn't you come this morning? Clear out! Get out of my sight. Come back tomorrow!" But I shall say to him: "Pavel Ivanych! Mr Doctor, sir! Your honour!" Get up there, blast you! Hup!'

The turner lashes the horse's back and without looking at the old woman continues to mumble into his beard:

' "Your honour! I swear, as God's my witness . . . here's the cross on it, I set out at first light I did. How could I get here before, if the Lord . . . the holy mother of God . . . was wroth and sent down this blizzard? You can see yourself what it's like . . . Finer horses 'n this wouldn't get through and you can see for yourself, mine's not a horse, it's a bleeding disgrace!" Then Pavel Ivanych'll frown and holler "I know you lot! You've always got an answer! Especially you, Grishka! I worked you out long ago! I bet you called in at half-a-dozen pubs on the way!" So I says: "Your honour! What do you take me for, a villain and a heathen or something? Do you think I'd go off round the pubs, with my old girl here giving up her ghost to God, with her dying? For mercy's sake, sir! May they rot, the pubs, the lot of 'em!" Then Pavel Ivanych'll tell them to carry you into the hospital. And I'll go down at his feet . . . "Pavel Ivanych!" I'll say. "Your honour! We're everlasting grateful to you! Forgive us fools and sinners, don't be hard on us, us peasants! I know we deserve to be thrown out on our necks, but you're so kind, you're going to all this trouble and getting your feet wet in the snow!" Then Pavel Ivanych'll look at me so as you'd think he was going to clout me, and he'll say: "Instead of bashing your head up and down at my feet, you'd do better to stop swilling vodka like a bloody fool, and have a bit of feeling for your old woman. You deserve a thrashing!" – "Yes, a good thrashing, Pavel Ivanych, God help me, a thrashing's what I need! But why shouldn't we bow down low to you, if you're all such benefactors and fathers to us? Your honour, sir! Mark my words – I swear before God now – you can spit in both eyes if I tell a lie: as soon as my Matryona here, you know – recovers, finds her feet again, I'll make anything for your worship that you care to ask me for! A cigarette-case if you want, from real Karelian birch . . . or croquet balls . . . or I can turn you skittles just like those foreign ones . . . I'll make anything you want! I won't take a kopeck off you! In Moscow they'd rook you four roubles for a cigarette-case like that, but I won't take a kopeck." Then the doctor'll laugh and say: "All right, all right . . . I believe you! It's a pity you're such a drunkard, that's all . . ." I know how to handle the gents, Matryona me old mate. There isn't a gent I can't get round. Just so long as the Lord keeps me on this road all right. Cor, what a blizzard! My eyes are full of it.'

And the turner rambles endlessly on. Chattering away mechanically like this at least helps smother the heavy feeling he has inside him. There are many words on the tip of his tongue, but even more thoughts and questions milling in his head. Misfortune has caught the turner unawares, when he was least expecting it, and now he simply cannot come to, pull himself together, work out what has happened. Till now he had lived an unclouded, unruffled existence, in a state of drunken semi-consciousness, knowing neither grief nor joy, and now he suddenly feels this terrible ache. Without warning, the carefree layabout and drunk has found himself in the position of a man with a task to do, a worried man, a man in a hurry and even battling with the elements.

The turner recalls that the misfortune began the previous evening. When he came home yesterday evening, dead drunk as usual, and by long-established tradition started swearing and throwing his fists about, the old woman looked at her ruffian in a way she had never looked at him before. Usually the look in her aged eyes was tormented, meek, like that of a dog that is underfed and often beaten, but now she stared at him sternly and unwaveringly, as saints on icons do, or people dying. Those strange, ill-boding eyes were the start of the misfortune. Stunned, the turner begged his neighbour's horse from him and now was taking the old woman to the hospital, in the hope that Pavel Ivanych would use his powders and ointments to give her back her old look.

'And if, er . . .' he mumbles, 'if Pavel Ivanych asks you, Matryona, if I beat you, you say "Never, sir!" Nor I shan't, any more. Here's the cross on it. And I didn't ever beat you for spite, did I? I just beat you, like. I feel sorry for you, I do. Another man might not feel much, but here am I taking you to hospital . . . doing my best for you. Ah, this snow, this snow! Thy will be done, Lord, only grant we stay on the road, that's all . . . Your side hurt, does it? Matryona, why won't you say anything? Does your side hurt, I say?'

He finds it odd that the snow does not melt on the old woman's face, odd that her face seems to have stretched out unusually long, to have taken on a greyish-white, dirty waxen colour, and come over serious and forbidding.

'Ha, you're a fool, Matryona!' mutters the turner. 'I'm saying all this on my soul, before God, and you just . . . Well, you're a fool, that's what! I've a mind not to take you to Pavel Ivanych after all!'

The turner lets go of the reins and ponders. To glance round at the old woman is too terrible: he can't do it! To ask her some question and get no answer is also terrible. At last, to put an end to his uncertainty, without looking round he feels for her cold hand and lifts it up. Her arm falls back like a cudgel.

'She's dead then . . . What a business!'

And the turner cries; not so much from pity as from frustration. He thinks to himself, how quickly everything in this world is over! His misfortune had scarcely begun before it had reached its conclusion. He had had no time to live with the old woman again, to talk to her properly, feel sorry for her, before she was dead. He had lived with her for forty years – yet these forty years had passed by in a kind of fog. Through all his drinking, brawling and poverty he had lost sight of life itself. And, as ill luck would have it, the old woman had died at the very time when he felt pity for her, when he felt that he could not live without her, that he had wronged her grievously.

'She used to go begging round the village, too!' he remembers. 'I used to send her out myself to beg bread from people. What a business . . . She should have lived another ten years, the fool, or she'll think I was really like that. Holy mother, where the devil do I think I'm going? It's not a doctor she needs now, it's a burial. Whoaa! Back!'

The turner brings the sled round and clouts the little horse with all his might. The road is getting worse from hour to hour. Now the yoke is completely invisible. Occasionally, the sled runs over a young fir-tree, for a second the turner glimpses some dark object which scratches him across the hands, then his vision is filled once more with swirling white.

'To live life over again . . .' thinks the turner.

He remembers that some forty years ago Matryona was young, beautiful, light-hearted, and came from a rich household. They had married her to him because they were so taken with his craftsmanship. Everything pointed to a happy life together, but the trouble was, he seemed never to have woken up again after getting drunk at the wedding and collapsing onto the stove. He can remember the wedding, but what came after he can't for the life of him remember, except drinking, lying about on the stove, and brawling. So forty years had gone to waste.

The white clouds of snow gradually begin to go grey. Dusk is closing in.

'Where do I think I'm going?' he rouses himself with a start. 'I've got to bury her, and I'm still taking her to the hospital . . . I'm going barmy!'

The turner brings the sled round once more and once more starts whipping the horse. The little nag summons up all her strength and with a snort breaks into a very slow trot. Again and again the turner lashes her across the back . . . Behind him he can hear something clumping, and although he won't look round he knows it is the corpse's head knocking against the sled. The air gets darker and darker, the wind colder and more biting . . .

'To live life over again . . .' thinks the turner. 'I'd get myself a new lathe, take in orders . . . and then give the money to the old girl. I would!'

And suddenly the reins drop from his grasp. He tries to find them again, to pick them up; but his hands won't move . . .

'That's all right . . .' he thinks. 'The horse'll get there on her own, she knows the way. I need a nap now . . . Before we get round to the burial, the funeral service, I could do with a kip.'

The turner shuts his eyes and dozes. A little while later he hears the horse stop. He opens his eyes and sees in front of him something dark, like a hut or a hayrick . . .

He wants to get off the sled and find out what it is, but there is such a weariness in all his limbs that he'd rather freeze than move from where he is . . . So he sinks back peacefully in sleep.

He wakes up in a large room with painted walls. Bright sunlight is streaming in through the windows. The turner sees people in front of him and immediately wants to show them he's a respectable man who knows what's what.

'A funeral, brothers, a funeral for my old woman!' he says. 'Go and fetch the priest –'

'Yes yes, all right!' someone's voice interrupts him. 'Just lie there and keep still!'

'Saviour! Pavel Ivanych!' exclaims the turner in amazement, seeing the doctor in front of him. 'Your honour! My benefactor!'

He wants to leap up and throw himself down at the feet of Medicine, but can feel that his arms and legs won't obey him.

'Your honour! My legs – where are my legs? Where are my arms?'

'You can say goodbye to your arms and legs . . . You got them frostbitten! Now, now . . . what are you crying for? You've had your life and be thankful! You've had your three score, haven't you? That'll do you, then!'

'But the pity of it! . . . Your honour, the pity of it all! I'm sorry, sir, I'm sorry, but just give me another five or six years . . .'

'What for?'

'The horse isn't mine, I've got to give it back . . . And to bury my old woman . . . Ah, how soon everything in this world is over! Your honour, Pavel Ivanych! I'll make you a cigarette-case from Karelian birch, sir, my very best! I'll turn some croquet balls for you . . .'

The doctor shrugs impatiently and walks out of the ward. That's it, then, turner!

1886

Romance with Double-Bass

Pitsikatoff was making his way on foot from town to Prince Bibuloff's country villa where 'a musical evening with dancing' was to take place in celebration of the engagement of the Prince's daughter. A gigantic double-bass in a leather case reposed on Pitsikatoff's back. He was walking along the bank of a river whose cooling waters rolled on if not majestically, then at least most poetically.

'How about a dip?' he thought.

In the twinkling of an eye he had taken off his clothes and immersed his body in the cooling stream. It was a glorious evening, and Pitsikatoff's poetic soul began to attune itself to the harmony of its surroundings. And imagine what sweet emotions filled his spirit when, swimming a few yards upstream, he beheld a beautiful young woman sitting on the steep bank fishing! A mixture of feelings welled up and made him stop and catch his breath: memories of childhood, regret for the past, awakening love . . . Love? But was he not convinced that for him love was no longer possible? Once he had lost his faith in humanity (his beloved wife having run off with his best friend, Sobarkin the bassoon), a sense of emptiness had filled his breast and he had become a misanthrope. More than once he had asked himself: 'What is life? What is it all for? Life is a myth, a dream . . . mere ventriloquy . . .'

But now, standing before this sleeping beauty (there could be no doubt she was asleep), suddenly, against his will, he felt stirring in his breast something akin to love. He stood a long time before her, devouring her with his gaze . . .

Then, sighing deeply, he said to himself: 'Enough! Farewell, sweet vision! It's time I was on my way to his Excellency's ball . . .'

He took one more look at the fair one and was just about to swim back when an idea flashed into his mind.

'I'll leave her a token!' he thought. 'I'll tie something to her line . . . It'll be a surprise – "from an unknown admirer".'

Pitsikatoff quietly swam to the bank, culled a large bouquet of wild flowers and waterlilies, bound them together with goosefoot and attached them to the end of the line.

The bouquet sank to the bottom, pulling the gaily painted float after it.

Good sense, the laws of Nature and the social station of my hero would seem to demand that the romance should come to an end at this point, but (alas!) the author's destiny is inexorable: because of circumstances beyond the author's control the romance did not end with the bouquet. In defiance of common sense and the entire natural order, our poor and plebeian Pitsikatoff was fated to play an important role in the life of a rich and beautiful young gentlewoman.

On reaching the bank, Pitsikatoff got a shock. His clothes were gone. Stolen . . . While he had been gazing in admiration at the fair one, anonymous villains had pinched everything except his double-bass and his top-hat.

'Accursed Fate!' he exclaimed. 'Oh Man, thou generation of vipers! It is not so much the deprivation of my garments that perturbs me (for clothing is but vanity), as the thought of having to go naked and thereby offending against public morality.'

He sat down on his instrument case and began to think how he was going to get out of this dreadful situation. 'I can't go to Prince Bibuloff's without any clothes,' he mused. 'There will be ladies present. What is more, the thieves have stolen not only my trousers, but also the rosin I had in my trouser pocket!'

He thought long and painfully, until his head ached.

'Aha!' – at last he'd got it – 'not far from here there's a little bridge surrounded by bushes. I can sit under there till nightfall and then make my way in the dark to the nearest cottage . . .'

And so, having adopted this plan, Pitsikatoff put on his top-hat, swung the double-bass onto his back and padded off towards the bushes. Naked, with his musical instrument slung over his shoulders, he resembled some ancient mythological demigod.

But now, gentle reader, while our hero sits moping under the bridge, let us leave him for a while and turn to the young lady who was fishing. What has become of her? When the fair creature awoke and could see no sign of her float she hurriedly tugged on the line. The line tautened, but neither float nor hook appeared. Presumably Pitsikatoff's bouquet had become water-logged and turned into a dead weight.

'Either I've caught a big fish,' thought the girl, 'or the line has got entangled.'

After another couple of tugs she decided it was the latter.

'What a pity!' she thought. 'They bite so much better towards dusk. What shall I do?'

In the twinkling of an eye the eccentric young lady had cast aside her diaphanous garments and immersed her beauteous person in the cooling stream right up to her marble-white shoulders. The line was all tangled up in the bouquet, and it was no easy matter extricating the hook, but perseverance triumphed in the end, and some fifteen minutes later our lovely heroine emerged from the water all glowing and happy, holding the hook in her hand.

But a malevolent fate had been watching out for her too: the wretches who had stolen Pitsikatoff's clothing had removed hers as well, leaving behind only her jar of bait.

'What am I to do?' she wept. 'Go home in this state? No, never! I would rather die! I shall wait until nightfall, then walk as far as old Agatha's cottage in the dark and send her to the house for some clothes . . . And in the meantime I'll go and hide under the little bridge.'

Our heroine scuttled off in that direction, bending low and keeping to where the grass was longest. She crept in under the bridge, saw a naked man there with artistic mane and hairy chest, screamed, and fell down in a swoon.

Pitsikatoff got a fright too. At first he took the girl for a naiad.

'Perhaps 'tis a water-sprite,' he thought, 'come to lure me away?', and felt flattered by the notion, since he had always had a high opinion of his appearance. 'But if it is not a sprite but a human being, how is this strange metamorphosis to be explained? What is she doing here under the bridge, and what has befallen her?'

As he pondered these questions the fair one recovered consciousness.

'Do not kill me!' she whispered. 'I am the Princess Bibuloff. I beseech you! They'll give you lots of money! I was disentangling my fishing-hook just now and some thieves stole my new dress and shoes and everything!'

'Mademoiselle,' Pitsikatoff replied plaintively, 'they've stolen my clothes too – *and* the rosin I had in my trouser pocket!'

Usually people who play the double-bass or the trombone are not very inventive, but Pitsikatoff was a pleasant exception.

'Mademoiselle,' he said after a pause, 'I see that my appearance embarrasses you. You must agree, though, that there is just as good reason for me to stay under here as for you. But I have had an idea: how would it be if you were to get into the case of my double-bass and close the lid? Then you wouldn't see me . . .'

So saying, Pitsikatoff dragged the double-bass out of its case. Just for a moment he wondered whether he might be profaning Art by using his case thus, but his hesitation did not last long. The fair one lay down in the case and curled up in a ball, while he fastened the straps with a feeling of pleasure that nature had endowed him with such intelligence.

'Now, mademoiselle, you cannot see me,' he said. 'You can lie there and relax, and when it gets dark I shall carry you to your parents' house. I can come back here for the double-bass afterwards.'

When darkness fell Pitsikatoff heaved the case with the fair one inside onto his shoulders and padded off towards Bibuloff's villa. His plan was that he should walk as he was to the nearest cottage, get some clothing there, and then go on . . .

'It's an ill wind that blows nobody good . . .' he thought, bending under his burden and stirring up the dust with his bare feet. 'No doubt Bibuloff will reward me handsomely for the deep concern that I have shown over his daughter's fate.'

'I trust you are comfortable, mademoiselle?' he enquired with a note of gallantry in his voice like that of a gentleman inviting a lady to dance a quadrille. 'Please don't stand on ceremony. Do make yourself at home in there.'

Suddenly the gallant Pitsikatoff thought he saw ahead of him two figures shrouded in darkness. Peering more closely he assured himself that it was not an optical illusion: there really were two figures walking ahead and – they were carrying bundles of some kind . . .

'The thieves!' it flashed through his mind. 'I bet that's who it is! And they're carrying something – must be our clothes!'

Pitsikatoff put the case down at the side of the road and chased after the figures.

'Stop!' he shouted. 'Stop thief!'

The figures looked round, and seeing they were pursued, took to their heels. The Princess continued to hear the sound of rapid footsteps and cries of 'Stop, stop!' for a long time, then all was quiet.

Pitsikatoff was quite carried away by the chase, and no doubt the fair one would have been lying out there at the roadside for a long time to come, had it not been for a lucky chance. It so happened that Pitsikatoff's two colleagues, Dronin the flute and Flamboisky the clarinet, were making their way along the road at that same time. Tripping over the double-bass case, they looked at each other with expressions of surprise and puzzlement.

'A double-bass!' said Dronin. 'Why, it's old Pitsikatoff's! How could it have got here?'

'Something must have happened to him,' Flamboisky decided. 'Either he's got drunk or he's been robbed . . . Anyway we can't leave his instrument lying here. Let's take it with us.'

Dronin heaved the case onto his back and the musicians walked on.

'What a ruddy weight!' the flautist kept groaning all the way. 'I wouldn't play a monster like this for all the tea in China . . . Phew!'

When they arrived at Prince Bibuloff's villa they deposited the case at the place reserved for the orchestra and went off to the buffet.

By now the chandeliers and candelabras were being lit. Princess Bibuloff's fiancé, Counsellor Sikofantoff, a nice handsome official from the Ministry of Communications, was standing in the drawing-room with his hands in his pockets, chatting to Count Tipplovitch. They were talking about music.

'You know, Count,' said Sikofantoff, 'in Naples I was personally acquainted with a violinist who could do absolute marvels. You'll hardly believe it, but he could get the most fantastic trills out of a double-bass – an ordinary double-bass – stupendous! He could play Strauss waltzes on the thing!'

'Come now, that's scarcely –' the Count objected.

'I assure you he could. He could even play Liszt's Hungarian rhapsody! I shared a hotel room with him and to pass the time I got him to teach me Liszt's Hungarian rhapsody on the double-bass.'

'Liszt's Hungarian . . ..? Come now . . . you're pulling my leg.'

'Ah, you don't believe me?' laughed Sikofantoff. 'Then I'll prove it to you straight away. Let's get an instrument!'

Bibuloff's prospective son-in-law and the Count made for the orchestra. They went over to the double-bass, quickly undid the straps and . . . oh, calamity!

But at this point, while the reader gives free rein to his imagination in picturing the outcome of this musical debate, let us return to Pitsikatoff . . . The unfortunate musician, not having caught up with the thieves, went back to the spot where he had left his case but could see no sign of his precious burden. Lost in bewilderment, he walked up and down several times in vain, and decided he must be on the wrong road . . .

'How awful!' he thought, tearing his hair and feeling his blood run cold. 'She'll suffocate in that case. I've murdered her!'

Pitsikatoff tramped the roads till midnight in search of the case and then, exhausted, retired under the bridge.

'I'll look for it in the morning,' he decided.

But his dawn search proved equally fruitless, and he decided to stay under the bridge again until nightfall . . .

'I shall find her!' he muttered, taking off his top-hat and tearing his hair. 'Even if it takes me a whole year – I'll find her!'

* * *

And to this day the peasants who live in those parts will tell you that at night near the little bridge you can sometimes see a naked man all covered in hair and wearing a top-hat . . . and occasionally from beneath the bridge you can hear the melancholy groaning of a double-bass.

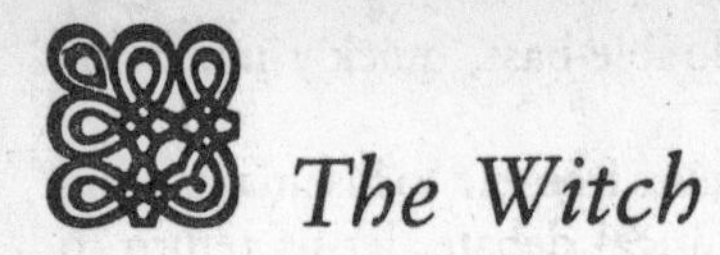

The Witch

It was nearing midnight. Subdeacon Savely Gykin lay on the huge bed in his watchman's lodge adjoining the church. He was wide awake, although it was his habit to drop off at the same time as the hens. From one end of a greasy patchwork quilt his coarse ginger hair peeped out; his big unwashed feet stuck up at the other. He was listening. His lodge was built into the church wall, and its one and only window looked out on open country. Out there a veritable battle was raging. Who was hounding whom, and for whose destruction all this pother had been stirred up in nature, it was hard to say, but judging by the sinister unending roar, someone was getting very short shrift. A vanquishing force was chasing someone across the countryside, kicking up a row in the forest and on the church roof, banging its fists viciously on the window, ranting and raving, while its victim howled and whimpered . . . The pitiful cries could be heard outside the window, then above the roof, then in the stove. They sounded not like cries for help but of despair; all hope was gone, it was too late. The snow-drifts were covered with a thin crust of ice; tear-drops trembled on them and upon the trees, while the roads and pathways were swimming in a dark sludge of mud and melted snow. In a word, the earth was thawing, but because of the dark night the sky had not noticed this, and was still pouring down fresh snow-flakes on the melting earth for all it was worth. And the wind was rampaging like a drunk . . . It would not let this snow settle on the ground but whirled it about in the darkness at its whim.

Gykin listened hard to this music and scowled. The fact was that he knew, or at least had a strong suspicion, what all the racket outside the window was leading up to and who was responsible for it.

'Oh yes, I know!' he mumbled, ticking someone off with his finger beneath the quilt. 'I know all right!'

On a stool by the window sat Raïsa Nilovna, the subdeacon's wife. A tin lamp standing on another stool cast a flickering watery light, as if shy and uncertain of itself, over her broad shoulders, the beautiful, inviting curves of her body, and her thick plait that reached to the ground. She was sewing some sacks out of coarse hessian. Her hands moved quickly, but the rest of her body, her eyes, brows, full lips and white neck, engrossed in the mechanical, monotonous work, were absolutely still and might have been asleep. Only from time to time did she raise her head to ease her weary neck, glance quickly over to the window where the blizzard was raging, and then bend over the hessian again. Her beautiful face with its dimpled cheeks and turned-up nose expressed nothing at all, no desires, no joy, no sadness; just as a beautiful fountain expresses nothing when it is not playing.

But now she came to the end of a sack, cast it aside, stretched luxuriously and turned her dull motionless gaze to the window . . . The snowflakes made brief white blobs on the window-panes, which were swimming with tears. Each flake would fall on the glass, take a look at the subdeacon's wife and melt . . .

'Come and lie down!' grunted the subdeacon.

His wife did not reply. Suddenly, though, her eyelashes flicked and her eyes sprang to life. Savely, who had been studying her expression closely all the time from beneath his quilt, stuck his head out and asked:

'What's up?'

'Oh nothing . . . sounds like someone's coming,' she replied in a soft voice.

The subdeacon flung the quilt off with his arms and legs, knelt on the bed, and stared blankly at his wife. The lamp cast its timid glow over his hairy, pock-marked face and flickered upon his coarse, tousled hair.

'Can you hear it?' his wife asked.

Through the monotonous wail of the snow-storm he caught a barely perceptible sound, a thin tinkling whine, like the drone of a mosquito when it is trying to land on your cheek and is angry at being prevented.

'It's the post,' grunted Savely, sitting back on his heels.

The post-road was three versts away from the church. When a strong wind was blowing from that direction, the inhabitants of the lodge could hear the bell of the mail-coach ringing.

'Goodness, fancy anyone wanting to be out in this weather!' sighed the subdeacon's wife.

'Their work's official. They do what they're told . . .'

The whining note hung briefly in the air, then stopped.

'They've passed!' said Savely, lying down.

But before he had time to cover himself with the quilt, his ears detected the unmistakable sound of the bell. The subdeacon glanced anxiously at his wife, sprang out of bed and began waddling up and down in front of the stove. The bell sounded for a while, then stopped once more, as if it had fallen off.

'Gone again . . .' muttered the subdeacon, halting and peering intently at his wife.

But just at that moment the wind beat on the window and carried the thin tinkling whine with it . . . Savely turned pale, croaked and again began flopping about the floor in his bare feet.

'They're being led astray!' he rasped, with a fierce look at his wife. 'You hear me? Led astray! I know what's going on all right! D'you think – do you think I don't see it?' he spluttered. 'I see it all, damn you!'

'See what?' his wife asked in a soft voice, not taking her eyes off the window.

'That it's all your doing, you devil! Your doing, damn you! You caused this storm, you made the post lose its way – you did it all, all!'

'You're off your head, silly,' his wife remarked calmly.

'I've been noticing things for a long time! First day we were married, I knew there was bitch's blood in you!'

'Ugh!' Raïsa exclaimed with a start, hunching her shoulders and crossing herself. 'Cross yourself too, idiot!'

'Once a witch, always a witch,' Savely went on in a hollow, tearful voice, hastily blowing his nose on the hem of his nightshirt. 'You may be my wife, you may count as clergy, but I'd say what you really are even at confession . . . Why, it stands to reason, so help me! Last year we had a blizzard on the Eve of Prophet Daniel and the Three Young Men – and what happened? That craftsman dropped in to warm himself. Then on the day of Alexis the Man of God the ice broke up on the river and in came the constable . . . Spent the whole night here nattering with you, damn him, and when he left in the morning and I took a good look at him, he had rings under his eyes and his cheeks were all hollow! Eh? During the Summer Fast there was two thunder-storms and each time the gamekeeper came in to spend the night. I saw it all, curse him! All of it! Yes, that's made her blush! Redder than a beetroot!'

'You never saw anything . . .'

'Oh yes I did! And this winter before Christmas on the Ten Martyrs of Crete, when that snow-storm lasted all day and night –

remember? – the Marshal's clerk lost his way and finished up here, the blighter . . . Fancy you falling for a miserable little clerk like that! He wasn't worth stirring up God's weather for! A snotty-nosed little devil not two foot off the ground, his mug covered in pimples and his neck all awry . . . If he'd been handsome, it'd make sense, but he was as ugly as sin!'

The subdeacon paused for breath, wiped his mouth and cocked his ear. There was no sound of the bell, but then a sudden gust of wind leapt over the roof and the tinkling started again in the darkness outside.

'Same thing now!' Savely went on. 'The post hasn't lost its way by accident. Spit in my eye if they aren't looking for you! Oh, the devil knows his job, he's a good helpmate! Round and round he'll lead them and land them up here. Oh yes! I see your game! You can't hide it from me! Devil's chatter-box, lustful pagan! As soon as the storm began, I knew what you were up to.'

'What an idiot!' laughed his wife. 'Do you really think in that stupid head of yours that I cause bad weather?'

'Hm . . . You can laugh! Maybe you do, maybe you don't, but what I know is this: as soon as your blood begins to itch, there's bad weather, and as soon as there's bad weather, some stupid fool or other gets blown in here. Without fail! So it must be your doing!'

To add weight to his words, the subdeacon placed one finger on his brow, closed his left eye and began intoning:

'O folly incarnate! O accursed Judas! If thou art a human being and not a witch, stop and ask yourself: suppose they weren't craftsmen, gamekeepers or clerks, but the devil in human form? Eh? What about that?'

'Savely, this is nonsense,' Raïsa sighed and looked at her husband pityingly. 'When my Papa was alive and lived here, all kinds of people used to come to him to be cured of the fever. They came from the village, the settlements and the Armenian farmsteads. They used to come here every day – and no one called them devils, did they? But now if anyone so much as drops in once a year to warm up when the weather's rough, you think it's the end of the world, you dolt, and start getting all sorts of ideas.'

The logic of his wife's argument affected Savely. He planted his bare feet wide apart, lowered his head, and pondered. His suspicions had not yet become firm convictions, and his wife's natural, unconcerned tone had thrown him completely off balance; nevertheless, after a little thought he shook his head and said:

'It's never old men or cripples, either – it's always young ones who want to come in here for the night . . . So why's that? Nor's it just warmth they're after, they're up to mischief. No, woman, there's no creature on earth more cunning than womankind! There's not an ounce of real brain in you, a sparrow's got more intelligence, but as for your guile – your devilish guile – may the Holy Mother of God preserve us! There's the bell again! The storm was only just starting, but I knew exactly what you were up to! You've been witching, you spideress!'

'Oh leave off, damn you!' said his wife, losing patience. 'Why have you got your teeth into me?'

'I'll tell you why. If anything happens tonight – God forbid that it should, but if it does . . . if it does – are you listening to me? – then I'm going off first thing tomorrow morning to Dyadkovo to see Father Nikodim and tell him everything. It's like this, I'll say, I beg you to forgive me, Father Nikodim, but she's a witch. How do I know? Mm . . . you wish me to tell you? Very well then. It's like this, I'll say. Then you'll be for it, woman! You'll be punished not only on the Day of Judgment, but in this life, too! There are prayers in the prayer-book specially for dealing with the likes of you!'

Suddenly there was a bang on the window, so loud and out of the ordinary that Savely turned pale and his knees buckled with fright. His wife jumped up and also turned pale.

'For God's sake, let us in to the warm!' came a deep, shaking voice. 'Who's in there? Let us in, will you, we've lost our way!'

'Who is it?' asked the subdeacon's wife, too scared to look at the window.

'The post!' a second voice replied.

'So your devilling's worked!' said Savely, turning aside. 'I was right then . . . Well, just you watch it!'

The subdeacon jumped up and down a couple of times, sprawled onto the bed and turned his face to the wall with an angry snort. Soon he felt a cold blast in the back. The door creaked and the tall figure of a man, plastered in snow from head to foot, appeared in the doorway. Standing behind was another figure, equally white . . .

'Shall I bring in the bags?' asked the second figure in a deep hoarse voice.

'Can't leave them out there!'

So saying, the first figure began to untie his hood, but without waiting till it was undone, he wrenched it off along with his peak cap and hurled them both angrily towards the stove. Then he pulled off his greatcoat, threw it in the same direction and without a word of greeting began to stride about the room.

He was a fair-haired young post-officer in a shabby old uniform and dirty yellowish-brown boots. After warming himself by pacing to and fro, he sat down at the table, stretched his dirty boots out towards Raïsa's sacks and propped his head up on his fist. His face, pale but with red blotches, still bore traces of the pain and terror he had just come through. Distorted with rage, still bearing the fresh traces of recent physical and mental suffering, and with snow melting on the eyebrows, moustache and small round beard, it was beautiful.

'What a dog's life!' grumbled the postman, his eyes roaming all over the walls as if he could not believe he was in the warm. 'We almost had it! But for your light, I don't know what would have happened . . . To hell with this dog's life! When's it all going to end? Where are we then?' he asked, lowering his voice and glancing up quickly at the subdeacon's wife.

'Gulyayevsky Hill, General Kalinovsky's estate,' she replied, startled, and blushed.

'Hear that, Stepan?' the postman turned to the driver, who had stopped in the doorway with a large leather bag on his back. 'We're on Gulyayevsky Hill!'

'Cor . . . way off!'

After uttering the last two words in the form of a hoarse, broken sigh, the driver went out again, and soon after came in with another, smaller, mailbag; then he went out once again and this time came back with the postman's sabre on a wide belt, rather like the long flat sword with which Judith is depicted on popular woodcuts before the couch of Holofernes. Having piled the bags along the wall, he went and sat down in the outer passage and lit his pipe.

'Maybe you'd care for some tea after your journey?' asked the subdeacon's wife.

'No time for tea-drinking!' frowned the postman. 'We must warm up quickly and move on, otherwise we'll be late for the mail-train. Ten minutes and we must be off. Only I'm afraid we're going to need someone to come along as guide . . .'

'It's an infliction, this weather,' sighed the subdeacon's wife.

'Y-es . . . And you – what do you do here?'

'Oh, we live here, we're attached to the church . . . We're members of the clergy . . . That's my husband over there! Savely, get up and say hello! This used to be a separate parish, but eighteen months ago they closed the church down. Of course, when the family lived on the estate and there were people here, it was worth keeping the church open, but you can imagine, once they went, what was there for the clergy to live on, seeing as how the nearest village is Markovka, and that's more than five versts away! Now Savely's on the unattached list and . . . and does the watchman's job. He's responsible for keeping an eye on the church . . .'

And there and then the postman also learned that if Savely were to go and see the General's wife and ask her for a note to the Bishop, he would be given a good living; but he wouldn't go to see the General's wife, because he was lazy and scared of people.

'All the same, we still count as clergy . . .' added the subdeacon's wife.

'What do you live on?' asked the postman.

'There's a hay meadow and vegetable plots that go with the church. Not that we get much out of them . . .' sighed the subdeacon's wife. 'Father Nikodim from Dyadkovo, he's an old grasper, he celebrates here on St Nicholas summertide and St Nicholas wintertide, and in return he takes practically everything for himself. There's no one who'll stick up for us!'

'Liar!' rasped Savely. 'Father Nikodim is a holy man, a luminary of the church, and whatever he takes, he's entitled to.'

'You've an angry one there!' chuckled the postman. 'Been married long?'

'Three years last Sunday before Lent. My Papa used to be subdeacon here and when his life was drawing to its close, to make sure the living was passed on to me, he went to the Consistory and asked them to send me an unmarried subdeacon as a bridegroom. And I married him.'

'Aha, so you killed two birds with one stone!' said the postman to Savely's back. 'A job and a wife in one go.'

Savely's foot twitched impatiently and he pressed himself closer to the wall. The postman got up from the table, stretched and sat down on a mailbag. Then, after a moment's thought, he plumped up the mailbags, transferred the sabre to a different position and stretched himself out full-length with one leg reaching to the floor.

'A dog's life,' he muttered, putting his hands behind his head and closing his eyes. 'I wouldn't wish it on the boldest Tartar.'

All was soon silent. The only sounds were of Savely wheezing and the postman breathing slowly and evenly in his sleep and emitting a deep, prolonged 'k-hhhh' each time he breathed out. Every so often some kind of little wheel creaked in his throat, or his leg jerked and brushed against the mailbag.

Savely rolled over beneath the quilt and gazed slowly round the room. His wife was sitting on the stool looking at the postman's face, her cheeks pressed between the palms of her hands. Her eyes were staring, as if she had been taken by surprise and had a fright.

'What are you gawping at?' Savely whispered angrily.

'Never you mind! Go to sleep!' his wife replied, without taking her eyes off the fair head.

Savely emptied his lungs in one angry breath and turned abruptly to the wall. Three minutes later he rolled over restlessly again, knelt up in bed, sat back with his hands on the pillow, and peered suspiciously at his wife. She was still staring at the visitor, motionless. Her cheeks looked paler and her eyes burned with a strange fiery light. The subdeacon made a noise in his throat, crawled across the bed on his stomach, went over to the postman and put a piece of cloth over his face.

'What's that for?' asked his wife.

'To keep the light off his eyes.'

'The light? Why not put it out altogether then?'

Glancing sceptically at his wife, Savely bent down to blow out the lamp, but straightway checked himself and flung up his hands.

'If that's not the devil's own cunning!' he exclaimed. 'Eh? I ask you, is there a creature on earth more cunning than you women?'

'Ahh, you black-robed devil!' hissed his wife, grimacing with annoyance. 'Just you wait!'

And settling herself more comfortably, she went back to gazing at the postman.

No matter that his face was hidden. It was not so much this man's face that she found absorbing, as his general appearance, his novelty. His chest was broad and powerful, his hands slender and beautiful, his legs straight and muscular, much more beautiful and manly than Savely's 'two little stubs'. There was simply no comparison.

'I may be a black-robed unclean spirit,' Savely said after standing there a while, 'but it's no good them sleeping here . . . No . . . Their work's official – we'll be the ones get the blame if we hold them up.

They've a job to do and they must do it, it's no good them sleeping . . . Hey, you!' Savely shouted into the outer passage. 'You, driver . . . what's your name? Want me to guide you? Get up, it's no good you sleeping in charge of the mail!'

And in his temper Savely darted towards the postman and tugged at his sleeve.

'Sir, sir! If you're going, go, if not, then you . . . You oughtn't to be asleep.'

The postman leapt up, sat down again, looked round the room bleary-eyed and lay down once more.

'You've got to be off,' Savely gabbled away, tugging at his sleeve. 'What's the mail for, eh, if not to get to places in good time? I'll guide you.'

The postman opened his eyes. Warmed and enervated by the sweetness of first sleep, still not fully awake, he had a hazy vision of the white neck and steady voluptuous gaze of the subdeacon's wife, closed his eyes and smiled, as if it were all a dream.

'How can they travel in weather like this?' he heard a woman's soft voice say. 'What they need is a good long sleep!'

'And the mail?' Savely said in alarm. 'Who'll take that then? Are you going to? You?'

The postman opened his eyes again, looked at the way the dimples were moving on the face of the subdeacon's wife, remembered where he was, understood what Savely was saying. The thought of having to drive on in the cold dark night sent a chill through his whole body, and he shuddered.

'Five more minutes' sleep won't matter . . .' he yawned. 'We've missed the connection anyway . . .'

'We might just make it!' came a voice from the outer passage. 'You never know, if we're lucky the train may be late, too.'

The postman stood up, stretched luxuriously and started to put on his greatcoat.

At the sight of the visitors preparing to leave, Savely positively neighed with pleasure.

'Give us a hand then!' the driver shouted to him, heaving a mailbag off the floor.

The subdeacon darted forward and helped him drag all the mail outside. The postman began unpicking the knot on his hood. And the subdeacon's wife looked deep into his eyes, as if she intended stealing right into his soul.

'Stay and have some tea . . .' she said.

'I'd be glad to,' he conceded, 'but they're all ready. We've missed the connection anyway.'

'Do stay then!' she whispered, looking down and touching his sleeve.

The postman finally undid the knot and flung the hood hesitantly over his arm. He felt warm standing by the subdeacon's wife.

'What a . . . lovely neck you have . . .'

And he touched her neck with two fingers. She did not resist, so with his whole hand he stroked her neck, her shoulder . . .

'You beauty . . .'

'Don't go . . . stay and have some tea.'

'Hey you, Black Pudding!' came the driver's voice from outside. 'What do you think you're doing? Lay them crossways.'

'Don't go . . . Hark at that wind howling!'

And the postman, who was still not fully awake and had not had time to shake off the enchantment of languid young sleep, was suddenly overwhelmed by a desire which makes one forget mailbags, mail-trains . . . absolutely everything. With a frightened glance at the door, as if wanting to hide or run away, he seized the subdeacon's wife by the waist, and had just leaned over to put out the lamp when there came the tramp of boots in the outer passage and the driver appeared in the doorway . . . Savely was peeping round his shoulder. The postman hastily dropped his arms and looked thoughtful.

'All ready!' said the driver.

The postman paused briefly, roused himself once and for all with a jerk of the head, and followed the driver out. The subdeacon's wife was left on her own.

'Well get in then and show us the route!' she heard a voice say.

First one bell began to ring sluggishly, then another, and the tinkling notes sped forth from the lodge in a long fine chain.

When they had very gradually died away, the subdeacon's wife sprang up and began walking nervously to and fro. At first she was pale, then she flushed all over. Her face disfigured with hate, her breathing coming in starts, her eyes flashing with a fierce, wild anger, she paced up and down like a tigress in a cage being tormented with a red-hot iron. For a minute she stopped and looked around at the place where she lived. Almost half the room was taken up by the bed, which stretched the whole length of the wall and consisted of a dirty feather-mattress, hard grey pillows, the quilt, and various nameless old bits and pieces. The bed was an ugly, shapeless lump, very much like that which stuck up on Savely's head whenever the latter felt an urge to put oil on his hair. In the space from the end of the bed to the door, which opened into the cold outer passage, stood the dark stove with its pots and hanging rags. Everything – including Savely, when he was present – was impossibly dirty, greasy and grimy, so that it struck one as strange to see the white neck and fine, delicate skin of a woman amid such surroundings. The subdeacon's wife ran over to the bed and flung out her hands as if wanting to sweep all this aside, to stamp on it and trample it to dust, but then the thought of coming into contact with the dirt seemed to scare her, she jumped back and began pacing again . . .

When Savely returned some two hours later, plastered in snow and worn out, she was already lying in bed undressed. Her eyes were shut, but from the faint twitching of the muscles on her face he could tell that she was still awake. On his way home he had vowed to say nothing and to leave her alone until morning, but now he could not resist the temptation to say something wounding.

'So much for your sorcery – he's gone!' he said with a malicious smirk.

She did not reply, but her chin quivered. Savely slowly undressed, climbed over her and lay down next to the wall.

'And tomorrow I shall explain to Father Nikodim what sort of a wife you are!' he muttered, curling up in a ball.

His wife rolled over to face him, her eyes flashing.

'You've got the living,' she said, 'what more do you want? If you want a wife, go and look for one in the forest! What sort of wife am I? May you drop dead! Why should I be lumbered with an idle, bumbling oaf like you, so help me?'

'That'll do . . . Go to sleep!'

'Oh how wretched I am!' she sobbed. 'But for you I might have married a merchant or a gentleman, even! But for you I'd love my husband now! Why weren't you buried in a snowdrift, why weren't you frozen to death out there on the highroad – you tyrant!'

The subdeacon's wife cried for a long time. Eventually she gave a deep sigh and quietened down. Outside, the storm was still raging. Something was crying in the stove, the chimney and round every wall, but to Savely the crying seemed to be within him, in his own ears. That evening had finally convinced him that his theories were right. He no longer had any doubt that his wife was in league with the devil and could make winds and post-troikas do as she wished. But to his utter dismay, this mysteriousness, this wild, supernatural power lent the woman lying beside him an especial, incomprehensible charm that he had not been aware of before. Because in his stupid fashion he had unconsciously poeticised her, she now seemed whiter, sleeker, more inaccessible . . .

'Witch!' he muttered to himself indignantly. 'Repulsive witch!'

But when she had fallen quiet and begun to breathe evenly, he reached out a finger and touched the back of her head . . . and held her thick plait in his hand. She didn't feel it . . . Then he became bolder and stroked her neck.

'Get off!' she yelled and gave him such a thump on the nose with her elbow that he saw stars.

The pain in his nose soon passed but his torment continued.

Grisha

Grisha, a chubby little boy born two years and eight months ago, is out for a walk in the park with his nanny. He is wearing a long felt pelisse, a scarf, a big cap with a fur bobble, and warm overshoes. He feels hot and stuffy, and to make matters worse the April sun is shining with cheerful abandon straight into his eyes and making his eyelids smart.

Everything about Grisha's ungainly appearance and timid, uncertain steps, expresses extreme bewilderment.

Hitherto the only world known to Grisha has been a rectangular one, with his bed in one corner, Nanny's trunk in another, the table in the third and the icon-lamp burning in the fourth. If you look under the bed, you can see a doll with one arm missing, and a drum, and if you look behind the trunk, you can see all sorts of different things: cotton-reels, pieces of paper, a box without a lid, and a broken toy clown. Apart from Nanny and Grisha, Mamma and the cat often appear in this world. Mamma looks like a doll, and the cat looks like Papa's fur coat, only the fur coat doesn't have eyes and a tail. From this world, which is called the nursery, a door leads to the space where they eat and drink tea. Here Grisha's high chair stands and on the wall hangs the clock, whose sole purpose is to swing its pendulum and strike. From the dining-room you can go through into a room with red armchairs. There is a dark stain here on the carpet which they still point to and wag their fingers at Grisha. Beyond this room is another one, which Grisha must not enter, and where Papa is sometimes to be seen – a most mysterious kind of person! Nanny and Mamma are easy to understand: they are there to dress Grisha, to feed him and put him to bed, but what Papa is there for – Grisha has no idea. Then there's another mysterious person, and that is Auntie, who gave Grisha the drum. Sometimes she's there, sometimes she's not. Where does she disappear to? Grisha has looked several times under the bed, behind the trunk and under the settee, but she was never there . . .

In this new world, though, where the sun hurts your eyes, there are so many Papas, Mammas and Aunties that you don't know which one to run up to. But the oddest, funniest things of all are the horses. Grisha looks at the way their legs move and is completely baffled. He looks at Nanny to see if she is going to explain it for him, but Nanny says nothing.

Suddenly he hears a terrible tramping sound . . . A crowd of soldiers is bearing straight down upon him, marching in step through the park. Their faces are red from the steam baths and under their arms they are carrying bundles of birch twigs. Grisha turns cold with horror and looks enquiringly at Nanny to see if they are dangerous. But Nanny doesn't run away or burst into tears, so they can't be dangerous after all. Grisha watches the soldiers go past and starts marching along in time with them.

Two big cats with pointed faces dash across the path, their tongues lolling out and their tails curling upwards. Grisha thinks he must start running, too, and hurries after them.

'Hey!' shouts Nanny, grabbing hold of him roughly by the shoulders. 'Where do you think you're going? Just you behave yourself!'

By the path another nanny is sitting with a little tub of oranges on her knees. As he walks past, Grisha quietly helps himself to one.

'What do you think you're up to?' shouts his companion, smacking him on the fingers and snatching away the orange. 'Stupid child!'

Grisha would love to pick up that piece of glass which he now sees lying at his feet and gleaming like the lamp in the corner of the room, but he's afraid of getting another smack on the fingers.

'My humble respects!' – he suddenly hears a loud, deep voice say almost above his ear, and sees a tall man with bright buttons.

Much to Grisha's joy, this man offers Nanny his hand and stands there talking to her. The brilliant light of the sun, the noise of the carriages, the horses, the bright buttons – all this is so astonishingly new and unfrightening that Grisha's whole being fills with delight and he starts chuckling.

'Come on! Come on!' he shouts at the man with the bright buttons, tugging at his coat-tails.

'Come on where?' the man asks.

'Come on!' Grisha insists. What he wants to say is that it would be nice to take Papa, Mamma and the cat along with them as well; but his tongue says something completely different.

After a while Nanny leaves the park and takes Grisha into a large courtyard, where there is still snow lying about. The man with the bright buttons follows, too. Carefully they pick their way round the blocks of snow and the puddles, then they go down a dark, dirty staircase and enter a room. It's very smoky inside, there's a strong smell of cooking, and a woman is standing by the stove frying some chops. The cook and Nanny kiss each other, then they and the man sit down on a bench and start talking quietly. Wrapped up in his warm clothes, Grisha begins to feel unbearably hot and stuffy.

'What's all this for?' he thinks, as he looks round.

He sees a dark ceiling, an oven-prong with curly horns, and a stove which looks like a big black hole . . .

'Ma-a-ma!' he wails.

'Now stop that!' shouts Nanny. 'You'll just have to wait!'

The cook places on the table a bottle, three glasses and a pie. The two women and the man with bright buttons clink their glasses and drink several times, and the man keeps embracing first Nanny, then the cook. And then all three of them start singing quietly.

Grisha stretches his hand out towards the pie and is given a small piece. As he eats it, he watches Nanny drinking . . . He feels like a drink, too.

'Me, Nanny, me!' he pleads.

The cook lets him have a sip from her glass. His eyes start, he frowns, coughs and for a long time afterwards waves his arms about, while the cook looks at him and laughs.

Back home again, Grisha starts telling Mamma, the walls and his bed about where he has been today and what he's seen. He talks more with his face and hands than with his tongue. He shows them the sun shining brightly and the horses trotting along, the horrible stove and the cook drinking.

That evening he just can't get to sleep. The soldiers with their birch twigs, the big cats, the horses, the piece of glass, the tub of oranges, the bright buttons – all these are rolled into one and press on his brain. He turns from side to side, babbles away and eventually, unable to bear his state of excitement any longer, starts to cry.

'You've got a temperature,' says Mamma, placing the palm of her hand on his forehead. 'I wonder how that came about?'

'Stove!' howls Grisha. 'Go away, horrid stove!'

'It's probably something he's eaten . . .' Mamma decides.

And so Grisha, bursting with impressions of the new life he has just discovered, is given a teaspoonful of castor-oil by his Mamma.

Kids

Papa, Mamma and Aunt Nadya are all out. They've gone to a christening party at the house of that old officer who rides about on the little grey horse. Grisha, Anya, Alyosha, Sonya and the cook's son, Andrey, are sitting round the dining-room table playing lotto, waiting for them to return. To tell the truth, it's well past their bedtime; but how can you be expected to go to sleep without finding out from Mamma what the new baby was like, and what kind of supper they were given? The table, lit by a hanging lamp, is covered with a colourful assortment of numbers, nutshells, bits of paper and glass counters. In front of each player are two cards and a pile of counters for covering the numbers. In the middle of the table is a gleaming white saucer with five one-kopeck pieces, and next to it a half-eaten apple, a pair of scissors and a plate in which they are supposed to put the nutshells. The children are playing for money. The stake is one kopeck. If anybody cheats, the rule is they're out of the game at once. The players have the dining-room to themselves. Agafya Ivanovna, the children's nanny, is downstairs in the kitchen teaching the cook how to cut out a dress pattern, while Vasya, their elder brother, who is in the fifth form at school, is reclining in a state of boredom on a sofa in the lounge.

They are passionately involved in the game. Judging from his face, the most passionately involved in Grisha – a small nine-year-old with a completely shaven head, chubby cheeks and fleshy lips like a negro's. He's already in the preparatory class at school, so he's looked upon as the most grown-up and the cleverest. Grisha is playing purely and simply for the money. But for those kopecks in the saucer, he'd have been asleep long ago. He keeps darting anxious, jealous glances at the other players' cards with his hazel-coloured eyes. Envy, fear of losing, and the financial considerations that fill his shaven head, prevent him from sitting still and concentrating. He is like a cat on hot bricks. Once he has won, he scoops the money up greedily and shoves it straight into his pocket. His eight-year-old sister, Anya, with her sharp little chin and gleaming, intelligent eyes, is similarly afraid of losing. Flushed and pale by turns, she watches the other players' every move. The kopecks mean nothing to her. For Anya winning is a matter of personal prestige. For the other sister, six-year-old Sonya, who has a curly head of hair and the kind of complexion that you see only in very healthy children, expensive dolls and on the lids of sweet boxes, it is the actual process of playing that is absorbing. Her face is a picture of bliss. No matter who wins, she shrieks with laughter and claps her hands with equal abandon. Alyosha, a round, chubby little chap, keeps puffing and blowing and goggling at his cards. For him, self-interest and prestige do not enter into it. He hasn't been shooed away from the table or put to bed – and is thankful for that. He's a quiet type to look at, but inside he's a proper little devil. It's not so much the lotto that interests him, as the misunderstandings that are bound to occur during the game. If one player hits another or calls him names, he's absolutely delighted. He should have popped out for a certain purpose long ago, but he won't leave the table for a moment in case someone steals his counters or his kopecks. Since he only knows numbers under ten and those ending in nought, Anya is covering his numbers for him. The fifth player, the cook's son, Andrey, a sickly dark-skinned boy wearing a calico shirt and with a bronze cross round his neck, stands there motionless and gazes dreamily at the numbers. He is quite unconcerned with who wins or loses, being completely absorbed in the mathematics of the game, in its simple logic: what a lot of different numbers there are in the world, and how extraordinary that they don't all get mixed up!

The children take it in turn to act as caller, except for Sonya and Alyosha. To avoid monotony, a great many special terms and funny nicknames have been worked out for the numbers. For instance, number seven is always called 'the poker', eleven 'two little sticks', seventy-seven is 'Semyon Semyonych', ninety – 'grandpa', and so on. The game proceeds at a lively pace.

'Thirty-two!' shouts Grisha, pulling the small yellow cylinders out of his father's hat. 'Seventeen! The poker! Twenty-eight – shut the gate!'

Anya notices that Andrey has missed number twenty-eight on his card. At any other time she would have pointed this out to him, but now that her personal prestige is lying there in the saucer with her kopeck, she is secretly triumphant.

'Twenty-three!' Grisha continues. 'Semyon Semyonych! Number nine!'

'A cockroach, a cockroach!' screams Sonya, pointing to an insect running across the table. 'Help!'

'Don't hurt him,' says Alyosha in his deep voice. 'Maybe he's got babies . . .'

Sonya watches the cockroach and thinks: how tiny those cockroach babies must be!

'Forty-three! Number one!' continues Grisha, suffering agonies because Anya already has two rows of four. 'Number six!'

'Lotto! Lotto!' shouts Sonya, flashing her eyes coquettishly and shrieking with laughter.

All the others' faces drop.

'Show us!' says Grisha, turning towards Sonya with a look of hatred.

As the most grown-up and the cleverest Grisha always has the last word. What he says, goes. A long time is spent thoroughly checking Sonya's numbers, and to the extreme disappointment of her fellow-players it turns out that she has not been cheating. They start a new game.

'You'll never guess what I saw yesterday!' says Anya, as if to herself. 'Old Philip pulled his eyelids right back and his eyes went all red and horrible, just like the Devil's.'

'I saw him too,' says Grisha. 'Number eight! There's a boy at school can move his ears. Twenty-seven!'

Andrey looks up at Grisha, ponders for a moment and says:

'I can wiggle my ears, too . . .'

'Go on then, wiggle them!'

Andrey moves his eyes, lips and fingers about, and thinks his ears are moving too. Laughter all round.

'I don't like that old Philip,' says Sonya, with a sigh. 'Do you know, he came into the nursery yesterday when I had nothing on but my night-dress . . . I felt so *embarrassed*!'

'Lotto!' yells Grisha all of a sudden, grabbing the money from the saucer. 'Lotto! Check if you like!'

The cook's son looks up with a wan expression.

'I'll have to stop playing now,' he says quietly.

'Why?'

'Because I've – I've run out of money.'

'Can't play if you've no money,' says Grisha.

Andrey rummages through his pockets once more just to make quite certain. But when he fails to find anything except crumbs and a chewed-up pencil-stub, his lower lip trembles and he blinks in distress. Any moment now he'll burst into tears . . .

'I'll put in a kopeck for you,' says Sonya, unable to bear his expression of suffering. 'Only mind you give it me back later.'

The stakes are placed and the game continues.

'Can you hear bells?' asks Anya, wide-eyed.

They all stop playing and stare at the dark window with open mouths. Beyond the darkness glimmers the reflection of the lamp.

'You're hearing things.'

'When it's night they only ring bells in the cemetery . . .' says Andrey.

'What do they do that for?'

'So that robbers won't break into the church. They're scared of bells.'

'Yes, but what do robbers want to break into the church for?' asks Sonya.

'To murder the watchmen, of course.'

A minute passes in silence. Then they glance at one another,

shudder and carry on playing. This time Andrey wins.
'Cheat!' blurts out Alyosha in his deep voice.
'No I'm not, you liar!'
Andrey turns pale, his lower lip trembles, and wallop! – he gives Alyosha one right on the head. Alyosha glares with rage, jumps up, puts one knee on the table, and wallop! – gives Andrey one right on the cheek. They each give the other one more slap in the face and burst out howling. All these dreadful goings-on are too much for Sonya, she too begins to cry, and the dining-room resounds to a cacophony of sobs. Do not imagine, though, that this puts an end to the game. Five minutes later the children are laughing away again and chatting peaceably. Their faces are tear-stained, but this doesn't stop them smiling. And Alyosha is positively happy: there's been a good squabble after all!
Into the dining-room comes Vasya, the fifth-former. He looks sleepy and disgruntled.
'What a disgrace!' he thinks, as he watches Grisha squeezing his pocketful of jingling kopecks. 'Fancy letting children have money! And fancy allowing them to play games of chance! Really, I don't know what education is coming to. It's a downright disgrace.'
But the children are playing with such relish that he too feels an urge to sit down with them and try his luck.
'Hang on,' he says, 'I'll come and have a game.'
'Put your kopeck in first!'
'All right,' he says, rummaging in his pockets. 'I haven't got a kopeck, but here's a rouble. I'll put in a rouble.'
'No, no, no, it must be a kopeck!'
'Don't be silly, a rouble's worth more than a kopeck.' explains the fifth-former. 'Whoever wins can give me change.'
'No, no, we're sorry, but you can't play!'
The fifth-former shrugs his shoulders and goes into the kitchen to get some change from the servants. But there isn't a kopeck to be had in the kitchen either.
'You'll just have to change a rouble for me,' he tackles Grisha again on his return. 'I'll give you commission. No? Then I'll buy ten kopecks from you for a rouble.'
Grisha looks up suspiciously at Vasya. Is it some kind of trick? Is he being swindled?
'Don't want to,' he says, keeping a tight hold on his pocket.
Vasya begins to lose his temper and shout at the players, calling

them oafs and dimwits.

'It's all right, Vasya, I'll put a kopeck in for you,' says Sonya. 'You can sit down.'

The fifth-former takes a seat and places two cards in front of him. Anya starts calling the numbers.

'I've dropped a kopeck!' Grisha suddenly announces in alarm. 'Stop the game!'

They unhook the lamp and crawl under the table to look for the kopeck. They grab at old bits of food and nutshells, they bang their heads together, but there's no sign of the kopeck. They start looking all over again and carry on searching until finally Vasya snatches the lamp from Grisha and puts it back in position. Grisha goes on searching in the dark.

But at last the kopeck has been found. The players sit down and are about to resume playing.

'Sonya's asleep!' announces Alyosha.

With her curly head resting on her arms, Sonya is enjoying a sweet, untroubled slumber, as though she'd fallen asleep an hour ago. She dropped off by accident, while the others were looking for the kopeck.

'Come and lie down on Mamma's bed,' says Anya, leading her out of the dining-room. 'This way!'

They all troop out with Sonya, and some five minutes later Mamma's bed presents a curious spectacle. Sonya is lying there asleep. Beside her is Alyosha, snoring softly. With their heads resting on the younger children's legs, Grisha and Anya are also sleeping. Andrey, the cook's son, has managed to find room for himself on the bed, too. Scattered all around lie the kopecks, their fascination quite forgotten until the next game. Pleasant dreams!

Revenge

Mr Leo Turmanov, an ordinary fellow, with a tidy little sum in the bank, a young wife and a dignified bald patch, was playing vint at a friend's birthday party. After a particularly bad hand which made him break into a cold sweat, he suddenly remembered that it was high time he had some more vodka. He got up, tiptoed his way between the tables with a dignified, rolling gait, negotiated the drawing-room where the young people were dancing (here he smiled condescendingly at a weedy young chemist and gave him a fatherly pat on the shoulder), then nipped smartly through a small door into the pantry. Here on a small round table stood bottles and vodka decanters, while on a nearby plate, amid the other delicacies, a half-eaten herring peeped out from its green trimmings of chive and parsley . . . After pouring himself some vodka and twiddling his fingers in the air as if about to make a speech, Leo knocked it back, pulled a frightful face, and had just stuck a fork into the herring when he heard voices on the other side of the wall . . .

'Yes, by all means,' a woman's voice was saying pertly. 'Only when is it to be?'

'My wife,' thought Leo. 'But who's she with?'

'Whenever you like, dear,' replied a deep, fruity bass. 'Today's scarcely convenient, tomorrow I'm busy the whole blessed day . . .'

'Why, that's Moorsky!' thought Turmanov, recognising the bass voice as that of a friend of his. '*Et tu, Brute!* So she's got her claws into you as well, has she? What a restless, insatiable creature! Can't let a day go by without some new affair!'

'Yes, I'm busy tomorrow,' the bass voice continued. 'But why not drop me a line instead? I'd look forward to that . . . Only we must decide how we're going to communicate, think up a good dodge. The ordinary post is scarcely convenient. If I write to you, your old paunch of a husband may intercept the letter from the postman, and if you write to me, it'll arrive when I'm out and my better half is sure to open it.'

'What shall we do then?'

'We must think up a good dodge. It's no use relying on the servants, either, because Double-Chins is bound to have your maid and footman under his thumb . . . Where is he, by the way, playing cards?'

'Yes. Still keeps losing, the poor fool!'

'Unlucky at cards, lucky in love,' said Moorsky, laughing. 'Now here's what I suggest, my pet . . . Tomorrow evening, when I leave the office, I shall walk through the park at exactly six o'clock on my way to see the keeper. What you must do, love, is put your note by six o'clock at the latest inside that marble urn – you know, the one to the left of the vine arbour . . .'

'Yes, yes, I know the one . . .'

'It'll be novel, poetic and mysterious . . . Old Pot-Belly won't find out, nor will my dearly beloved. All right?'

Leo downed another glass and made his way back to the card-table. His discovery had not shocked or surprised him or even upset him at all. The days when he became worked up, made a scene, used bad language and even fought duels, were long since past; he had given that up and now turned a blind eye to his wife's giddy affairs. But all the same he felt put out. Such phrases as 'Old Paunch', 'Double-Chins' and 'Pot-Belly' were a blow to his self-esteem.

'What a scoundrel that Moorsky is!' he thought, chalking up his losses. 'Meet him in the street and he's all smiles, pats you on the stomach, pretends he's your best friend – and now look at the names he comes out with! Calls me friend to my face, but behind my back I'm nothing but "Paunch" and "Pot-Belly" . . .'

As his ghastly losses kept mounting, so his feeling of injured pride grew . . .

'Upstart,' he thought, angrily breaking the piece of chalk. 'Whipper-snapper . . . If I didn't want to keep out of it, I'd give you Double-Chins!'

Over supper he couldn't stand having to look at Moorsky's face, but the latter seemed to be going out of his way to pester him with questions: had he been winning? why was he so down in the mouth? etcetera. And he even had the nerve – speaking as an old friend, of course – to reproach Turmanov's wife in a loud voice for not looking after her husband's health properly. As for his wife, she just gave him her usual come-hither look, laughed cheerfully and chattered away innocently, so that the devil himself would never have suspected her of being unfaithful.

Returning home, Leo felt angry and dissatisfied, as if he'd eaten an old pair of galoshes instead of veal at supper. He might have managed to restrain himself and forget all about it, had not his wife's chatter and smiles constantly reminded him of 'Paunch', 'Fattie', 'Pot-Belly' . . .

'I'd like to slap the blighter's cheeks,' he thought. 'Insult him in public.'

And he thought how pleasant it would be to give Moorsky a thrashing, to wing him in a duel like a sparrow . . . have him turfed out of his job, or put something foul and revolting in the marble urn – like a dead rat, for example . . . Or how about stealing his wife's letter from the urn in advance, and substituting for it some smutty poem signed 'Eliza', or something of that kind?

Turmanov paced up and down the bedroom for a long time, indulging in similar pleasing fancies. Suddenly he stopped and clapped his hand to his head.

'Got it, I've got it,' he exclaimed, and his whole face beamed with pleasure. 'That'll be perfect, ab-so-lutely perfect!'

When his wife had gone to sleep, he sat down at his desk and after much thought, disguising his handwriting and concocting various mistakes, wrote as follows:

'To the merchant Dulinov. Dear Sir! If before six this evening the twelth of september you have not dipposited two hundrid roubles in the marbel vase what stands in the park to the left of the vine arber you will be killed and your abbingdashery shop blown up.'

On completing the letter, Leo jumped for joy.

'What a brainwave!' he muttered, rubbing his hands. 'Superb! Old Nick himself couldn't have thought up a better revenge. The old merchant boy's sure to take fright and run straight round to the police, and they'll be lying in wait at six in the bushes . . . then as soon as you go poking round for your letter, lad, they'll nab you! He'll get the shock of his life! And while they're sorting it all out, just think what the scoundrel will have to go through, sitting there in the cells . . . Oh, excellent!'

Leo stuck on the stamp and took the letter round to the post-box himself. He fell asleep with a most blissful smile on his lips and slept more sweetly than he had done for years. When he woke up next morning and remembered his plan, he purred merrily and even chucked his unfaithful wife under the chin.

On his way to work and then sitting at his office desk, he kept on smiling and picturing to himself Moorsky's horror when the trap was sprung . . .

After five he could bear it no longer and hurried off to the park to feast his eyes on the desperate plight of his enemy.

'A-hah . . .' he said to himself, as he passed a policeman.

On reaching the vine arbour, he hid behind a bush and gazing avidly at the urn, settled down to wait. His impatience knew no bounds.

Moorsky appeared on the stroke of six. The young man was obviously in a most excellent frame of mind. His top-hat was perched jauntily on the back of his head, and his coat was thrown wide open, so that not just his waistcoat but his very soul seemed to be displayed to the world. He was whistling and smoking a cigar . . .

'Now we'll see about Double-Chins and Pot-Belly!' thought Turmanov, with malicious glee. 'Just you wait!'

Moorsky went up to the urn and casually put his hand inside . . . Leo half rose, fastening his eyes on him . . . The young man pulled out of the urn a small packet, examined it this way and that, and shrugged his shoulders; then he unsealed it hesitantly, shrugging his shoulders yet again; and then the expression on his face changed to one of complete astonishment: the packet contained two multi-coloured hundred-rouble notes!

Moorsky studied these notes for a long time. Eventually, still shrugging his shoulders, he stuffed them into his pocket and said: '*Merci*!'

The unfortunate Leo heard that word. All the rest of the evening he spent standing opposite Dulinov's shop, shaking his fist at the sign and muttering indignantly:

'Coward! Money-grubber! Jumped-up little merchant! Chicken! Pot-bellied little coward! . . .'

Easter Night

I was standing on the bank of the Goltva, waiting for the ferry to come over from the other side. At normal times the Goltva is a river of no great pretensions, taciturn and pensive, glinting meekly from behind thick rushes; now, a whole lake lay spread before me. The rampant spring waters had swept over both banks and flooded large areas on either side, capturing marshes, hay fields and vegetable plots, so that it was quite common to encounter on the surface lone poplars and bushes sticking out like grim crags in the darkness.

The weather struck me as magnificent. It was dark, yet even so I could see the trees, the water, and human beings . . . The world was lit by stars, bestrewing every corner of the sky. I don't think I have ever seen so many stars. Literally, you couldn't have stuck a pin between them. There were ones as big as goose eggs and others as tiny as hempseed . . . Each and every one of them, from great to small, had come out to parade for the festival, washed, refurbished and jubilant, and each and every one was quietly twinkling. The sky lay reflected in the water; the stars bathed in its dark depths and trembled with the faint ripples on the surface. The air was warm and still . . . Far away on the other bank, in impenetrable dark, several bright red fires were blazing furiously. . .

Close by me stood the dark silhouette of a peasant in a tall hat and holding a short, knobbly staff.

'The ferry's taking a long time, isn't it?' I said.

'Yes, about time it was here,' the silhouette answered.

'Are you waiting for the ferry too?'

'No . . .' yawned the peasant, 'I'm just waiting for the luminations. I'd go, but I ain't got the five kopecks for the ferry.'

'I'll give you them.'

'Thank you kindly sir, but I'd rather you put up a candle for me there in the monastery, with those five kopecks . . . That'll be more interesting, with me standing here. Where's that ferry got to – has it vanished or something?'

The peasant went down to the water's edge, seized the ferry rope, and yelled:

'Ieronim! Ieron-i-m!'

As though in answer to his shout, a long peal from a great bell came to us from the other bank. The peal was rich and deep, like the thickest string on a double-bass: it was as though the darkness itself had given a hoarse cough. Immediately a shot rang out from a cannon. It rolled away in the darkness and petered out somewhere far behind me. The peasant took off his hat and crossed himself.

'Christ is Risen!' he said.

Hardly had the waves from the first peal of the bell died on the air, when a second one resounded, hard on it a third, and suddenly the darkness was filled with a continuous, vibrant din. Beside the red fires new ones blazed up, and they all started moving together and flickering restlessly.

'Ieroni-m!' came a long echoing cry.

'They're shouting for him from the other bank,' said the peasant. 'So the ferry's not there either. He's fallen asleep, our Ieronim.'

The fires and the velvety tolling of the bell were calling me . . . I was beginning to get impatient and fidgety. Finally, though, peering into the dark distance, I saw the silhouette of something very similar to a gallows. It was the long-awaited ferry. It was approaching with such slowness that had it not been for the gradual sharpening of its outlines, one might have thought it was standing still, or, indeed, going towards the other bank.

'Come on, Ieronim!' shouted my peasant. 'There's a gentleman waiting!'

The ferry crept up to the bank, lurched, and creaked to a halt. On it, holding the rope, stood a tall man in a monk's cassock and a conical cap.

'What kept you?' I asked him, leaping onto the ferry.

'Forgive me for the Lord's sake,' replied Ieronim quietly. 'Anyone else?'

'No, just me . . .'

Ieronim grasped the rope with both hands, bent himself into the shape of a question-mark, and let out a groan. The ferry creaked and lurched. The silhouette of the peasant in the tall hat began slowly to recede from me: so the ferry was under way. Soon Ieronim straightened up and began to work the rope with one hand. We gazed silently at the bank towards which we were floating. There the 'luminations' the peasant was waiting for had already begun. At the water's edge barrels of tar were blazing like enormous bonfires. Their reflections, as ruddy as a rising moon, crept out towards us in long wide strips. The burning barrels lit up their own smoke and the long shadows of people flitting about by the fires, but the area to either side of the barrels and beyond them, whence came the velvety tolling of the bell, was all dense black gloom still. Suddenly, slashing the darkness, a rocket shot up to the sky in a golden streamer; it described an arc, and as if smashing against the sky disintegrated in a crackle of sparks. A roar went up from the bank, like a distant 'hurrah'.

'Beautiful!' I said.

'Yes, beautiful beyond words!' sighed Ieronim. 'It's that kind of night, sir! Another time and we wouldn't even pay any attention to rockets, but tonight we rejoice at every vain thing. And where might you be from?'

I told him.

'Mmm. . .it's a joyful day today. . .' continued Ieronim in a sighing little high-pitched voice like that of someone recovering from an illness. 'The sky rejoices, and the earth, and all that is under the earth. All creation is celebrating. Only tell me, good sir: why is it that even in the midst of great rejoicing a man cannot forget his sorrows?'

I was afraid that this unexpected question was inviting me to join in one of those protracted, uplifting discussions that monks who are idle and bored are so partial to. I was not much disposed to conversation, so I merely asked:

'What sorrows do you have, father?'

'Usually the same as everyone else's, your honour, good sir, but this day a particular sorrow has befallen the monastery: at the liturgy itself, during the lessons, Nikolay the monk died . . .'

'Well, it's God will!' I said, affecting the monastic tone. 'We all must die. Shouldn't you rather be rejoicing? . . . They say that anyone who dies at Easter, or during Eastertide, is sure to go to the kingdom of heaven.'

'That's true.'

We fell silent. The silhouette of the tall-hatted peasant merged with the features of the bank. The tar barrels blazed higher and higher.

'The scriptures make clear to us the vanity of sorrow, as does contemplation,' Ieronim broke the silence. 'But why will the soul still grieve and not listen to reason? Why does one want to weep so bitterly?'

Ieronim shrugged his shoulders, turned to me, and spoke rapidly:

'If it was me had died, or someone else, perhaps no one would have so much as noticed, but it was Nikolay who died! Nikolay, of all people! It's hard to believe, even, that he's no longer in the world! I stand here on the ferry and I keep thinking to myself that his voice is going to call out to me from the bank. So that I wouldn't be scared on my own on the ferry, he would always come down to the riverbank and hail me. He would get out of bed every night specially. A kind soul he was! God knows, how kind and considerate! Many a mother's not as kind to her own children as Nikolay was to me! The Lord save his soul!'

Ieronim took hold of the rope, but immediately turned to me again.

'Oh, and what a brilliant mind, your honour!' he said liltingly. 'What sweet and melodious speech! It was just as they'll be singing soon at the mass: "O how loving-kind! O most sweet is Thy voice!" And apart from all his other human qualities, he had an extraordinary gift!'

'What was that?' I asked.

The monk eyed me carefully, then, as if persuaded that I could be trusted with a secret, he chuckled.

'He had the gift of writing canticles . . .' he said. 'It was a miracle, sir, no less! You'll scarcely believe it if I tell you. Reverend Father, our archimandrite, is from Moscow, our Father Vicar graduated from the Kazan Academy, and we have learned monks in orders here, and elders, but let me assure you, sir, there isn't one of them who could write things himself – yet Nikolay, a simple monk, a mere deacon, who hadn't studied anywhere and was nothing at all to look at, he could! It was a miracle, a veritable miracle!'

Ieronim clasped his hands and forgetting all about the rope, continued excitedly:

'Our Father Vicar finds it difficult putting sermons together, when he was writing the history of our monastery he made our lives a misery and had to drive into town a dozen times. Nikolay, though, could write canticles! Canticles! That's a different matter from a sermon or a history!'

'Are canticles so hard to write, then?' I asked.

'V-ery hard . . .' said Ieronim with a roll of the head. 'It doesn't matter how wise or saintly you are, if God hasn't given you the gift. Monks who don't know what they're talking about reckon all you have to do is know the life of the saint you're writing it to, and model it on all the other canticles. But that's not correct, sir. Of course, anyone who writes a canticle has to know the saint's life inside out, down to the last minutest detail. He must consult the other canticles, too, to know how to begin and what to write about. To give you an example, the first collect-hymn always begins with the words "Most High Elect" or "The Chosen One" . . . The first *ikos* must always begin with an angel. I don't know if you're interested, but in the canticle to Jesus the Most Sweet the *ikos* begins like this: "Angels' Creator and Lord of Hosts!", in the canticle to the Most Holy Mother of God it's "An Angel was sent down from the Heavens to be a Messenger", and to St Nicholas the Miracle-Worker – "Angel in form, though in substance an Earthly Being", and so on. It always begins with an angel. Of course, you do have to consult the other canticles, but it isn't the saint's life or how the canticle compares with other ones that matters – it's the beauty and sweetness of the thing. Everything in it must be graceful, brief, and pregnant with meaning. Every tiny line must breathe a softness, a gentleness, a tenderness; there mustn't be a single word that's coarse, harsh, or out of place. You must write in such a way that the worshipper rejoices in his heart and weeps, and his mind is shaken and he's all a-tremble. In the canticle to the Holy Mother of God there are the words: "Rejoice, O Thou too high for the mind of man to scale: rejoice, O Thou too deep for the eyes of Angels to fathom!" Elsewhere in the same canticle it says: "Rejoice, O Tree of fairest Fruit that nourishest the faithful: rejoice, O Tree of benign Canopy that shelterest the multitudes!" '

As though taking fright at something, or suddenly overcome with shame, Ieronim covered his face with his hands and rocked his head from side to side.

'Tree of fairest Fruit . . . Tree of benign Canopy . . .' he muttered to himself. 'To find such words! Only the Lord bestows such a power! For brevity he'd link several words and thoughts together – and how smooth and pregnant he succeeds in making them! "Thou art a light-enduing Beacon to the people . . ." it says in the canticle to Jesus the Most Sweet. "Light-enduing"! You won't find that word in conversation or in books – yet he managed to think it up, to find it in his own mind! As well as smoothness and felicitousness, sir, every line must also be adorned in divers ways – with flowers and lightning and wind and sun and all the objects of the visible world. And you have to compose every exclamation so that it falls smoothly and easily on the ear. "Rejoice, thou Lily that dwellest in the heavens!" it says in the canticle to St Nicholas the Miracle-Worker. Not just "Lily of heaven", but "Lily that *dwellest* in the heavens!" That way it's smoother and sweeter on the ear. And that's how Nikolay used to write, too! Just like that! Oh, I can't begin to tell you how he used to write!'

'Well, in that case it's a pity he's died,' I said. 'But let's carry on across, father, or we shall be late . . .'

Ieronim started out of his thoughts and scurried to the rope. On the bank all the bells were beginning to peal out. Probably the procession was already under way near the monastery, for the whole of the dark area beyond the tar barrels was now dotted with moving lights.

'Did Nikolay have his canticles printed?' I asked Ieronim.

'How could he?' he sighed. 'And it would have seemed strange, too. For what purpose? No one in our monastery's interested in that sort of thing. They don't approve. They knew that Nikolay wrote them, but they ignored them. Nowadays, sir, no one thinks very highly of new writings!'

'They're prejudiced against them?'

'That's right. If Nikolay had been an elder, well then perhaps the brotherhood would have taken some interest, but he wasn't yet forty. There were those that laughed at his writing, and even held it a sin.'

'Why did he write, then?'

'Well, more for his own consolation. Of all the brotherhood I was the only one who actually read his canticles. I'd slip along to him without letting the others see and he'd be so glad that I took an interest. He would hug me, stroke my head, and call me affectionate names, as though I were a little child. He would shut up his cell, sit me down next to him, and we'd read away . . .'

Ieronim left the rope and came up to me.

'He and I were like friends, somehow,' he whispered, looking at me with gleaming eyes. 'Wherever he went, I went too. When I wasn't there, he would miss me. And he loved me more than anyone else, and all because I used to weep over the canticles he wrote. It's touching to think of! Now I feel just like an orphan or a widow. You see, they're all good, kind, devout people in our monastery, but . . . none of them has that softness and gentility, they're more like commonfolk. They all talk loudly and clump their feet, they make a lot of noise and are always clearing their throats, whereas Nikolay always spoke quietly, affectionately, and if he noticed that someone was sleeping or praying, then he would creep past as though he were a little fly, or a gnat. And his face was loving and compassionate . . .'

Ieronim gave a deep sigh and took up the rope again. By now we were approaching the bank. We were drifting out of the darkness and the stillness of the river straight into an enchanted realm full of choking smoke, crackling light and uproar. Round the tar barrels one could now clearly see people moving. The flickering of the fire gave their red faces and forms a strange, almost fantastic, appearance. Occasionally among the heads and faces one glimpsed the muzzles of horses, as motionless as if cast in red copper.

'They'll be singing the Easter Canon in a moment . . .' said Ieronim, 'but Nikolay isn't there, so there's no one to really take it in . . . Nothing that was written was sweeter to him than that canon. He would enter into every word of it! You're going to be there, sir, so you listen closely to what they sing: it'll take your breath away!'

'Aren't you going to be in the church yourself?'

'I can't, sir . . .I've got to work the ferry . . .'

'But can't someone take over from you?'

'I don't know . . . Someone should have relieved me at eight, but they haven't, as you see! . . . And I must confess, I'd like to be in church . . .'

'You are a monk?'

'Yes . . . that is, I'm a lay-brother.'

The ferry ran into the bank and stopped. I thrust a five-kopeck piece into Ieronim's hand and jumped ashore. Immediately, a cart with a little boy and a sleeping peasant woman in it trundled creakily onto the ferry. Ieronim, who was lit faintly by the fires, took up the rope, bent himself double, and set the ferry in motion . . .

I took a few steps through mud, then was able to walk on a soft, freshly trodden path. This footpath led to the dark, cavern-like gates of the monastery through clouds of smoke and a jumbled mass of people, unharnessed horses, carts and britchkas. The whole assortment was creaking, snorting and laughing, and over it all played a ruddy light and the billowy shadows of the smoke . . . It was utter chaos! And to think that in this crush they could still find room to load a small cannon and to sell gingerbreads!

On the other side of the wall, in the precinct, no less of a commotion was going on, but there was a greater sense of order and dignity. The air smelt of juniper leaves and benzoin incense. People talked loudly, but there was no sound of laughter or horses' snorting. Around the tombstones and crosses huddled people with Easter cakes and bundles. Evidently many of them had come from far away to have their Easter cakes blessed, and were now weary. Young lay-brothers scampered to and fro over the cast-iron slabs that lay in a solid strip from the gates to the church door, their boots ringing on the metal. In the belfry, too, they were bustling about and shouting.

'What a night of turmoil!' I thought. 'How superb!'

It was tempting to see the same turmoil and sleeplessness in everything around, from the night dark to the iron slabs, the crosses on the graves and the trees beneath which people were bustling. But nowhere were the excitement and turmoil so evident as inside the church. At the entrance a ceaseless struggle was going on between the ebb and the flow. Some were going in, others coming out and shortly returning, only to stand for a while and move off again. People were darting aimlessly all over the place, apparently looking for something. A wave would start from the entrance and travel the length of the church, unsettling even the front rows where the solid, respectable people were standing. There could be no question of concentrated prayer. There were no prayers at all, only sheer, spontaneous childlike joy seeking a pretext to burst out and express itself in any form of movement, be it only the non-stop roaming and jostling.

The same extraordinary activity strikes you in the Easter service itself. The sanctuary gates are wide open in all the side-chapels, and dense clouds of incense float about the chandelier in the nave; all around you are lights and the blaze and crackle of candles . . . There is no provision for readings; the singing goes on briskly and cheerfully to the very end of the service; after each hymn of the canon, the clergy change their vestments and come out to cense, and this is repeated nearly every ten minutes.

I had just squeezed in, when a wave surged up from the front and hurled me back. Before me passed a tall, portly deacon holding a long red candle; behind him hurried the archimandrite, grey-haired, wearing a gold mitre, and swinging his censer. Once they had disappeared, the crowd pushed me back to my previous place. But in less than ten minutes another wave surged and again the deacon appeared. This time he was followed by the Father Vicar, the very one whom Ieronim had described as writing the history of the monastery.

Merging with the crowd and infected by the universal jubilation and excitement, I felt unbearable pity for Ieronim. Why would no one relieve him? Why couldn't someone less feeling and less impressionable be sent to the ferry?

'Cast thine eyes about thee, O Zion, and behold!' they were singing in the choir. 'For lo! from the West and from the North, and from the Sea and from the East, as to a light by God illumined, have thy children assembled unto thee . . .'

I looked at the faces. They were all radiant with triumph; but not a single person was listening to and taking in what was being sung, and none of them was feeling his 'breath taken away'. Why would no one relieve Ieronim? I could imagine this Ieronim standing humbly somewhere by the wall, hunched up and snatching greedily at the beauty of each sacred phrase. All that was now glancing past the ears of those standing about me, he would have drunk in thirstily with his sensitive soul, he would have drunk himself into ecstasies – till his breath was taken away – and there would not have been a happier man in the whole building. Now, though, he was plying back and forth on the dark river and grieving for his dead brother and friend.

Behind me another wave surged forward. A stout, smiling monk fiddling with a rosary and looking over his shoulder squeezed past me sideways, clearing the way for a lady in a hat and velvet cloak. Behind the lady, holding a chair above our heads, hurried a monastery servant.

I came out of the church. I wanted to have a look at the dead Nikolay, the unacclaimed writer of canticles. I strolled round the precinct, where a row of monks' cells stretched along the monastery wall, I looked in through several windows, and, seeing nothing, turned back. Now I do not regret not having seen Nikolay; goodness knows, perhaps if I had seen him I should have lost the image that my imagination now paints of him. I picture this attractive, poetical man who would come out at night to call to Ieronim, who besprinkled his canticles with flowers, stars and sunbeams, and was completely alone and not understood, as shy, pale, with soft, meek and sad features. As well as intelligence, his eyes surely glowed with affection and that barely restrainable childlike rapture that I had heard in Ieronim's voice, when he quoted to me pieces from the canticles.

When we emerged from the church after mass, the night was already gone. Morning was breaking. The stars had faded and the sky was now a sombre greyish-blue. The cast-iron slabs, the tombstones and the buds on the trees were coated with dew. It was distinctly fresh. Beyond the monastery wall there was no longer the animation that I had seen at night. The horses and people looked weary, sleepy, they scarcely moved, whilst all that was left of the tar barrels was a few heaps of black ash. When a person feels weary and wants to sleep, he thinks that nature is experiencing the same state. It seemed to me that the trees and the young grass were sleeping. It seemed that even the bells were not ringing so loudly and cheerfully as in the night. The turmoil was over and of the excitement only a pleasant languor remained, a craving for warmth and sleep.

Now I could see the river and both its banks. Above it, here and there, drifted humps of thin mist. A grim chill wafted from the river. When I jumped onto the ferry, someone's britchka was already standing on it, and a couple of dozen men and women. The rope, which was damp and, it seemed to me, sleepy, stretched away far across the broad river and disappeared in places in the white mist.

'Christ is Risen! Anyone else?' asked a quiet voice.

I recognised Ieronim's voice. Now the darkness of the night no longer prevented me from making out the monk's appearance. He was a tall, narrow-shouldered man of about thirty-five, with large rounded features, half-closed, listlessly-peering eyes, and an unkempt little spade beard. He looked extremely sad and weary.

'Haven't they relieved you yet?' I asked in surprise.

'Me?' he asked back, turning his numbed, dew-covered face to me, and smiling. 'There's no one to take my place now till morn. They'll all be going to the father archimandrite soon to break the fast.'

He and a strange little peasant in an orange fur hat resembling one of the limewood tubs they sell honey in, applied themselves to the rope, gave a groan in unison, and the ferry moved off.

We floated across, disturbing on our way the lazily rising mist. Everyone was silent. Ieronim worked the rope mechanically with one hand. For a long time his meek, bleary eyes roamed all over us, then he brought his gaze to rest on the rosy, black-browed face of a young merchant's wife, who was standing on the ferry next to me, hunched up silently in the enveloping mist. He did not take his eyes off her face the whole way.

There was little that was masculine in that prolonged gaze. In the woman's face I feel Ieronim was searching for the soft and loving features of his late-lamented friend.

The Little Joke

Noon, on a clear winter's day . . . The frost is hard, the air crackles, and silvery crystals cover the curls on Nadenka's brow and the light down on her lip. She is holding my arm. We are standing at the top of a hill: from our feet to the ground below stretches a smooth incline, like a mirror in which the sun is looking at itself. Beside us is a little toboggan, covered in bright red cloth.

'Come on, let's go down, Nadezhda Petrovna!' I implore her. 'Just once! No harm'll come to us, I assure you, we shall be quite safe.'

But Nadenka is afraid. The whole distance from her little overshoes to the bottom of the hill of ice seems to her a terrible, unfathomable abyss. She catches her breath, she can't breathe when she looks down, when I so much as suggest sitting on the toboggan. And whatever will it be like if she dares to fly down into the abyss! She will die, she will go mad.

'Please, please!' I say. 'You mustn't be afraid! It's sheer cowardice!'

In the end, Nadenka yields, although I can see from her face that she still yields in fear of her life. I seat her pale and trembling on the toboggan, I put my arm around her, and together we hurtle into the abyss.

The toboggan goes like a bullet. It slices through the air and the wind beats in our faces, roars, whistles in our ears, tears at us, and nips us painfully in its rage, as though it wanted to wrench our heads off. The blast is so strong we can't even breathe. It is as though the devil himself had got us in his clutches and was dragging us roaring down to hell. Everything round us merges into one long strip rushing by . . . Another moment, it seems, and we shall perish!

'I love you, Nadya!' I say under my breath.

The toboggan runs quieter and quieter now, the roar of the wind and the hiss of the runners are no longer so terrible, we can breathe freely again, and finally we are at the bottom. Nadenka is neither dead nor alive. She is pale, scarcely able to breathe . . . I help her to get up.

'I shall never ever do that again!' she says, looking at me wide-eyed with terror. 'Not for anything in the world! I nearly died!'

After a while, however, she comes to herself again and looks me questioningly in the eyes: did I say those four words, or did she just think she heard them, in the rushing wind? I stand beside her, smoking, and am carefully examining my glove.

She takes my arm and for a long time we walk about the bottom of the hill. The mystery obviously gives her no peace. Were those words said or not? Yes, or no? Yes, or no? The question is one that touches her self-esteem, her honour, her life, her happiness, it's a question of life and death, the most important question in the whole world. Nadenka looks impatiently, sadly, penetratingly into my face and answers my questions haphazardly, waiting to see if I will speak first. Oh, the emotions that play across that dear face! I can see that she is struggling with herself, she desperately wants to say something, to ask something, but she can't find the words, she feels awkward, scared, her very joy prevents her . . .

'You know what?' she says, not looking at me.

'What?' I ask.

'Let's . . . let's go down again.'

So we climb up the steps beside the hill. Again I seat Nadenka pale and trembling on the toboggan, again we hurtle into the terrible abyss, again the wind roars and the runners hiss, and again just as we are travelling fastest and the noise of the toboggan is at its height, I say under my breath:

'I love you, Nadenka!'

When the toboggan comes to a halt, Nadenka glances quickly back up the hill, then stares me in the face for a long time and listens hard to my indifferent, emotionless voice, and all of her, even her muff, her very hood, her whole figure, expresses the most extreme perplexity. And written all over her face is:

'What's going on? Who said *those* words? Was it him, or did I just think I heard them?'

The uncertainty nags her, she can't bear not to know. The poor girl doesn't answer my questions, frowns, is on the point of bursting into tears.

'Perhaps we should be going home?' I ask.

'I . . . I quite like tobogganing,' she says, blushing. 'Couldn't we go down once more?'

She 'likes' tobogganing, yet just as before, when she sits down on the toboggan she is pale, can scarcely breathe for fear, and is trembling all over.

We go down a third time, and I can see that she is looking at my face to see if my lips move. But I put a handkerchief to my mouth, cough, and just as we reach the middle of the slope I manage to say the words:

'I love you, Nadya!'

And the mystery remains a mystery! Nadenka is silent, thinking about something . . . When I accompany her home from the slopes, she tries to make us take our time, slows down her pace, and keeps waiting to see if I will say those words to her. And I can see her soul suffering, I can see she is making a tremendous effort to stop herself saying:

'It couldn't possibly have been the wind that said them! And I don't want it to have been the wind, either!'

The next morning I receive a note, which reads: 'If you are going to the slopes today, please call for me. N.' And thenceforth I start going out to the slopes with Nadenka every day, and each time as we hurtle downwards on the toboggan I say under my breath the same words:

'I love you, Nadya!'

Before long Nadenka has grown addicted to this phrase, as though it were wine, or morphine. She can't live without it. True, she is as frightened of flying down the hill as ever, but now the fear and danger add a special charm to these words about love, words which remain a mystery as before, and make her soul ache. She still suspects the same two of saying them – myself and the wind . . . Which of these two is declaring his love for her, she does not know, but obviously she doesn't care, either: any vessel's good enough, when you just want to get drunk.

Once, at midday, I went out to the slopes alone. Mingling with the crowd, I suddenly see Nadenka come up to the hill and start looking round for me . . . Then she timidly climbs the steps up the side . . . Oh, it's so frightening to go down on one's own, so frightening! She is pale as the snow, trembling, looks as though she is climbing the scaffold, yet she climbs on without looking back, quite resolved. So at last she has decided to find out for herself whether she will still hear those amazing, sweet words when I am not there. I watch her sit on the toboggan, face pale and mouth parted in fear; she closes her eyes, and, bidding the Earth farewell forever, moves off . . . ZHZHZHzhzhzhshshsss . . . hiss the runners. Whether Nadenka hears those words, I don't know . . . All I see is that she gets off the toboggan looking quite faint and exhausted. And I can see from her face that she doesn't know herself whether she heard anything or not. Her fear as she was plummeting downwards made her incapable of hearing, of distinguishing the sounds, taking anything in . . .

But now March comes, and with it the spring . . . The sun becomes gentler. Our hill of ice darkens, loses its shine, and finally melts away. We stop going out tobogganing. Now there is nowhere left for poor Nadenka to hear those words, and no one to say them, either, for the wind is silent and I am about to leave for Petersburg for a long time, if not for ever.

At dusk one evening, a couple of days before my departure, I am sitting in our garden, which is separated from Nadenka's house by a high fence topped with nails . . . It is still fairly cold, there is still snow beneath the manure on the garden, the trees are dead, but spring is already in the air, and the rooks caw noisily as they settle for the night. I go over to the fence and peep through a crack in it for a long time. I see Nadenka come out onto the porch and gaze sadly, yearningly into the sky . . . The spring breeze is blowing straight into her pale, dejected face . . . It reminds her of the wind that roared past us those times on the slope, when she used to hear those four words, and her face grows sad, so sad, and a tear trickles down her cheek . . . And the poor girl stretches out her hands as though begging the breeze to send her those words again. And I wait for the wind to pick up, and just at that moment I say in a low voice:

'I love you, Nadya!'

Goodness, what a change that brings to Nadenka! She gives a little scream, smiles all over her face, and stretches her arms out to the wind, joyful, full of happiness, beautiful.

I go off and start to pack . . .

That was a long time ago. Now Nadenka is married: she was given away to – or herself chose, it makes no difference – the secretary of a court of wards of the nobility, and has three children. She hasn't forgotten how we used to go tobogganing every day and how the wind whispered to her 'I love you, Nadenka'; now this is the happiest, tenderest and most beautiful memory of her life . . .

And now that I am older, I cannot understand why I said those words, why I played that joke on her . . .

The Objet d'Art

Holding under his arm an object carefully wrapped up in No.223 of the *Stock Exchange Gazette*, Sasha Smirnoff (an only son) pulled a long face and walked into Doctor Florinsky's consulting-room.

'Ah, my young friend!' the doctor greeted him. 'And how are we today? Everything well, I trust?'

Sasha blinked his eyes, pressed his hand to his heart and said in a voice trembling with emotion:

'Mum sends her regards, Doctor, and told me to thank you . . . I'm a mother's only son and you saved my life – cured me of a dangerous illness . . . and Mum and me simply don't know how to thank you.'

'Nonsense, lad,' interrupted the doctor, simpering with delight. 'Anyone else would have done the same in my place.'

'I'm a mother's only son . . . We're poor folk, Mum and me, and of course we can't pay you for your services . . . and we feel very bad about it, Doctor, but all the same, we – Mum and me, that is, her one and only – we do beg you most earnestly to accept as a token of our gratitude this . . . this object here, which . . . It's a very valuable antique bronze – an exceptional work of art.'

'No, really,' said the doctor, frowning. 'I couldn't possibly.'

'Yes, yes, you simply must accept it!' Sasha mumbled away as he unwrapped the parcel. 'If you refuse, we'll be offended, Mum and me . . . It's a very fine piece . . . an antique bronze . . . It came to us when Dad died and we've kept it as a precious memento . . . Dad used to buy up antique bronzes and sell them to collectors . . . Now Mum and me are running the business . . .'

Sasha finished unwrapping the object and placed it triumphantly on the table. It was a small, finely modelled old bronze candelabrum. On its pedestal two female figures were standing in a state of nature and in poses that I am neither bold nor hot-blooded enough to describe. The figures were smiling coquettishly, and altogether seemed to suggest that but for the need to go on supporting the candlestick, they would leap off the pedestal and turn the room into a scene of such wild debauch that the mere thought of it, gentle reader, would bring a blush to your cheek.

After glancing at the present, the doctor slowly scratched the back of his ear, cleared his throat and blew his nose uncertainly.

'Yes, it's a beautiful object all right,' he mumbled, 'but, well, how shall I put it? . . . You couldn't say it was exactly tasteful . . . I mean, décolleté's one thing, but this is really going too far . . .'

'How do you mean, going too far?'

'The Arch-Tempter himself couldn't have thought up anything more vile. Why, if I were to put a fandangle like that on the table, I'd feel I was polluting the whole house!'

'What a strange view of art you have, Doctor!' said Sasha, sounding hurt. 'Why, this is a work of inspiration! Look at all that beauty and elegance – doesn't it fill you with awe and bring a lump to your throat? You forget all about worldly things when you contemplate beauty like that . . . Why, look at the movement there, Doctor, look at all the air and *expression*!'

'I appreciate that only too well, my friend,' interrupted the doctor, 'but you're forgetting, I'm a family man – think of my small children running about, think of the ladies.'

'Of course, if you're going to look at it through the eyes of the masses,' said Sasha, 'then of course this highly artistic creation does appear in a different light . . . But you must raise yourself above the masses, Doctor, especially as Mum and me'll be deeply offended if you refuse. I'm a mother's only son – you saved my life . . . We're giving you our most treasured possession . . . and my only regret is that we don't have another one to make the pair . . .'

'Thank you, dear boy, I'm very grateful . . . Give Mum my regards, but just put yourself in my place – think of the children running about, think of the ladies . . . Oh, all right then, let it stay! I can see I'm not going to convince you.'

'There's nothing to convince me of,' Sasha replied joyfully. 'You must stand the candelabrum here, next to this vase. What a pity there isn't the pair! What a pity! Goodbye, then, Doctor!'

When Sasha had left, the doctor spent a long time gazing at the candelabrum, scratching the back of his ear and pondering.

'It's a superb thing, no two ways about that,' he thought, 'and it's a shame to let it go . . . But there's no question of keeping it here . . . Hmm, quite a problem! Who can I give it to or unload it on?'

After lengthy consideration he thought of his good friend Harkin the solicitor, to whom he was indebted for professional services.

'Yes, that's the answer,' the doctor decided. 'As a friend it's awkward for him to accept money from me, but if I make him a present of this object, that'll be very *comme il faut*. Yes, I'll take this diabolical creation round to him – after all, he's a bachelor, doesn't take life seriously . . .'

Without further ado, the doctor put on his coat, picked up the candelabrum and set off for Harkin's.

'Greetings!' he said, finding the solicitor at home. 'I've come to thank you, old man, for all that help you gave me – I know you don't like taking money, but perhaps you'd be willing to accept this little trifle . . . here you are, my dear chap – it's really rather special!'

When he saw the little trifle, the solicitor went into transports of delight.

'Oh, my word, yes!' he roared. 'How do they think such things up? Superb! Entrancing! Wherever did you get hold of such a gem?'

Having exhausted his expressions of delight, the solicitor glanced round nervously at the door and said:

'Only be a good chap and take it back, will you? I can't accept it . . .'

'Why ever not?' said the doctor in alarm.

'Obvious reasons . . . Think of my mother coming in, think of my clients . . . And how could I look the servants in the face?'

'No, no, no, don't you dare refuse!' said the doctor, waving his arms at him. 'You're being a boor! This is a work of inspiration – look at the movement there . . . the *expression* . . . Any more fuss and I shall be offended!'

'If only it was daubed over or had some fig leaves stuck on . . .'

But the doctor waved his arms at him even more vigorously, nipped smartly out of the apartment and returned home, highly pleased that he'd managed to get the present off his hands . . .

When his friend had gone, Harkin studied the candelabrum closely, kept touching it all over, and like the doctor, racked his brains for a long time wondering what was to be done with it.

'It's a fine piece of work,' he reflected, 'and it'd be a shame to let it go, but keeping it here would be most improper. The best thing would be to give it to someone . . . Yes, I know – there's a benefit performance tonight for Shashkin, the comic actor. I'll take the candelabrum round to him as a present – after all, the old rascal loves that kind of thing . . .'

No sooner said than done. That evening the candelabrum, painstakingly wrapped, was presented to the comic actor Shashkin. The whole evening the actor's dressing-room was besieged by male visitors coming to admire the present; all evening the dressing-room was filled with a hubbub of rapturous exclamations and laughter like the whinnying of a horse. Whenever one of the actresses knocked on the door and asked if she could come in, the actor's husky voice would immediately reply:

'Not just now, darling, I'm changing.'

After the show the actor hunched his shoulders, threw up his hands in perplexity and said:

'Where the hell can I put this obscenity? After all, I live in a private apartment – think of the actresses who come to see me! It's not like a photograph, you can't shove it into a desk drawer!'

'Why not sell it, sir?' advised the wig-maker who was helping him off with his costume. 'There's an old woman in this area who buys up bronzes like that . . . Just ask for Mrs Smirnoff – everyone knows her.'

The comic actor took his advice . . .

Two days later Doctor Florinsky was sitting in his consulting-room with one finger pressed to his forehead, and was thinking about the acids of the bile. Suddenly the door flew open and in rushed Sasha Smirnoff. He was smiling, beaming, and his whole figure radiated happiness . . . In his hands he was holding something wrapped up in newspaper.

'Doctor!' he began, gasping for breath. 'I'm so delighted! You won't believe your luck – we've managed to find another candelabrum to make your pair! . . . Mum's thrilled to bits . . . I'm a mother's only son – you saved my life . . .'

And Sasha, all aquiver with gratitude, placed the candelabrum in front of the doctor. The doctor's mouth dropped, he tried to say something but nothing came out: he was speechless.

The Chorus-Girl

Once, when she was younger and prettier and still had a good voice, she was entertaining an admirer of hers, Nikolay Petrovich Kolpakov, at her summer datcha. They were sitting at the back in the entresol. The weather was unbearably hot and sultry. Kolpakov had just finished his meal. He had drunk a whole bottle of cheap port and was feeling bad-tempered and out of sorts. Both of them were bored; they were waiting for the heat to die down before taking a walk.

Suddenly there was a ring at the front door. They were not expecting anyone and Kolpakov, who was in shirtsleeves and slippers, jumped up and looked at Pasha.

'Must be the postman, or maybe one of the girls,' said the singer.

Kolpakov was not afraid of being seen by postmen or Pasha's girl friends, but to be on the safe side he gathered up his clothes and went into the connecting room, while Pasha ran to open the door. To her great astonishment, instead of the postman or one of her friends, an unknown woman was standing there, young, beautiful, dressed like a lady and judging by her appearance highly respectable.

The stranger was pale and breathing heavily, as if she had just climbed a long flight of stairs.

'What can I do for you?' asked Pasha.

The lady did not reply at once. She took a step forward, slowly looked round the room and sat down, as if too tired or unwell to remain standing; then her pale lips quivered for a long time, as she tried to form her words.

'Is my husband with you?' she finally asked, raising her large eyes, their lids red from crying, and looking at Pasha.

'Husband?' Pasha managed to whisper and suddenly felt so scared that her arms and legs turned cold. 'Husband?' she repeated, beginning to tremble.

'My husband . . . Nikolay Petrovich Kolpakov.'

'N-no, madam . . . I . . . I don't know any husband.'

A minute went by in silence. Several times the stranger passed a handkerchief across her pale lips, and to stop herself trembling inside she kept holding her breath, while Pasha stood rooted to the spot in front of her, gazing at her in fear and bewilderment.

'So you say he's not here?' the lady asked in a voice now firm, and smiled oddly.

'I – I don't know who you're talking about.'

'You loathsome, foul creature . . .' muttered the stranger, looking Pasha up and down with hatred and revulsion. 'Yes, foul – that's what you are. At last I can have the pleasure of telling you so!'

Pasha had the feeling that to this lady in black, with the angry eyes and slender white fingers, she really did look foul and disfigured, and she began to feel ashamed of her plump red cheeks, her pock-marked nose and the quiff of hair that refused to be combed back. And it seemed to her that if she were thin and not made up and did not have the quiff, she might have concealed the fact that she was not respectable, and would not have felt so terrified and ashamed standing in front of this mysterious, unknown lady.

'Where is my husband?' continued the lady. 'Not that it matters to me whether he's here or not – but I should tell you they've found out the money's missing and they're looking for Nikolay Petrovich. They mean to arrest him. That's what you've succeeded in doing!'

The lady stood up and began walking about the room in great agitation. Pasha gazed at her and was too scared to understand anything.

'They'll find him today and arrest him,' said the lady, giving a sob of wounded pride and vexation. 'I know who's got him into this awful mess! You foul, base woman! Disgusting, mercenary creature!' (The lady's lips twisted and her nose wrinkled up with revulsion.) 'I am weak – listen to me, you base woman! – I am weak . . . you are stronger than I am . . . but there is One who will stand up for me and my children! God sees everything! He is just! He will make you pay for every tear of mine, for all my sleepless nights! The time will come when you will remember me!'

Another silence followed. The lady walked up and down the room wringing her hands, while Pasha continued to stare blankly at her in bewilderment, unable to follow the lady's words but anticipating something dreadful.

'I don't know what you're talking about, madam,' she said and suddenly burst into tears.

'You liar!' shouted the lady and her eyes flashed at her angrily. 'I know everything! I've known about you for a long time! I know he's been coming here every day for the past month!'

'So what? What if he has? I have many visitors but I don't force anyone. It's a free world.'

'But don't you see, they've found out the money's missing! He's been embezzling other people's money from the office! For the sake of a . . . a woman like you, he was even prepared to break the law. Listen,' said the lady in a decisive tone, stopping in front of Pasha. 'You cannot have any principles, you exist solely in order to promote evil, that's your aim in life, but I cannot believe you have fallen so low as to lose all trace of human feeling! He has a wife and children . . . If he is convicted and sent to Siberia, the children and I will starve to death – do you realise that? But there is still a way open to save him and us from penury and humiliation. If I pay in nine hundred roubles today, they'll leave him alone. Only nine hundred roubles!'

'Nine hundred roubles?' Pasha asked quietly. 'I-I don't know what you mean . . . I didn't take them.'

'I'm not asking you for nine hundred roubles. You don't have any money and I wouldn't touch it if you had. I'm asking you for something else . . . Usually, men give women like you expensive presents. Simply give me back the presents you've had from my husband!'

'But, madam, the gentleman never gave me any presents!' squealed Pasha, beginning to follow.

'So where is the money? He's got through his own money, my money and other people's . . . Where's it all gone? Listen to me, I beg you! I was worked up just now and said a lot of unpleasant things to you, but I apologise. I know you must hate me, but if you are capable of sympathy, put yourself in my position! Give me back the presents, I implore you!'

'Mm . . .' said Pasha, shrugging her shoulders. 'I'd be glad to, but as God's my judge, the gentleman never gave me anything. That's the truth. Ah no, you're right,' the singer added, flustered. 'He did once bring me two little things. You can have them if you like . . .'

Pasha opened one of the small drawers in her dressing-table and took out a hollow gilt bracelet and a thin little ring with a ruby.

'Here you are,' she said, handing the objects to the visitor.

The lady flushed and her face trembled. She was insulted.

'These are no good,' she said. 'I'm not asking you for charity, I'm asking you for what doesn't belong to you . . . for what you squeezed out of my husband by exploiting your position – that weak, unfortunate man . . . When I saw you with him on Thursday at the landing-stage, you were wearing expensive brooches and bracelets. So don't try playing the innocent with me! I'm asking you for the last time: will you give me back the presents or not?'

'You're a funny one, you really are,' said Pasha, beginning to take offence herself. 'I swear to you, I never had anything from your Nikolay Petrovich other than the ring and the bracelet. All he ever brought me was fancy pastries.'

'Fancy pastries,' said the stranger with a bitter smile. 'At home the children are starving, and here you're eating fancy pastries. So you absolutely refuse to give me back the presents?'

Receiving no reply, the lady sat down and began staring straight ahead, thinking.

'What am I to do now?' she said. 'If I can't get the nine hundred roubles, he's finished, and the children and me with him. Which am I to do: kill this vile creature or go down on my knees to her?'

The lady pressed her handkerchief to her face and burst into tears.

'I implore you!' she said through her sobs. 'You're the one who's ruined and destroyed my husband, you must save him . . . You may have no sympathy for him, but the children . . . what of them? What have they done to deserve this?'

Pasha had a picture of small children standing on the street crying with hunger, and she too burst into tears.

'But what can I do, madam?' she said. 'You say I'm a vile creature and I've ruined Nikolay Petrovich, but I'm telling you the gospel truth . . . I swear I haven't had anything out of him. Motya's the only one in our chorus with a rich man to keep her, the rest of us just live from hand to mouth. Nikolay Petrovich is an educated, refined gentleman, so, I made him welcome. We're not allowed to say no.'

'It's the presents I'm asking for! Give me the presents! I'm crying, I'm humiliating myself . . . Do you want me to go down on my knees to you? Do you?'

Pasha gave a frightened shriek and threw up her arms. She felt that this pale, beautiful lady, who was expressing herself so nobly that she might have been on stage, really was capable of going down on her knees to her, precisely because she was so proud and noble and wanted to exalt herself and humiliate the chorus-girl.

'All right,' said Pasha, jumping up and wiping her eyes. 'I'll give you the presents. All right. Only they aren't from Nikolay Petrovich . . . I had them from other visitors. But if that's how you want it . . .'

Pasha went over to a chest of drawers, pulled out the top one, took out a diamond brooch, a coral necklace, several rings and a bracelet, and handed them all to the lady.

'I never had a thing from your husband, but you take them: take them and grow rich!' Pasha continued, offended by the lady's threat to go down on her knees to her. 'And if you're his respectable, lawful wedded wife, how come you couldn't keep him? It stands to reason! I didn't seek him out, he came to me ...'

Through her tears the lady looked the objects over and said:

'Where are the rest? ... These won't fetch five hundred.'

In a fit of emotion Pasha furiously tossed out a gold watch, a cigarette-case and a pair of cuff-links from the drawer, threw up her hands and said:

'That's the lot ... You can search the place if you like!'

The visitor sighed, picked up the objects with trembling hands, wrapped them in a handkerchief, and without so much as a word or even a nod, left.

The door from the next room opened and Kolpakov came in. He was pale and was shaking his head nervously from side to side, as if he had just swallowed something very bitter; tears were glistening in his eyes.

'Presents! What presents?' said Pasha, flying at him. 'When did you ever give me anything?'

'Oh what do presents matter?' Kolpakov replied and shook his head. 'My God – she cried in front of you, humiliated herself ...'

'What presents did you ever give me, I'm asking you?' Pasha shouted.

'My God, a decent, proud, pure being like that was even prepared to kneel down before this ... this whore! And I brought her to it! I let it happen!'

He seized his head in his hands and groaned:

'No, I shall never forgive myself! Never! Get away from me, you – you trash!' he shouted with loathing, backing away from Pasha and pushing her aside with trembling hands. 'She was about to go down on her knees, and to whom? To you! Oh God!'

Dressing quickly and stepping round Pasha in his disgust, he made his way to the door and left.

Pasha lay down and sobbed loudly. She was already beginning to regret giving away her things in the heat of the moment, and she felt hurt. She remembered how three years ago, for no rhyme or reason, a merchant had given her a beating, and sobbed even louder.

Dreams

Two village constables – one black-bearded, stocky, and with such peculiarly short legs that from behind they appear to start much lower down than everyone else's, the other long, thin and straight as a stick, with a sparse little dark-red beard – are escorting to the nearest town a tramp who will not divulge his name. The first waddles along looking from side to side, one moment chewing a straw, the next his own sleeve, slapping his thighs and humming to himself, and in general has a happy-go-lucky air; the other, despite his drawn face and narrow shoulders, looks solid, serious and substantial, and in build and bearing his whole figure resembles that of an Old Believer priest or a warrior of the kind one sees on very old icons; 'for the increase of his wisdom God has extended his brow', i.e. he is going bald, and this emphasises the similarity even more. The first is called Andrey Ptakha, the second Nikandr Sapozhnikov.

The person they are escorting does not at all conform to the popular notion of a tramp. He is a puny little man, feeble and sickly-looking, with small, drab, extremely nondescript features. His eyebrows are scanty, his look mild and submissive, and his beard hardly shows through, although the tramp must be over thirty. He treads timidly, stooping and with his hands tucked into his sleeves. The collar of his threadbare little serge coat, which is not that of a peasant, is turned right up, touching his cap, so that only a red point of a nose ventures to look out on the world. He speaks in a thin, high-pitched, wheedling voice, constantly clearing his throat. It is hard, very hard, to think of him as a tramp concealing his identity. He looks more like some impoverished, down-and-out son of a priest, a clerk dismissed for drunkenness, or a merchant's son or nephew who has tried his meagre talents on the stage and is now going home to play out the last act of the parable of the prodigal son; perhaps, judging from the grim perseverance with which he is battling against the impossible autumn mud, he is a fanatic – some monastic servant roaming the monasteries of Russia in stubborn search of 'a life of peace free from all sin', which he never finds . . .

By now the travellers have been going a long time, but still they cannot get off the small patch of earth on which they are walking. In front of them stretches thirty feet of mud-bound, brownish-black road, behind them as much again, and beyond, wherever you look, is an impenetrable wall of white mist. They walk and walk, but the earth is still the same, the wall gets no closer, and the patch remains a patch. A jagged white piece of cobblestone, a gully, or a sheaf of hay someone has dropped, appears for a moment, a dingy puddle gleams briefly, then all of a sudden a shadow of uncertain outline looms ahead unexpectedly; the closer to it they get, the smaller and darker it becomes; closer still, and the travellers make out a leaning post with the number of versts half erased, or a pathetic little birch tree, drenched and bare like a wayside beggar. The birch tree whispers something with its remaining yellow leaves, one leaf breaks off, and floats lethargically to the earth . . . Then there is nothing but mist again, mud, and the brown grass along the edges of the road. On the grass hang bleary, cheerless tears. These are not the tears of quiet joy that the earth weeps as it welcomes and bids farewell to the summer sun, and which it gives the quails, the corncrakes and the slender, long-billed curlew to drink at dawn! The travellers' feet drag in the heavy, clinging mud. Every step is hard work.

Andrey Ptakha is somewhat agitated. He keeps eyeing the tramp and striving to understand how a living, sober human being can fail to remember his own name.

'But you're a Russian Orthodox, aren't you?' he asks.

'I am,' the tramp answers mildly.

'Hm! . . . So you were christened then?'

'Of course – I'm not a Turk, am I? I go to church, I fast for the sacrament, I only eat what's proper in Lent, I observe all the practiculars of religion . . .'

'Well then, what's your name?'

'Call me what you will, lad.'

Ptakha shrugs his shoulders and in utter bewilderment slaps his thighs. The other constable, though, Nikandr Sapozhnikov, maintains a lofty silence. He is not as naive as Ptakha and evidently has a very good idea of the kind of reasons that might induce a normal Orthodox person to conceal his name from people. His face is manifestly cold and severe. He walks apart, does not deign to chat idly with his fellows, and seems to be trying to demonstrate his gravity and wisdom to all and sundry, even the mist.

'God knows what to make of you!' Ptakha continues to press. 'You're neither peasant nor gent, but a sort of in-between . . . The other day, I was washing some sieves in the pond when I caught this creepy-crawly thing – so long, the size of your finger, with gills and a tail. First I thought it was a fish, then I looked at it and – blow me if it didn't have little paws! It weren't a fish, it weren't a viper, damned if I know what it was . . . And you're just the same . . . What's your official status?'

'I'm a peasant, I'm of peasant stock,' sighs the tramp. 'My mamma was a house serf. I don't much look like a peasant, I know, because that was how fate treated me, kind sir. My mamma was a nursemaid to the gentry and had every comfort and I'm, well, her flesh and blood, and I lived with her in the big house. She pampered me and spoilt me and set her heart on lifting me out of the lower orders and making a gentleman of me. I slept in a bed, every day I ate a proper dinner, and I wore trousers and half-boots like any little lord. Whatever my mamma had to eat, I had the same; if they gave her cloth for a dress, she'd make clothes for me out of it . . . Oh, we lived well! The sweets and gingerbreads I scoffed in the days of my childhood – if you sold them now, they'd buy you a decent horse. My mamma taught me to read and write, she made me fear God from an early age, and she trained me so well that now I can't bring myself to use any ungenteel, peasant word. I don't drink vodka, either, lad, and I dress neat, and know how to behave properly in good society. If she is still alive, then God give her health, and if she's died, then grant rest unto her soul, O Lord, in thy kingdom where all the righteous do find rest!'

The tramp bares his head, with its sparse tufts of bristles, raises his eyes, and signs himself twice with the cross.

'Bring her, O Lord, to a verdant pasture, a place of repose!' he intones in a voice more like an old woman's than a man's. 'Teach her, O Lord, thy servant Kseniya, thy statutes! If it weren't for my kind mamma, I'd be just a simple peasant with no clue about anything! Now though, lad, you can ask me about anything you like and I'll tell you – whether it's profane writings, or holy writ, your prayers or your catechism. And I live by the good Book, too . . . I harm no one, I keep my body in purity and chastity, I observe the fasts, I eat at the appointed times. Another man might have no pleasure in life but vodka and lewd talk, but if I have any spare time I sit down in a little corner and read a book. I read, and cry and cry . . .'

'What do you cry for?'

'They write so sadly! A book might not cost you more than five kopecks, yet you can cry and groan over it no end.'

'Is your father dead?' asks Ptakha.

'I don't know, lad. No harm in telling you – I don't know who my parent was. The way I see it, I was my mamma's illegitimate child. My mamma lived all her life with the gentry and didn't wish to marry an ordinary peasant –'

'So she set her sights on the master instead,' grins Ptakha.

'She transgressed, that she did. She was devout, God-fearing, but she did not preserve her maidenhood. It's a sin, of course, a great sin, no denying it, but then maybe there's noble blood in me as a result. Maybe I'm only a peasant in rank, underneath it I'm a noble gentleman.'

The 'noble gentleman' says all this in a soft, treacly high-pitched voice, furrowing his narrow little brow and emitting little squeaks through his frozen red nose. Ptakha listens, squints at him amazed, and never ceases shrugging his shoulders.

After walking nearly six versts, the constables and the tramp sit down on a mound to rest.

'Even a dog remembers its own name,' Ptakha mutters. 'I'm called Andryushka, he's called Nikandra – every man has his holy name, and that name must never be forgot! Never!'

'Who needs to know my name?' sighs the tramp, propping his cheek on his fist. 'And what good will it do me? Maybe, if they'd let me go where I like . . . but as it is it'd only make matters worse. My brothers in the faith, I know the law. Now I'm just a tramp, anonymous, and at worst they'll send me to East Siberia and give me thirty or forty lashes. But if I tell them my real name and status they'll pack me off to hard labour again. I know!'

'You mean to say you were doing hard labour?'

'I was, dear friend. Four years I went round with my head shaven and with irons on.'

'What were you there for?'

'For murder, kind sir! When I was just a lad, about eighteen or so, by accident my mamma put arsenic in the master's glass instead of soda and acid. There were lots of different medicine boxes in the storeroom, it wasn't difficult to muddle them up . . .'

The tramp sighs, wags his head, and says:

'She was devout all right, but who can really tell – another's soul is a dense forest! Maybe it was an accident, but maybe in her heart she couldn't bear the insult of the master taking another maidservant unto him . . . Maybe she put it in on purpose, who knows! I was young then and didn't understand it all . . . Come to think of it, the master did take another paramour, and my mamma was sorely put out about it. Nearly two years it took them to try us . . . My mamma was sentenced to twenty years' hard labour and myself just to seven, because I was under age.'

'Why did they sentence *you*?'

'As an accomplice. I took him the glass. That's how it always was: my mamma used to mix the soda, and I took it to him. Mind you, brothers, I'm only telling you this as one Christian to another, as I would before God, don't go telling anyone . . .'

'Oh, no one'll ask us,' says Ptakha. 'So you escaped from the penal colony, is that it?'

'I did, dear friend. There was about fourteen of us bolted. God bless them for it, they'd decided to run away themselves, and they took me with them. So you work it out, lad, and tell me honestly, why should I reveal my origins? They'll send me straight back to hard labour! And what kind of a convict am I? I'm delicate, I'm not very well, I like it to be clean where I eat and sleep. When I say my prayers, I like to light a little lamp or candle, and there must be no noise roundabout. When I do my bows to the ground, there must be no litter or spittle on the floor. And I do forty every morning and evening, you know, for my mamma.'

The tramp takes off his cap and crosses himself.

'But let 'em send me to East Siberia,' he says. 'I'm not afraid of that!'

'Is that better, then?'

'It's a completely different story! In the penal colony you're like crayfish stuffed in a basket – cramped and crushed together, you can't even draw breath, may the Holy Mother spare us such hell! You're a criminal, and that's how they treat you, worse than a dog. You can't eat or sleep or pray properly there. But it's different in a settlement. In a settlement the first thing that happens is I become a member of the community like everyone else. The authorities have to give me my share by law . . . oh yes! Land there, they say, costs no more than snow – you take as much as you want! They'll give me land to till, lad, land for my vegetables, and land to build on . . . I'll plough and sow just like other people, I'll keep cattle and the whole lot – bees, sheep, dogs . . . And a Siberian cat to stop the rats and mice eating my goods . . . I'll put up a log hut, brothers, I'll buy myself icons . . . God willing, I'll get married and have my own little children.'

The tramp mumbles all this looking not at his listeners but somewhere to one side. For all their naivety, he voices these fantasies with such sincerity and inner conviction that it is hard not to believe them. The tramp's little mouth has slanted into a smile, whilst his eyes and nose and whole face are set hard in blissful anticipation of that far-off happiness. The constables listen and regard him seriously, not without sympathy. They too believe.

'No, I'm not afraid of Siberia,' the tramp goes on mumbling. 'Siberia's all part of the same Russia, it's got the same God and Tsar as we have, they talk the same Orthodox tongue as you and me. Only there's more scope there, people are better off. Everything's better there. The rivers, for instance, are far better than the ones here! As for fish and game and what have you – it's teeming with them! And my Number One pleasure in life, brothers, is fishing. I'm happy to go without bread, so long as I can sit with a rod. I mean it. I fish with a rod and with pike-lines, I set creels, and when the ice is under way I fish with a cast-net. I'm not strong enough to lift it myself, so I pay a peasant five kopecks to do it for me. Lord, what sport that is! To catch a burbot or chub, say, is like coming across your own long-lost brother! And every fish has its own mentality, you know: one of them you catch with a live-bait, another with a grub, another with a frog or a grasshopper. You've got to know all about that! Take the burbot, for example. The burbot's not a choosy fish, she'll go for a ruffe even, whilst the pike is fond of a gudgeon and the asp a butterfly. As for chub, there's no better pleasure than fishing for them in a swift stream. You let out about seventy foot of line with no sinker, and a butterfly or beetle on the end, make sure the bait floats on top, then stand in the water with your trousers off, let it go downstream, and – jerk! – you've got a chub. Only you must watch he doesn't whip the bait off, the rascal. As soon as he jiggles your line, you must strike, don't hang about. Good grief, the fish I've caught in my time! When we were on the run and the other prisoners were asleep in the forest, I'd be wide awake itching to get down to the river. And the rivers there are broad and fast, and goodness the banks are steep! Along the banks it's nothing but dense forest. The trees are so tall you only have to look at their tops and your head swims. By prices hereabouts, each pine tree would fetch ten roubles or so.'

Overcome by the welter of day-dreams, artistically powerful

images of the past, and sweet presentiments of happiness, the poor man falls silent and merely moves his lips, as though whispering to himself. The blissful set smile does not leave his face. The constables are silent. They are deep in thought, their heads bowed. In the autumn stillness, when the cold grim mist off the land settles on your soul, when it looms before your eyes like a prison wall, and constantly reminds you how restricted is man's free will, it is sweet to think of broad, fast rivers with banks that are open to the sky, impenetrable forests and boundless steppes. Slowly and calmly the imagination paints you a picture of early morning, when the bloom of dawn still lingers in the sky, and a man no bigger than a speck is making his way along a steep, deserted river bank; the age-old masts of pines, piled high in terraces on either side of the torrent, stare grimly at the free man, and grumble moodily; roots, huge boulders and thorny bushes bar his way, but he is strong in body and bold of spirit, he does not fear pines, boulders, his own loneliness, or the rumbling echo that repeats his every step.

The constables paint to themselves pictures of a free life such as they have never lived. Perhaps they are dimly recalling images of something they heard of long ago, or perhaps they inherited their ideas of this free life with their own flesh and blood from distant forebears who were themselves free. Who knows?

The first to break the silence is Nikandr Sapozhnikov, who has not uttered a single word until now. Whether he has suddenly envied the tramp his illusory happiness, or feels in his heart that these dreams of happiness do not accord with the grey mist and the brownish-black mud – either way, he looks sternly at the tramp and says:

'Be that as it may, that's all well and good, brother, only you're not going to get to them places of freedom and plenty. You don't stand a chance. You'll have had it before you've gone three hundred versts. Look how weedy you are! You've only done six versts and you're struggling to get your wind!'

The tramp turns slowly towards Nikandr and the blissful smile vanishes from his face. He looks at the grave face of the constable apprehensively and sheepishly, evidently begins to recall something, and hangs his head. Again they are silent . . . All three are thinking. The constables are straining their imaginations to encompass what probably God alone can imagine, namely the terrible expanse that separates them from the realm of freedom. The tramp's head, though, is crowded with clear, distinct pictures that are more terrible by far than that expanse. Before him rise vivid images of all the legal delays, the transfer prisons and the penal colony prisons, the convicts' barges, the exhausting stops en route, the freezing hard winters, the illnesses and deaths of fellow-prisoners . . .

The tramp blinks sheepishly, brushes the tiny beads of sweat from his forehead with his sleeve, and blows out a long breath, as though he has just jumped out of a sweltering hot bath-house, then he wipes his forehead with the other sleeve, and looks around fearfully.

'Too right you won't get there!' agrees Ptakha. 'What kind of a walker are you? Look at yourself: all skin and bones! You'll die first, brother!'

'Of course he will! He doesn't stand a chance!' says Nikandr. 'They'll put him straight in the infirmary . . . I'm telling you!'

The man with no name looks in terror at the severe, impassive faces of his hostile companions and, without taking his cap off, hurriedly crosses himself, his eyes staring . . . He trembles all over, his head shakes, and the whole of him begins to writhe like a caterpillar that has been trodden on. . .

'Right, time to go,' says Nikandr, getting up. 'We've had our rest!'

A minute later and the travellers are trudging along the muddy road. The tramp has hunched himself up even more and shoved his hands even further into his sleeves. Ptakha is silent.

The Orator

One fine morning they buried Collegiate Assessor Kirill Ivanovich Babylonov. He died of two complaints so frequently encountered in our native land: a nagging wife and alcoholism. When the funeral procession moved off from the church on its way to the cemetery, one of the deceased's colleagues, a certain Poplavsky, hailed a cab and dashed round to his friend, Grigory Petrovich Vodkin. Vodkin is a young man, but has already made quite a name for himself. As many readers will know, he possesses a rare gift for making impromptu speeches at weddings, anniversaries and funerals. He can speak in any condition: half-asleep, on an empty stomach, drunk as a lord, or in a raging fever. Words flow as smoothly and evenly from his mouth as water from a drainpipe, and as copiously; black beetles in a tavern are not more numerous than the maudlin words in his vocabulary. He always speaks eloquently and at great length, so that sometimes, particularly at merchant weddings, the only way to stop him is to summon the police.

'I've come to ask you a favour, old man,' began Poplavsky, finding him at home. 'Put your coat on straight away and let's go. One of our lot has died, we're just seeing him off to the next world, and someone's got to whiffle a few words of farewell . . . We're banking on you, old man. We wouldn't have bothered you for one of the small fry, but this time it's our secretary – a pillar of the department, you might say. You can't bury a big shot like that without a speech.'

'Your secretary?' yawned Vodkin. 'The one who was always drunk?'

'Yes, him. There'll be pancakes and a good spread . . . cab fares on us. Come on, old son! Spin us some Ciceronian palaver by the grave, and we'll give you a right royal thank-you!'

Vodkin gladly agreed. He ruffled up his hair, put on a melancholy face and left with Poplavsky.

'I remember that secretary of yours,' he said, seating himself in the cab. 'You'd have to go a long way to find a bigger cheat and swindler, God rest his soul.'

'Now then Grisha, one shouldn't speak ill of the dead.'

'Of course not – *aut mortuis nihil bene* – but the man's still a crook.'

The friends caught up with the funeral procession and joined it. The dead man was being borne along slowly, so that before reaching the cemetery they had time to nip into several pubs and knock back a quick one for the good of Babylonov's soul.

At the cemetery a short service of committal was held. Mother-in-law, wife and sister-in-law, following established custom, wept profusely. As the coffin was being lowered into the grave, the wife even shouted: 'Stand back – let me join him!' – but did not, probably remembering the pension. Vodkin waited until everything had quietened down, then stepped forward, took in all his listeners at a glance, and began:

'Surely our eyes and ears deceive us? This grave, these tear-stained faces, this moaning and wailing: is it not all some terrible dream? Alas, it is no dream and our vision doth not deceive us! He whom we saw only the other day so cheerful, so youthfully fresh and pure, who only the other day, like the indefatigable bee, before our very eyes was bearing his honey to the hive of his country's common weal, he who – who – that man has now been reduced to dust, to an objective vacuum. Implacable Death placed its withering hand upon him at a time when, for all his ripeness of years, he was still at the height of his powers and full of the most radiant hopes. Oh, irreparable loss! Who can possibly replace him? We have no dearth of good civil servants, but there was only one Prokofy Osipych. He was devoted to his honourable duties heart and soul, never did he spare himself, many were the sleepless nights he spent, he was unselfish and incorruptible . . . How he despised those who tried to suborn him to the detriment of the common good, who sought with life's little comforts to lure him into betraying his duty! Why, with our very eyes we have seen Prokofy Osipych divide his meagre salary among his poorest colleagues, and you yourselves have just heard the wailing of the widows and orphans who depended upon his charity. Devoted as he was to the call of duty and to good works, he was a stranger to the joys of life and even turned his back on domestic felicity; as you know, he remained a bachelor to the end of his days! And who will replace him as a colleague? How clearly I can see before me now that tender, clean-shaven face, turned towards us with a kindly smile, how clearly I can hear the note of loving friendship in that gentle voice! May you rest in peace, Prokofy Osipych! Sleep well – thou true and faithful servant!'

As Vodkin proceeded, his listeners began to whisper among themselves. Everyone liked the speech, it even extracted a few tears, but there was a lot in it that seemed odd. First, no one could understand why the orator called the dead man Prokofy Osipovich, instead of Kirill Ivanovich. Secondly, everyone knew that the deceased had spent a lifetime warring with his lawful wedded wife and could not therefore be termed a bachelor; and thirdly, he had a bushy ginger beard and had never once used a razor, so that it was a mystery why the orator should describe him as clean-shaven. Perplexed, the listeners exchanged glances and shrugged.

'Prokofy Osipych!' continued the orator, staring raptly into the grave. 'Your face was plain – shall I say ugly? – you were stern and unbending, but we all knew that behind that outer shell there beat a heart of purest gold!'

Soon the audience began to notice something odd about the orator, too. His eyes were fixed on one point, he fidgeted restlessly and he himself began to shrug his shoulders. Suddenly he dried up, his mouth fell open in astonishment, and he turned round to Poplavsky.

'But he's alive!' he said, staring in horror.

'Who is?'

'Prokofy Osipych! He's standing over there by the headstone!'

'He's not the one who's dead, it's Kirill Ivanych!'

'But you said yourself your secretary had died!'

'Kirill Ivanych *was* our secretary – you've mixed them up, you clown! Prokofy Osipych was our secretary before, that's right, but he was transferred two years ago to the second section as head clerk.'

'Ah, God knows!'

'Why aren't you going on? This is getting embarrassing!'

Vodkin turned back to the grave and resumed with all his previous eloquence. Prokofy Osipych, an elderly civil servant with a clean-shaven countenance, was indeed standing by the headstone, looking at the orator and scowling.

'You put your foot in it there!' laughed the civil servants on their way back from the funeral with Vodkin. 'Fancy burying someone who's still alive.'

'A poor show, young fellow!' growled Prokofy Osipych. 'That kind of speech may be all right when someone's dead, but when they're still alive – it's just poking fun, sir! How did you put it, for heaven's sake? Unselfish, incorruptible, doesn't take bribes! To say that of a living person you have to be joking, sir. And who asked you, young man, to sound off about my face? Plain and ugly it may be, but why draw the attention of all and sundry to it? No sir, I'm offended!'

Vanka

Vanka Zhukov, a boy of nine apprenticed three months ago to Alyakhin the shoemaker, did not go to bed on Christmas Eve. He waited until his master and mistress and the older apprentices had left for the early morning service, then he fetched a little bottle of ink and a pen with a rusty nib from his master's cupboard, spread a crumpled sheet of paper in front of him, and began to write. Before forming the first letter, he looked round nervously several times at the doors and windows, glanced up at the dark icon, to left and right of which stretched shelves of lasts, and sighed brokenly. He was kneeling in front of a work bench, on which lay his sheet of paper.

'Dear Grandad Konstantin Makarych,' he wrote. 'I'm writing you this letter. I wish you a Happy Christmas and all God's blessings. I have no father or mummy, you're the only person I have left.'

Vanka turned to look at the dark window, in which flickered the reflection of his candle, and vividly imagined to himself his grandfather Konstantin Makarych, who worked as a night-watchman on the Zhivaryovs' estate. He was a skinny little old man of about sixty-five, but amazingly lively and nimble, with a face that was always laughing and drunken eyes. During the daytime he slept in the servants' kitchen or played the fool with the cooks; at night, wrapped in his voluminous full-length sheepskin, he went the rounds of the estate beating with his watchman's clapper. Behind him, their heads hung low, walked old Kashtanka and Loacher, named after the fish on account of his dark back and long, weasel-like body. Loacher is an extremely deferential and affectionate dog, he gives the same adoring look to friend and stranger alike, but his reputation is nil. Behind that deference and docility there lurks the most Jesuitical cunning. No one knows better than he how to creep up and nip you in the leg, slip into the ice-house, or steal a peasant's chicken. Many is the time he has nearly had his back legs broken, a couple of times he has been strung up, and every week he is beaten within an inch of his life; but he always bounces back.

Now Grandfather was sure to be standing at the gates of the village church, squinting at its bright red windows, stamping up and down in his big felt boots, and fooling about with the servants. His watchman's clapper hangs at his belt. He waves his arms around, hugs himself to keep warm, and with an impish old chuckle keeps going up to the housemaids and cooks and pinching them.

'Why don't we have some snuff?' he says, offering the girls his snuff-box.

The girls take a pinch and sneeze. This sends grandfather into indescribable raptures, he breaks into peals of merry laughter, and cries:

'Wipe the stuff off, it's freezing to you!'

They hold the box out to the dogs, as well. Kashtanka sneezes, shakes her muzzle about and walks away, offended. Loacher is too polite to sneeze and wags his tail instead. The weather is superb. The air is still, transparent, and crisp. It is a dark night, but the whole village can be seen clearly: the white roofs with plumes of smoke rising from their chimneys, the trees silvered with rime, the deep snowdrifts. The whole sky is strewn with gaily twinkling stars, and the Milky Way shines forth so clearly that you would think it had been washed and polished with snow for Christmas . . .

Vanka sighed, dipped his pen in the ink, and carried on writing:

'And yesterday I got a thrashing. The master dragged me out into the yard by my hair and walloped me with a strap, because I was rocking their baby in it's cradle and went and dropped off. And last week the mistress told me to gut a herring and I started from the tail so she took hold of the herring and wiped it's snout all over my mug. The older apprentices are always making fun of me they send me to the tavern for vodka and make me steal the master's gherkins and the master beats me with the first thing comes to hand. And there's nothing to eat here at all. They give me bread in the morning porridge for dinner and bread again for supper but the master and mistress they guzzle all the tea and cabbage soup. And they make me sleep in the passage and when their baby's crying I don't sleep at all but have to rock the cradle. Dear Grandad, for the Dear Lord's sake take me away from here take me home to the village I can't stand it any longer . . . I beg and beseech you and will pray for you always take me away from here or I'll die –'

Vanka's mouth trembled, he wiped his eyes with his grubby fist, and gave a sob.

'– I'll grind your snuff for you,' he continued, 'I'll pray to God for you, and if I do anything bad you can beat the hide off me. And if you're worried I won't have a job to do then I'll beg the steward to take Christian pity on me and let me clean boots or I'll take over from Fedka as shepherd-boy. Dear Grandpa, I can't stand it any longer its killing me. I was going to run away to the village, but I don't have any boots and I'm scared of the frost. And when I grow up I'll look after you in return and won't let anyone harm you and when you die I'll pray for your soul just as I do for Pelageya my mummy.

'Moscow is a very big town. All the houses are gents' houses and there are lots of horses but no sheep and the dogs aren't fierce at all. The boys don't go about with the star here at Christmas and they won't let people go up and sing in the choir and once I saw some hooks for sale in a shop window with line on them and for all sorts of fish, very fine they were too and there was even one strong enough to hold a forty-pound wels. Also I've seen shops with all sorts of guns like the master's at home they'd be about a hundred roubles each I reckon . . . Also in the butcher's shops there are black-cock and hazel grouse and hares but where they shoot them the butchers don't say.

'Dear Grandad, when they have the Christmas tree with presents on at the big house get one of the gold walnuts for me will you and put it away in the green chest. Ask Miss Olga Ignatyevna, say its for Vanka.'

Vanka let out a deep sigh and once more gazed at the window-pane. He remembered that it was always his grandfather who went into the forest to get the Christmas tree for the big house, taking Vanka with him. Oh what fun that was! Grandfather crackled, the frost crackled, and looking at them Vanka crackled too. Before felling the tree, his grandfather would smoke a pipe, take his time over a pinch of snuff, and laugh at little Vanka shivering there . . . The young fir-trees clothed in rime stood motionless, waiting to see which of them was to die. Then, goodness knows where from, a hare shoots across the snowdrifts like an arrow . . . Grandfather can never resist shouting:

'Catch him, catch him! Catch the bob-tailed rascal!'

After cutting down the fir-tree, grandfather would drag it off to the house. There they would set about decorating it . . . Miss Olga Ignatyevna, Vanka's favourite, bustled about most. When Vanka's mother Pelageya was still alive and worked for the Zhivaryovs as a housemaid, Olga Ignatyevna used to give Vanka sweets, and amused herself by teaching him to read, write, count to a hundred and even dance a quadrille. But when Pelageya died, the orphaned Vanka was packed off to his grandfather in the servants' kitchen, and thence to Moscow to Alyakhin the shoemaker . . .

'Come and fetch me dear Grandad,' Vanka continued. 'I beg you in Christ's name to take me away from here. Have pity on me a poor orphan or they'll go on clouting me and I'm hungry all day long and I'm so miserable I can't tell you I cry all the time. And once the master hit me on the head with a last and I fell down and nearly didn't wake up. My life's so awful worse than any dog's . . . Please give my love also to Alyona One-Eyed Yegorka and the coachmen and don't give my concertina away to anyone. I remain your grandson Ivan Zhukov. Dear Grandad come.'

Vanka folded the closely-written sheet in four and put it into an envelope that he had bought for a kopeck the previous day . . . He thought for a moment, dipped his pen, and wrote down the address:

The Village. To Grandad.

Then he scratched his head, thought again, and added: ' – Konstantin Makarych.' Pleased not to have been disturbed while writing, he grabbed his cap and without bothering to put a coat on over his shirt, dashed out into the street . . .

The men at the butcher's shop, in answer to his questions the day before, had told him that letters are dropped into post-boxes, then carried from the post-boxes to all the ends of the earth on mail troikas with drunken drivers and tinkling bells. Vanka ran up to the nearest post-box and pushed his precious letter through the opening . . .

An hour later, lulled by fond hopes, he was fast asleep. He dreamt he saw the stove. On it was sitting his grandfather, dangling his bare feet and reading the letter to the cooks . . . Round the stove walked Loacher, wagging his tail . . .

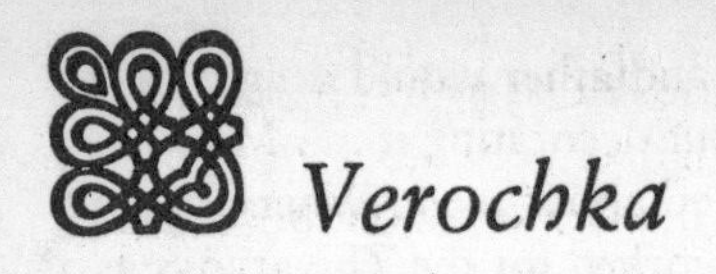

Verochka 1887

Ivan Alekseyevich Ognyov remembers how the glass door rang as he opened it that August evening and stepped out onto the verandah. He was wearing a light cape and the same broad-brimmed straw hat that is now gathering dust under his bed along with his Hessian boots. In one hand he was holding a large bundle of books and exercise-books, in the other a stout, knobbly walking-stick.

Standing in the doorway, guiding him with a lamp, was the owner of the house, Kuznetsov, a bald-headed old man with a long grey beard and a snow-white piqué waistcoat. He was smiling and nodding benignly.

'Goodbye, old friend!' Ognyov shouted to him.

Kuznetsov put the lamp down on a table and came out onto the verandah. Two long thin shadows strode across the steps to the flower-beds, wobbled and bumped their heads against the trunks of the lime-trees.

'Goodbye and thank you again, old chap!' said Ivan Alekseich. 'Thank you for being so generous, so kind and so affectionate . . . I shall never ever forget your hospitality. You're a fine person, your daughter's a fine person, and all of you here are so kind and cheerful and warm-hearted . . . You're such a marvellous crowd, I can't begin to tell you.'

Carried away by his emotions and by the effects of the home-brewed vodka he had just drunk, Ognyov intoned his words like a young priest, and was so overcome that he expressed his feelings more by blinking his eyes and twitching his shoulders than by words. Kuznetsov, who was also tipsy and emotionally overcome, leaned forward to the young man and exchanged kisses with him.

'I've become like a faithful old gun-dog to you!' Ognyov continued. 'Almost every day I've wandered over here, a dozen times I've stopped the night, and I shudder to think how much of your vodka I must have drunk. But what I'm most grateful to you for, Gavriil Petrovich, is your help and co-operation. Without you I should have been messing about here with my statistics until October. And that's what I'll say in my foreword: "I consider it my duty to express my gratitude to Chairman of the Rural Council of N., Kuznetsov, for his kind co-operation." What a fan-tastic future statistics has! Give Vera Gavrilovna my humblest regards, and tell the doctors, the two magistrates and your secretary that I shall never forget the help they gave me! And now, old friend, let us embrace each other in a final, farewell kiss.'

Overwhelmed with sentiment, Ognyov exchanged kisses once more with the old man and began to descend the steps. On the last one he looked round and asked:

'Shall we ever meet again?'

'Heaven knows!' replied the old man. 'I doubt it.'

'So do I. Nothing on earth will tempt you to Petersburg, and I don't expect I'll ever come to this district again. Farewell, then!'

'You could have left your books here!' Kuznetsov shouted after him. 'What do you want to drag that load around for? I could have got one of the servants to bring them tomorrow.'

But Ognyov was walking briskly away and no longer listening. Primed by the liquor, he felt at once cheerful, warm, and melancholy . . . As he walked along, he thought how often in life one comes across fine people, and how sad it is that of these encounters nothing remains but memories. A flock of cranes appears suddenly on the horizon, a faint breeze brings you their mournfully exultant cry, but a minute later, however avidly you peer into the blue distance, not a speck is to be seen, not a sound heard; so too human beings, with their faces and voices, appear briefly in our lives and disappear into our past, leaving nothing but a few trivial scraps of memory. After living in the N. district since early spring and visiting the kind-hearted Kuznetsovs almost every day, Ivan Alekseich had come to think of the old man, his daughter and the servants as his own family, had become familiar with every nook and cranny of the house, the cosy verandah, the twists in the paths, and the silhouettes of the trees above the kitchen and the bath-house; but as soon as he closed the garden gate behind him, all this would turn into a memory and lose its vital significance for ever, while in a year or two's time all these dear images would fade in his mind and be indistinguishable from the fruits and fancies of imagination.

'It's people who are most precious in life!' thought Ognyov, feeling very moved, as he strode along the path towards the gate. 'People!'

In the garden it was warm and quiet. The smell of still-flowering tobacco-plants, heliotrope and mignonette wafted to him from the beds. The spaces between the shrubs and tree-trunks were filled with a soft, airy mist suffused with moonlight, and Ognyov would long remember how wraith-like wisps stole one by one, slowly but perceptibly, across the pathways. The moon stood high above the garden, while below it translucent patches of mist raced towards the east. The whole world seemed to be made up of nothing but black silhouettes and floating white shapes, and Ognyov, who was seeing a misty moonlit August night for practically the first time in his life, felt that he was looking not at nature but at some stage set on which incompetent pyrotechnists, attempting to illuminate the garden with white Bengal lights, had stationed themselves behind the shrubs and succeeded in filling the air not only with light but with white smoke as well.

As Ognyov was approaching the garden gate, a dark shadow detached itself from the low paling fence and came towards him.

'Vera Gavrilovna!' he exclaimed joyfully. 'So that's where you are! I've been looking for you everywhere, I wanted to say farewell . . . I'm just off!'

'So soon? But it's only eleven o'clock.'

'No, I must be going. It's five versts there and I still have to pack. Got to be up early tomorrow . . .'

Standing in front of Ognyov was Kuznetsov's daughter Vera, a girl of twenty-one, as usual sad-looking, casually dressed and appealing. Girls who dream to themselves a lot and spend days on end lying around lazily reading everything that comes their way, who are bored and feel sad, generally do dress casually. This touch of informality lends an especial charm to those of them who are endowed with good taste and an instinct for beauty. Ognyov, at any rate, when he came to recall later how pretty Verochka was, could not picture her without the loose-fitting blouse, creased into deep folds at the waist but still not touching her figure, or the curl that had worked itself loose from her piled-up hair and was hanging over her brow, or the red knitted shawl with the shaggy bobbles round the edges, which in the evenings hung dejectedly on Verochka's shoulder like a flag in calm weather, and during the day lay crumpled up in the hall next to the men's caps or on a chest in the dining-room, where it was unceremoniously slept on by the old cat. The shawl and the creases in the blouse conveyed an air of relaxation and placid domesticity. Perhaps because Ognyov liked Vera, for him every button and frill that she wore held something warm, cosy and good, a naivety and poetry that are so conspicuously absent in women who are artificial, devoid of a feeling for beauty, and essentially cold.

Verochka had a good figure, a straight profile and attractive curly hair. Ognyov, who had not seen many women in his lifetime, thought her beautiful.

'So I'm leaving!' he said, bidding her farewell by the gate. 'Think kindly of me, won't you; and thank you for everything!'

In the same chanting voice in which he had talked to the old man, blinking and twitching his shoulders as before, he began to thank Vera for being so kind, hospitable and welcoming.

'I mentioned you every time I wrote home to my mother,' he said. 'If everyone in the world was like you and your papa, we'd be living in a seventh heaven! You're such a marvellous crowd here! So simple, warm-hearted and sincere.'

'Where are you off to now?' asked Vera.

'First to see my mother in Oryol and spend a couple of weeks with her, then back to work in Petersburg.'

'And after that?'

'After that? I'll be working right through the winter, then off again in the spring to the provinces somewhere to collect material. Well then, all the best, long life to you . . . think kindly of me. We shan't meet again.'

Ognyov bent over and kissed Verochka's hand. Then, at a loss for words, he straightened his cape, took a better grip on his bundle of books, and after a further pause said:

'What a lot of mist's collected!'

'Yes. Are you sure you haven't left anything?'

'Left anything? I don't think so . . .'

Ognyov stood there in silence for several seconds, then turned awkwardly towards the garden gate and went out.

'Just a moment,' said Vera, running after him, 'I'll come with you as far as our wood.'

They set off along the track. There were no trees to shut out the view now, so one could see the sky and the far distance. The whole of nature was veiled in a gauzy, transparent haze, which made its beauty all the more appealing. The thicker, whiter mist, lying unevenly round the ricks and bushes or floating in wisps across the track, hugged the ground, as if trying not to obscure the view. Through the haze the whole of the track could be seen as far as the wood, with dark ditches on either side in which grew small bushes that hindered the passage of the floating wisps. The dark strip of the

Kuznetsovs' wood began half a verst from the gate.

'Why's she come with me? I'll have to see her back,' thought Ognyov, but glancing at Vera's profile, he smiled affectionately and said:

'One doesn't feel like leaving on a night like this! It's a real romantic night, what with the moon, the silence and all the trimmings. Shall I tell you something, Vera Gavrilovna? I'm twenty-nine and I've never had a single romance. Not a single romantic episode in my whole life – so I only know about such things as garden trysts, avenues of sighs, and kisses at second-hand. It's not normal! When you're sitting in a room in town, you're not aware you've missed out on something, but here in the countryside you become very conscious of it . . . and it's rather hurtful!'

'And why are you like this?'

'I don't know. Probably because I've never had the time, but maybe because I've simply not come across the kind of women who . . . The fact is, I don't have many friends and I never go out.'

For about three hundred paces the young people walked along in silence. Ognyov kept glancing at Verochka's bare head and shawl, and one after another the memories of days in spring and summer came flooding back to him. Far from his dismal Petersburg room, revelling in nature, the kind attentions of good people and his favourite work, he had not been aware of one day following the next, how first the nightingale, then the quail, and a little later the corncrake, fell silent, presaging the end of summer . . . Time had sped by unnoticed, so life must have been easy and good . . . He began recalling aloud how unwillingly he had come here to N. district at the end of April, a young man of modest means unused to travel and to people, and how he was expecting to find boredom, loneliness and an indifference to statistics, which in his opinion now occupied the foremost position among the sciences. Arriving one April morning at the little district town of N., he had put up at the inn run by the Old Believer Ryabukhin, where for twenty kopecks a day he was given a clean, bright room with the condition that he smoke out of doors. After resting and finding out who was the Chairman of the Rural Council, he had immediately set off on foot to see Gavriil Petrovich. The route had taken him through four versts of luxuriant meadows and young woodland. Skylarks hovered beneath the very clouds, filling the air with silvery notes, while rooks sailed across the green-sprouting fields, flapping their wings solemnly and sedately.

'Gracious,' Ognyov had thought with surprise, 'do they always breathe this air here, or have they laid it on specially today for my arrival?'

Expecting a dry, official reception, he had entered the Kuznetsovs' house timidly, looking askance and tugging shyly at his beard. At first the old man furrowed his brow and did not understand how the Rural Council could be of use to this young man and his statistics, but when Ognyov gave him a full explanation of what statistical material was and where it was to be collected, Gavriil Petrovich perked up, beamed, and started to look at Ognyov's exercise-books with boyish curiosity . . . That same evening Ivan Alekseich was already dining with the Kuznetsovs. The potent vodka quickly went to his head, and as he watched the calm faces and lazy movements of his new friends, his whole body was filled with the sweet indolence that makes you feel like falling asleep, stretching yourself, or smiling. And the new friends studied him with kindly attention and asked him if his mother and father were still alive, how much he earned a month, and whether he often went to the theatre . . .

Ognyov recalled his journeys round the outlying districts, the picnics and fishing parties, and the group excursion to the nunnery to see the Abbess Martha, who gave each of the visitors a bead-purse; and he recalled those heated, interminable, typically Russian arguments, when the debaters, spluttering and banging their fists on the table, misunderstand and interrupt one another, contradict themselves at every turn without noticing, keep changing the subject and after two or three hours of argument, laugh it all off saying:

'Heaven knows what set us arguing! We started in sunshine and ended in rain.'

'Do you remember when you and I and the doctor rode over to Shestovo?' Ivan Alekseich said to Vera, as they approached the wood. 'That was the day we came across the holy fool. I gave him a five-kopeck piece and he crossed himself three times and threw it into the rye. Gracious, I'm taking so many impressions away with me that if one could turn them into a solid mass, they'd make a sizeable gold ingot! I don't understand why intelligent and sensitive people should want to herd together in the big cities and not come out here. Is there really more room to breathe and more truth to be found on the Nevsky and in those great big damp houses? I must say, my kind of life in furnished apartments, chock-a-block with artists, academics and journalists, has always struck me as totally false.'

Twenty paces from the wood was a narrow footbridge over a sunken lane, with small pillars at the corners. This was always used by the Kuznetsovs and their visitors as a brief stopping-place during evening walks. From here those so inclined could call out the echo from the wood, and the track could be seen disappearing into the dark cutting between the trees.

'Here we are at the bridge,' said Ognyov. 'Time for you to turn back . . .'

Vera stopped and drew a deep breath.

'Let's sit here for a while,' she said, sitting down on one of the pillars. 'Usually everyone sits down when people are saying farewell before a departure.'

Ognyov settled himself beside her on his pile of books and went on talking. She was breathing hard after the walk and was not looking at Ivan Alekseich but to one side, so that he could not see her face.

'And suppose we suddenly meet in ten years' time,' he was saying. 'What shall we be like then? You'll be the respected mother of a family, and I'll be the author of some respected, totally unread collection of statistics as fat as forty thousand others. We'll meet and remember the old days . . . Now we're experiencing the present, it absorbs and excites us, but when we meet then, we shan't remember the date or the month or even the year when we last saw each other on this bridge. You'll be a different person, I expect . . . don't you think you'll be a different person?'

Vera gave a start and turned her face towards him.

'What?' she asked.

'I was just asking you –'

'I'm sorry, I didn't hear what you were saying.'

Only now did Ognyov notice the change in Vera. She was pale, breathing in starts, and her trembling conveyed itself to her arms, lips and head, so that two curls rather than the usual one had escaped from her hair . . . She was evidently trying to avoid looking him straight in the eye, and in an effort to disguise her agitation kept adjusting her collar as if it were too tight, or shifting her red shawl from shoulder to shoulder . . .

'You must be cold,' said Ognyov. 'Sitting in the mist isn't exactly healthy. Let me see you *nach Hause*.'

Vera did not reply.

'What's the matter?' Ivan Alekseich asked with a smile. 'Why don't you say anything or answer my questions? Are you ill, or angry? Tell me.'

Vera pressed the palm of her hand firmly against the cheek that was turned towards Ognyov and immediately drew it away again sharply.

'It's terrible . . .' she whispered, with an expression of acute pain on her face. 'Terrible!'

'What's terrible?' asked Ognyov, shrugging his shoulders and making no secret of his astonishment. 'What's the matter?'

Still breathing hard and with shoulders trembling, Vera turned her back to him, looked at the sky for half a minute and said:

'I must have a talk with you, Ivan Alekseich . . .'

'I'm listening.'

'You may find this strange . . . You'll be surprised, but I can't help it . . .'

Ognyov shrugged his shoulders once more and prepared to listen.

'It's like this,' Verochka began, bowing her head and fiddling with a bobble on her shawl. 'You see, what I wanted to tell you . . . was that . . . You may find this strange and . . . silly, but I . . . I can't bear it any more.'

Vera's words turned into a vague mumble and suddenly broke off in sobs. The young girl hid her face in her shawl, bowed her head even lower and sobbed bitterly. Ivan Alekseich cleared his throat in embarrassment, and too taken aback to know what to say or do, looked about him helplessly. Being unused to sobs and tears, he felt his own eyes beginning to prickle.

'This is awful,' he began mumbling desperately. 'Vera Gavrilovna, whatever's the matter? Are you – are you ill, my dear? Has someone offended you? You must tell me, perhaps I can . . . I may be able to help . . .'

When, in an attempt to console her, he allowed himself to take her hands carefully away from her face, she smiled at him through her tears and said:

'I . . . I love you.'

These simple ordinary words were spoken in simple human language, yet Ognyov turned away from Vera in utter confusion, stood up, and felt his confusion change to fear.

The sad, warm, sentimental mood induced in him by the farewell and Kuznetsov's vodka had suddenly vanished, leaving an acutely unpleasant feeling of awkwardness in its stead. As if all his affections had been turned upside down, he almost glared at Vera, and now that she had declared her love for him and cast off that inaccessibility which so becomes a woman, she seemed to him shorter, plainer, darker.

'What a thing to happen,' he thought to himself, aghast. 'But do I – do I love her, or not? That's the problem!'

Vera, meanwhile, now that the most important and difficult thing had at last been said, was breathing easily and freely again. She too stood up and looking Ivan Alekseich straight in the face, spoke rapidly, ardently and without restraint.

Just as someone who has had a sudden fright cannot recall afterwards the order in which he heard the sounds of the disaster that stunned him, so Ognyov cannot remember Vera's words and sentences. All that he does remember is their general import, Vera herself and the feeling that her words produced in him. He remembers her voice, which sounded stifled and somewhat hoarse with emotion, and her unusually musical, passionate intonation. Crying, laughing, with tears glistening on her eyelashes, she told him that from the very first days of their acquaintance she had been struck by his originality and intellect, his kind, clever eyes, and the aims and tasks he had set himself in life; that she had fallen in love with him passionately, madly and deeply; that when she used to come into the house from the garden during the summer and saw his cape in the hall or heard his voice from a distance, she would feel her heart go numb at the prospect of happiness; even his feeblest jokes made her laugh, to her every number in his exercise-books appeared unusually wise and exalted, and his knobbly walking-stick was to her more beautiful than the trees themselves.

The wood, the wisps of mist and the dark ditches on either side of the track seemed to be hushed listening to her, but in Ognyov's heart something strange and disagreeable was taking place . . . Vera was enchantingly pretty as she declared her love, she spoke beautifully and passionately, but instead of the pleasure and joy at being alive that he would have liked to feel, he felt only sympathy for her, pain and regret that a good person should be suffering on his account. Whether he was prompted in this by abstract reason, or by that incurable habit of being objective which so often prevents people from really living, Heaven alone knows, but the fact remained that Vera's raptures and suffering seemed to him cloying, not to be taken seriously; yet at the same time feeling rebelled within him and whispered that so far as nature and personal happiness were concerned, everything that he was seeing and hearing now was more serious than all his statistics, books and half-truths put together . . . And he felt angry and reproached himself, though with what he did not exactly know.

To crown his embarrassment, he had absolutely no idea what to say, and to say something was essential. It was not within his power to say straight out 'I do not love you', and he could not say 'Yes', because, search as he might, he could find not the faintest glimmer . . .

He remained silent, and in the mean time she was saying that for her there was no greater happiness than to see him, to follow him, straight away if he liked, wherever he wished, to be his wife and helper, and that if he were to leave her, she would die of despair . . .

'I can't go on living here,' she said, wringing her hands. 'I'm sick of the house, this wood, the very air. I can't stand this perpetual calm, this aimless life, I can't stand the people here, they're all so colourless and insipid, you can't tell one from the other. They're all sincere and well-meaning, but that's because they're satisfied, they've nothing to suffer or struggle for . . . I want to go to those great big damp houses of yours, where people are suffering and ground down by hard work and privation . . .'

This too struck Ognyov as cloying and not really serious. When Vera had finished, he still had no idea what to say, but since he could not say nothing, he began mumbling:

'Vera Gavrilovna, I'm very grateful to you, although I feel I've done nothing to deserve this – this feeling – on your part. Secondly, as an honest man, I am bound to say that . . . that happiness is based on reciprocity, that is, when both parties . . . love equally . . .'

But Ognyov was immediately ashamed of his mumbling and fell silent. He felt that the expression on his face as he said these things was stupid, lifeless and apologetic, that it was false and strained . . . Vera must have been able to read in his face the truth, because she suddenly became serious, turned pale and bowed her head.

'You must forgive me,' Ognyov mumbled, unable to endure the silence any longer. 'I have so much respect for you, that . . . this is painful for me!'

Vera turned on her heel and walked rapidly towards the estate. Ognyov followed her.

'No, don't bother!' said Vera, waving him away with her hand. 'There's no need, I can go by myself . . .'

'Yes, but even so . . . I can't not see you back.'

Every single word he spoke struck Ognyov as trite and nauseating. His feeling of guilt increased with each step. He fumed, clenched his fists and cursed his coldness and ineptitude with women. In an attempt to rouse his feelings, he looked at Verochka's attractive figure, her plait and the prints left by her small feet on the dusty track, he relived her words and tears, but all this he found no more than touching; it did not inflame his soul.

'But one can't *make* oneself fall in love!' he told himself, and at the same time thought: 'And when am I going to fall in love without making myself? I'm nearly thirty! I've never met anyone better than Vera and I never will . . . Oh, damned old age! To be too old at thirty!'

Ahead of him Vera was walking faster and faster, not looking round and with head bowed. She seemed to him in her grief to have become thinner, narrower in the shoulders . . .

'I can just imagine what's going on inside her now,' he thought, looking at her back. 'She must feel so ashamed and miserable she wishes she were dead. Heavens, there's enough life and poetry and meaning in all this to melt a stone, but I'm – I'm just stupid and ridiculous!'

At the gate Vera glanced back at him for a moment, pulled the shawl more tightly round her hunched shoulders, and hurried along the path.

Ivan Alekseich was left alone. He walked slowly back to the wood, pausing continually to look back at the gate, and his whole bearing seemed to express incredulity at what he had done. His eyes scanned the track for Vera's footprints, and he could not believe that a girl whom he liked so much had just declared her love to him, and he had so crudely and clumsily 'turned her down'! For the first time in his life he had learned from experience how little a man's actions depend on his good will, and had found himself in the position of a decent, sincere man, who against his will has caused cruel and unwarranted suffering to his neighbour.

His conscience worried him, and when Vera had disappeared from sight he began to feel that he had lost something very close and precious that he would never recover. He felt that with Vera part of his youth had slipped away, and that the minutes which he had just lived through so fruitlessly would never be repeated.

On reaching the little bridge, he paused and reflected. He wanted to discover the reason for his strange coldness. It was clear that it did not lie outside himself, but within. He frankly admitted that it was not the rational kind of coldness that clever people often boast of having, or the coldness of the foolish egoist, but simply an impotence of the soul, an inability to respond deeply to beauty, and the premature onset of old age due to his upbringing, his desperate struggle to earn a living and his bachelor existence in furnished rooms.

From the bridge he walked slowly, as if reluctantly, into the wood. Here, where the occasional sharp outlines of patches of moonlight showed through the thick black darkness, and he was conscious of nothing except his own thoughts, he felt a passionate longing to regain what he had lost.

And Ivan Alekseich remembers how he turned back. Spurring himself on with memories, forcing himself to conjure up Vera's image, he strode quickly towards the garden. The track and garden were both free of mist now, the bright, high moon looked down as if newly washed, but in the east it was still misty and overcast ... Ognyov remembers his cautious footsteps, the dark windows and the heavy scent of heliotrope and mignonette. The familiar Caro, wagging his tail in friendly greeting, came up and sniffed his hand ... He was the only living creature who saw Ognyov walk twice round the house, stand for a while beneath Vera's darkened window, then give up and leave the garden with a deep sigh.

An hour later he was already in the town. Weary and dejected, he leaned his body and burning face against the gates of the inn, and banged on the knocker. Somewhere in the town a dog woke up and barked, and as if in answer to Ognyov's knock, someone struck the piece of iron hanging by the church ...

'Gadding about at night again ...' grumbled the Old Believer innkeeper as he opened the gates for him in a long garment like a woman's nightdress. 'You ought to be praying to God.'

Ivan Alekseich went into his room, sank down on his bed and for a long, long time stared at the lamp. Then he shook his head and began packing ...

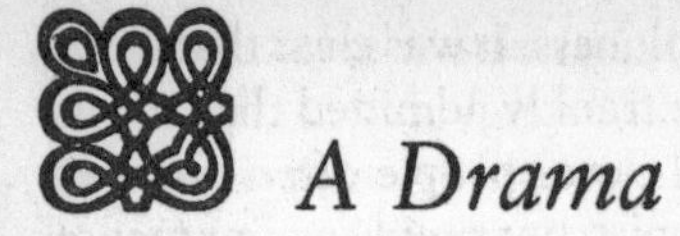

A Drama

'If you please, sir, there's this lady wants to speak to you,' announced Luka. 'She's been waiting a good hour . . .'

Pavel Vasilyevich had just finished lunch. Hearing of the lady, he frowned and said:

'To hell with her! Say I'm busy.'

'But she's been here four times already, sir. Says she simply must speak to you . . . Almost in tears, she is.'

'Hm . . . Oh well, all right, ask her into the study.'

Taking his time, Pavel Vasilyevich put on his frock-coat, picked up a pen in one hand and a book in the other, and giving the appearance of being extremely busy, walked into the study. His visitor had already been shown in: a large stout lady with fleshy red cheeks and wearing glasses, clearly a person of extreme respectability and more than respectably dressed (she was wearing a four-flounced bustle and a tall hat surmounted by a ginger bird). On seeing the master of the house, she rolled her eyes heavenward and clasped her hands together as if in prayer.

'You won't remember me, of course,' she began in a kind of mannish falsetto, visibly agitated. 'I-I had the pleasure of making your acquaintance at the Khrutskys . . . My name is Medusina . . .'

'Ah . . . aha . . .mm . . . Do take a seat! And how can I be of service to you?'

'Well, you see, I . . . I . . .' the lady continued, sitting down and becoming even more agitated. 'You won't remember me . . . My name is Medusina . . . You see, I'm a great admirer of your talent and always read your articles with such enjoyment . . . Please don't think I say that to flatter – Heaven forbid – I'm only giving credit where credit's due . . . I read every *word* of yours. I am not a complete stranger to authorship myself . . . That's to say, I naturally wouldn't dare call myself a writer . . . but nevertheless I have added my own drop of honey to the comb. I've had three children's stories published at various times – you won't have read them, of course . . . and a number of translations . . . and my late brother worked on *The Cause*.'

'Aha . . . mm . . . And how can I be of service to you?'

'Well, you see,' (Medusina looked down bashfully and blushed) 'knowing your talent . . . and your views, Pavel Vasilyevich, I should like to find out your opinion, or should I say, seek your advice. I must tell you that I have recently – *pardon pour l'expression* – conceived and brought forth a drama, and before sending it to the censor, I should like to have your opinion.'

Fluttering about like a trapped bird, Medusina began rummaging nervously in her skirts and pulled out a huge fat exercise-book.

Pavel Vasilyevich liked only his own articles, and whenever he had to read or listen to other people's, he always felt as if the mouth of a cannon were being aimed straight at his head. Scared by the sight of the exercise-book, he said quickly:

'Very well, leave it with me . . . I'll read it.'

'Pavel Vasilyevich!' moaned Medusina, rising to her feet and clasping her hands together as if in prayer. 'I know how busy you are, how every minute is precious to you . . . and I know that in your heart of hearts you must be cursing me at this moment, but please let me read my drama to you now . . . Please!'

'I'd be delighted,' stammered Pavel Vasilyevich, 'but my dear lady, I'm . . . I'm busy . . . I'm about to – about to leave town.'

'Pavel Vasilyevich,' the good lady groaned, and her eyes filled with tears. 'I'm asking for a sacrifice. Call me brazen and importunate, but be magnanimous! I'm leaving for Kazan tomorrow and that's why I'd like to hear your opinion today. Spare me your attention for half an hour – just half an hour! I implore you!'

Pavel Vasilyevich was a spineless fellow and did not know how to refuse; so when the lady seemed on the point of bursting into tears and falling on her knees, he lost his nerve and mumbled helplessly:

'Very well then, please do . . . I'm listening . . . I can spare half an hour.'

With a squeal of delight, Medusina took off her hat, settled herself more comfortably and began to read. First she read how a maid and a footman, as they were tidying up a magnificent drawing-room, had a long conversation about their young mistress, Anna Sergeyevna, who had just built a school and a hospital for the village peasants. When the footman had gone off, the maid delivered a monologue on the theme that 'knowledge is light and ignorance darkness'; then Medusina brought the footman back into the drawing-room and made him recite a long monologue on their master, the General, who could not abide his daughter's convictions, intended to marry her to a rich Groom of the Chamber, and believed that the salvation of the peasantry lay in total ignorance. After the servants had made their exit, the young lady herself entered and informed the audience that she had lain awake all night thinking of Valentine Ivanovich, the son of the impecunious schoolmaster, who assisted his sick father with no thought of reward. Valentine had studied all the sciences, but believed neither in love nor friendship, had no aim in life and longed for death, and therefore she, the young lady, had to save him.

Pavel Vasilyevich listened and thought back fondly to his sofa. He glared at Medusina, felt his eardrums being battered by her strident voice, took in nothing and thought to himself:

'Why pick on me? . . . Why should I have to listen to your drivel? Is it my fault you've written this "drama"? Heavens, look how fat that exercise-book is! This is torture!'

Pavel Vasilyevich glanced at his wife's portrait which hung between the windows, and remembered that she had instructed him to buy four yards of braid, a pound of cheese and some toothpaste, and bring them back with him to their datcha.

'Hope to goodness I haven't lost the sample for the braid,' he thought. 'Where did I put it? In my blue jacket, I think . . . Those wretched flies have sprinkled full stops all over her portrait again. I must tell Olga to wipe the glass . . . She's on to Scene Twelve, so it'll soon be the end of Act One. How could anyone be inspired in this heat, let alone a mountain of flesh like her? Instead of writing dramas, she'd be better off drinking iced soup and having a nap in the cellar . . .'

'You don't find this monologue a trifle long?' Medusina asked suddenly, looking up.

Pavel Vasilyevich had not heard the monologue. Caught off his guard, he answered so apologetically that one might have thought the monologue had been written by him, not the lady.

'No, indeed, not in the least . . . It's most charming.'

Medusina beamed with happiness and continued reading:

'*Anna*. Analysis has eaten into your soul. You ceased too soon living by the heart and put all your faith in the intellect. *Valentine*. What do you mean by the heart? It's a concept in anatomy. As a conventional term to describe what are referred to as the feelings, I refuse to acknowledge it. *Anna (in confusion)*. And love? Is that too only a product of the association of ideas? Tell me frankly: have you ever loved? *Valentine (bitterly)*. Let us not open up old wounds,

wounds yet barely healed. (*Pause.*) What are you thinking about? *Anna*. It seems to me that you are unhappy.'

During the course of Scene Sixteen Pavel Vasilyevich yawned, and his teeth inadvertently produced the kind of noise that dogs make when they are snapping at flies. Scared by the impropriety of this noise, he tried to cover it up by assuming an expression of rapt attention.

'Scene Seventeen. When on earth's it going to finish?' he thought. 'Good God, if this torment goes on another ten minutes, I'll have to shout for help. This is too much!'

But now at last the good lady began reading faster and more loudly, raised her pitch and announced: 'Curtain.'

Pavel Vasilyevich breathed a sigh of relief and was about to get up, but straight away Medusina turned over the page and carried on reading;

'Act Two. The stage represents the village street. Right a school, left a hospital. On the steps of the hospital sit the village lads and lasses.'

'Pardon me for interrupting,' said Pavel Vasilyevich, 'but how many acts are there altogether?'

'Five,' answered Medusina, and straight away, as if fearing her listener might leave the room, hurried on: 'Valentine is looking out of a window in the school. Upstage villagers can be seen taking their goods and chattels into the village tavern.'

Like a condemned man who knows he cannot be reprieved, Pavel Vasilyevich abandoned all hope, gave up wondering when the play would end, and was concerned only to keep his eyes from sticking together and to preserve the expression of interest on his face. The future, when this lady would finish reading and depart, seemed so remote that he could not even contemplate it.

'A-blah-bla-bla-bla . . .' Medusina's voice reverberated in his ears. 'Blah-bla-bla . . . Zzzzz . . . . . '

'I forgot to take my soda,' he thought. '. . . Er, what was that? Oh yes, my soda . . . I've probably got a stomach ulcer . . . It's an extraordinary thing, Smirnovsky guzzles vodka all day long, and his stomach's still all right . . . Some little bird's settled on the window-sill . . . A sparrow . . .'

Pavel Vasilyevich forced himself to keep his aching, drooping eyelids apart, yawned without opening his mouth and looked at Medusina. She was becoming blurred, started wobbling, grew three heads, towered up and touched the ceiling . . .

'*Valentine*. No, you must allow me to go away . . . *Anna* (*alarmed*). But why? *Valentine* (*aside*). She blanched! (*To Anna*.) Do not force me to explain my reasons. I would rather die than let you know those reasons. *Anna (after a pause)*. You cannot leave now . . .'

Medusina began to swell again, expanded to gigantic proportions and merged with the grey atmosphere of the study; all he saw now was her mouth opening and closing; then suddenly she became very small, like a bottle, started to wobble and together with the desk receded to the far end of the room . . .

'*Valentine (holding Anna in his arms)*. You have resurrected me, you have shown me life's purpose! You have revived me as the spring rain revives the awakening earth! But it is too late – ah, too late! An incurable malady gnaws at my breast . . .'

Pavel Vasilyevich gave a start and stared at Medusina with dull, bleary eyes; for a whole minute he gazed at her fixedly, as if in a complete stupor . . .

'Scene Eleven. Enter the Baron and a police officer with witnesses. *Valentine*. Take me away! *Anna*. I am his! Take me too! Yes, take me too! I love him, love him more than my own life. *The Baron*. Anna Sergeyevna, does your father's suffering mean nothing to you –'

Medusina began to swell again . . . Gazing round wildly, Pavel Vasilyevich half rose, gave a deep-chested, unnatural yell, seized a heavy paperweight from the table and completely beside himself, swung it round with all his strength at Medusina's head . . .

'Tie me up, I've killed her!' he said when the servants ran in a minute later.

He was acquitted.

Typhus

Young Lieutenant Klimov was travelling in a smoking compartment of the mail train from Petersburg to Moscow. Opposite him sat an elderly man with the clean-shaven face of a ship's master, a well-to-do Finn or Swede to judge by his appearance, who spent the entire journey sucking on his pipe and going over the same topic of conversation:

'Ha, you are officer! My brother also is officer but he is sailor. He is sailor stationed at Kronstadt. Why are you going to Moscow?'

'I'm stationed there.'

'Ha! And are you family man?'

'No, I live with my aunt and sister.'

'My brother also is officer, sailor, but he is family man, has wife and three children. Ha!'

The Finn seemed constantly astonished by something, gave a broad, fatuous grin every time he exclaimed 'Ha!', and kept puffing away at his stinking pipe. Klimov, who was feeling unwell and found it hard work answering his questions, loathed him from the bottom of his heart. He imagined how pleasant it would be to snatch the hissing pipe out of his hands and fling it under the seat, then drive the Finn himself into another carriage.

'They're a disgusting race, these Finns . . . and the Greeks,' he thought. 'A useless, superfluous, disgusting race. They just take up living space. What use are they?'

And the thought of Finns and Greeks made him feel a kind of nausea all over. By way of comparison he tried to think about the French and Italians, but for some reason the only images that these races conjured up in his mind were of organ-grinders, naked women and the foreign oleographs that hung above his aunt's chest of drawers at home.

Altogether, the officer did not feel his normal self. Even though he was occupying the whole of a seat, he somehow could not make his arms and legs comfortable on it, his mouth felt dry and sticky, and a thick fog filled his mind; his thoughts seemed to be wandering about not only inside his skull but outside it as well, among the seats and passengers shrouded in gloom. Through his clouded mind, as in a dream, he heard the mutter of voices, the clatter of wheels, the banging of doors. Bells rang, the guard blew his whistle, and passengers scurried along the platform – all more frequently than usual. Time flew by quickly, imperceptibly, so that the train seemed to be stopping at a station every minute, and metallic voices were constantly shouting from outside:

'Mail aboard?'

'All aboard!'

The stove-attendant seemed to come in too often to glance at the thermometer, and the noise of trains passing in the other direction and the rumble of wheels as they crossed a bridge seemed to go on without a break. The noises and whistles, the Finn, the tobacco smoke – all these, mixed up with those menacing, fleeting, shadowy images, whose shape and meaning are beyond the recall of a healthy person, pressed in on Klimov like an intolerable nightmare. In terrible anguish he raised his heavy head and looked at the lantern, in whose rays shadows and misty spots were swirling; he wanted to ask for some water, but his parched tongue would scarcely move and he was barely strong enough to answer the Finn's questions. He tried to settle himself more comfortably and go to sleep, but to no avail; the Finn dropped off several times, woke up and re-lit his pipe, addressed him with his inevitable 'Ha!' and dropped off again, but the lieutenant was still quite unable to find a comfortable position for his legs, and the menacing images still floated before his eyes.

At Spirovo he got out and went into the station for a glass of water. Some people were sitting at a table, having a quick meal.

'How can they bear to eat?' he thought, trying not to breathe in the smell of fried meat or look at the chewing mouths, all of which disgusted him to the point of nausea.

A beautiful lady was carrying on a loud conversation with a military man in a red peak-cap and showing a set of magnificent white teeth whenever she smiled; the smile, the teeth and the lady herself produced in Klimov the same feeling of disgust as the smoked bacon and fried cutlets. He could not understand how the military man in the red cap could possibly bear to sit beside her and look at her healthy, smiling face.

He finished his water and returned to the carriage. The Finn was sitting up smoking. His pipe was hissing and wheezing like a leaky galosh in wet weather.

'Ha!' he said with astonishment. 'What station is this?'

'I don't know,' Klimov replied, lying down and covering his mouth, so as not to inhale the acrid tobacco smoke.

'And when shall we be in Tver?'

'I don't know. I'm sorry, but I . . . I can't talk. I'm ill, I've caught a chill today.'

The Finn knocked his pipe out on the window-frame and began talking about his brother, the sailor. Klimov was not listening any more. He was thinking longingly of his soft, comfortable bed, his carafe of cold water and his sister Katya, who was so good at putting him to bed, soothing him and handing him his water. He even smiled as an image flashed through his mind of his batman Pavel, taking off his master's heavy, thickly-lined boots and placing the water on his bedside table. All he needed to do, he felt, was to lie down in his own bed and drink some water, and this nightmare would give way to a deep, healthy sleep.

'Mail aboard?' a hollow voice shouted from a distance.

'All aboard!' replied a deep voice almost beneath the window.

They were already two or three stations beyond Spirovo.

Time flew by quickly, in jumps, and the bells, the whistles and the stops seemed never-ending. In despair Klimov buried his face in the corner of the seat, wrapped his hands round his head and began thinking again about his sister Katya and his batman Pavel, but sister and batman became mixed up with the shadowy images, spun round with them, and disappeared. His hot breath, reflected off the back of the seat, burned his face, his legs were lying uncomfortably and his back was in a draught from the window, but no matter how agonising his position, he no longer had any wish to change it . . . A heavy, nightmarish inertia gradually overwhelmed him and fettered his limbs.

When he finally ventured to raise his head, the carriage was already light. The passengers were putting on their outdoor coats and moving about. The train was stationary. Porters in white aprons and wearing numbered discs were bustling round the passengers, grabbing their suitcases. Klimov put on his greatcoat and mechanically followed the other passengers out of the carriage, and it was as if someone other than himself were moving in his place, some stranger, and he felt that his fever, his thirst and those menacing images which had given him no sleep all night, had come out of the carriage with him. Mechanically he collected his luggage and hired a cab. The driver demanded a rouble and a quarter to take him to

Povarskaya Street, but he didn't haggle and took his seat on the sledge obediently and without demur. He was aware still of being overcharged, but money no longer had the slightest value for him.

At home Klimov was met by his aunt and sister Katya, a girl of eighteen. Katya greeted him holding an exercise-book and a pencil, and he remembered that she was preparing for her teacher's examination. Without replying to their questions and greetings, he walked blindly right through the apartment, panting feverishly, and on reaching his bed collapsed onto the pillow. The Finn, the red cap, the lady with the white teeth, the smell of fried meat and the flickering spots of light took over his senses completely, and he no longer knew where he was or heard the anxious voices round him.

When he came to, he saw that he was lying in his own bed, undressed, he saw the carafe of water and Pavel, but none of this made him feel any cooler, more relaxed or more comfortable. He still could not find the right position for his arms and legs, his tongue was sticking to the roof of his mouth, and he could hear the wheezing of the Finn's pipe. A doctor with a black beard was fussing by his bedside and his ample, solid back kept bumping into Pavel.

'Don't worry, lad,' he mumbled, 'don't worry! Well done, well done . . . Goot, goot . . .'

The doctor kept calling Klimov 'lad' and saying 'goot' instead of 'good' and 'ya' for 'yes'.

'Ya, ya, ya,' he babbled on. 'Goot, goot . . . Well done, lad . . . Keep your spirits up!'

The doctor's brisk, offhand way of speaking, his well-fed face and his condescending use of 'lad' irritated Klimov.

'Why do you keep calling me "lad"?' he groaned. 'Damned cheek!'

And the sound of his own voice scared him. It was such a dry, weak, singsong voice that he could not recognise it.

'Well done, well done,' mumbled the doctor, not in the least offended. 'Try not to get angry . . . Ya, ya, ya . . .'

Time flew by just as amazingly quickly at home as in the railway carriage. Daylight in the bedroom kept changing to dusk. The doctor seemed to be there all the time, saying 'ya, ya, ya' every minute. An unbroken procession of people filed through the bedroom. There was Pavel, the Finn, Captain Yaroshevich, Sergeant-Major Maksimenko, the red peak-cap, the lady with the white teeth, and the doctor. They were all talking, waving their arms about, smoking and eating. Once, in daylight, Klimov even saw his regimental priest,

Father Alexander, wearing his stole and with a prayer-book in his hands, standing at the foot of the bed mumbling something and looking more serious than Klimov had ever seen before. The lieutenant remembered that Father Alexander referred jovially to all the Catholic officers as 'Polacks', and wanting to make him laugh, he shouted:

'Father, Yaroshevich the Polack's run off to the Pole!'

But Father Alexander, a cheerful man who was easily amused, did not burst out laughing but became even more serious and made the sign of the cross over Klimov. At night two noiseless shadows came and went from the room in turn. They belonged to his aunt and his sister. His sister's shadow knelt down and began praying, and when she bowed to the icon, her grey shadow on the wall bowed with her, so that there were two shadows praying to God. All the time Klimov could smell fried meat and the Finn's pipe, but on one occasion he became aware of a strong smell of incense. His stomach began to heave and he shouted:

'The incense! Take away the incense!'

There was no reply. The only sounds were of priests chanting softly somewhere and of someone running down the main stairs...

When Klimov emerged from his delirium, there was not a soul in the bedroom. The morning sun was flooding through the lowered curtain, and a trembling beam, as fine and graceful as a rapier, was playing on the carafe. The clatter of wheels could be heard – so he knew the snow must have gone from the streets. The lieutenant looked at the beam of sunlight, at the familiar furniture and the door, and the first thing he did was to start laughing. His chest and stomach quivered with sweet, happy, tickling laughter. His whole being was seized from head to foot by a sensation of boundless happiness and joy at being alive, like that which the first man probably experienced when he was created and saw the world for the first time. Klimov longed passionately for movement, for people, for human speech. He was lying flat on his back, he could move nothing but his arms, but he scarcely noticed this and concentrated all his attention on little things. He delighted in his own breathing and laughter, delighted in the existence of the carafe, the ceiling, the sunbeam and the braid on the curtain. Even in a cramped little corner like the bedroom, God's world seemed to him beautiful, varied and magnificent. When the doctor appeared, the lieutenant thought what a marvellous thing medicine was, what a charming and sympathetic man the doctor was, and how good and interesting people were generally.

'Ya, ya, ya,' the doctor babbled on. 'Well done, well done . . . Now we're all right again . . . Goot, goot.'

The lieutenant was listening and laughing joyfully. He remembered the Finn, the lady with the white teeth, the smoked bacon, and suddenly he felt the urge to eat and smoke.

'Doctor,' he said, 'tell them to bring me a crust of rye bread and salt and . . . and some sardines.'

But the doctor refused, nor would Pavel obey his order and go for the bread. This was too much for the lieutenant, and he burst into tears like a spoilt child.

'Ah, poor little baby!' said the doctor, laughing. 'Hushaby, mummy's baby!'

Klimov also began laughing and after the doctor's departure fell sound asleep. He woke up with the same feeling of joy and happiness as before. His aunt was sitting by his bedside.

'Auntie!' he exclaimed blissfully. 'What's been the matter with me?'

'You've had typhus.'

'Really? But I feel fine now, fine! Where's Katya?'

'She's out. I expect she called in to see someone after her exam.'

The old lady said these words and bent down over the stocking she was knitting; her lips began to tremble, she turned aside and suddenly burst out sobbing.

'Oh Katya, Katya!' she said, in her despair forgetting all that the doctor had told her. 'Our angel's gone! Gone!'

She dropped the stocking and bent down to pick it up, and as she did so, her cap fell off her head. Looking at her grey hair and not understanding anything, Klimov felt scared for Katya and asked:

'But where is she? Auntie!'

The old lady, who was no longer thinking about Klimov but only of her own grief, said:

'She caught typhus from you and . . . and died. She was buried the day before yesterday.'

This terrible and unexpected news entered fully into Klimov's consciousness, but however terrible and compelling it might be, it could not overcome the feeling of animal joy that filled the lieutenant as he regained his strength. He cried, he laughed, and soon he began swearing because he was not allowed to eat.

It was only the week after, when he walked over to the window in his dressing-gown leaning on Pavel's arm, looked out at the dull spring sky and listened to the unpleasant clanging of some old rails being carried past in the street, that he felt sick at heart, burst into tears, and pressed his forehead against the window-frame.

'Lord, how unhappy I am,' he murmured. 'How unhappy!'

And his joy gave way to a feeling of mundane boredom and a sense of irreparable loss.

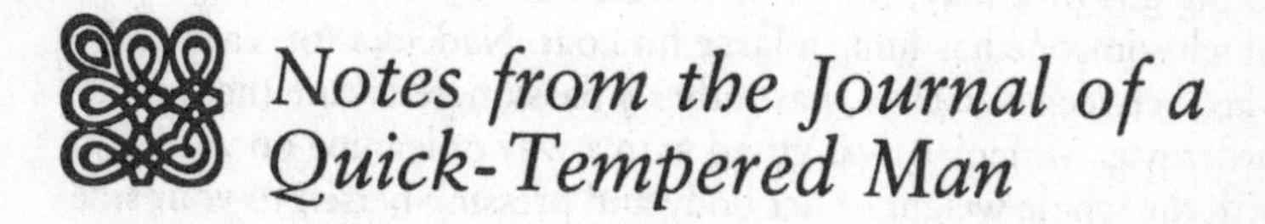

Notes from the Journal of a Quick-Tempered Man

I am a serious person with a philosophical turn of mind. An accountant by profession, I am studying fiscal law and writing a thesis entitled: 'The Dog-Tax: its Past and Future.' It's quite obvious I can have absolutely no interest in young ladies, love songs, the moon and suchlike nonsense.

At 10 a.m. my *maman* poured my coffee. I drank it and went out on to the balcony to get down to work on my thesis right away. I took a fresh sheet of paper, dipped my pen in the ink and put down the title: 'The Dog-Tax: its Past and Future.' Then, after thinking for a while, I wrote: 'Historical Survey. Judging from certain passing references to be found in Herodotus and Xenophon, the dog-tax arose from –'

But at that point I heard footsteps of a highly suspicious nature. Looking down from the balcony I saw a young lady with an elongated face and elongated figure. I believe she is called Nadenka or Varenka (however, that is absolutely irrelevant). She was looking for something, pretending not to have noticed me, and singing: 'Dost thou recall that melody so full, so full of bliss . . .'

I re-read what I had written and was about to continue when the young lady suddenly pretended she had just noticed me and said plaintively:

'Oh good morning, Nikolay Andreich! I'm awfully upset. I must have lost a bauble from my bracelet when I was out walking yesterday.'

I read the opening phrase of my thesis once again, touched up the crossbar on a 't' and was about to resume – but the young lady was not to be put off so easily.

'Nikolay Andreich,' she said, 'please come and see me back to the house. I'm so scared of passing that enormous dog of the Karelins I daren't go on my own.'

Well, there was no way out, so I replaced my pen and went down. Nadenka (or Varenka) took my arm and we set off towards her datcha.

Whenever it happens that I am obliged to walk arm-in-arm with a young girl or a lady, for some reason I always feel like a hook on which someone has hung a large fur coat. Nadenka (or Varenka) – who, between ourselves, has rather a passionate nature (her grandfather was Armenian) – is gifted with a way of leaning on your arm with the whole weight of her body and pressing herself to your side like a leech. So that was how we proceeded . . . As we walked past the Karelins' I saw their large dog. That reminded me of the dog-tax and I sighed wistfully as I recalled my opening sentence.

'Why are you sighing?' asked Nadenka (or Varenka), and herself breathed a deep sigh.

A word of explanation here. Nadenka or Varenka (but now I seem to recall that her name is, in fact, Mashenka) for some reason has got it into her head that I am in love with her, and therefore considers it her duty, on humanitarian grounds, always to look at me with compassion in her eyes and to minister verbally to my wounded soul.

She stopped and said: 'Oh, I know why you are sighing. You love someone, that's what it is! But in the name of our friendship I beg you to believe that the girl whom you love holds you in great respect! She cannot answer your affection with like, but is the fault hers if her heart has long belonged to another?'

Mashenka's nose flushed and began to look puffy, and tears welled up in her eyes. She obviously expected me to reply, but fortunately just at that moment we arrived at her house . . . Mashenka's *maman* was sitting on the verandah. She is a kind woman, but with some funny ideas. Observing the signs of emotion in her daughter's face, she gave me a long hard look and sighed, as if to say: 'Ah, youth, youth! Too innocent even to conceal your feelings!' Apart from her there were several variegated young ladies sitting on the verandah, and in their midst the fellow who lives in the datcha next door to mine – an ex-army officer wounded during the last war in the left temple and right hip. Like me, this unfortunate had made up his mind to devote the summer to literary activity. He was writing the 'Memoirs of a Military Man'. Like me, he would set about his honourable task every morning and never get further than writing: 'I was born in . . .' when some Varenka or Mashenka would appear beneath his balcony and carry off the wounded warrior under escort.

The whole party sitting on the verandah were preparing some kind of ghastly berries for jam-making. I bowed with the intention of leaving them, but the variegated damsels seized my hat with a squeal and insisted I stay. So I sat down. I was given a plateful of berries and a hairpin. I started stoning the berries.

The variegated young ladies were discoursing on the subject of men: Mr. A. was awfully sweet, Mr. B. was good-looking but not very attractive, Mr. C. wasn't good-looking but he was attractive, Mr. D. wouldn't be bad if his nose wasn't so like a thimble, and so on.

'And you, *monsieur Nicolas*,' Varenka's *maman* said turning to me, 'aren't good-looking but you are attractive. You've an interesting face . . . But of course,' she sighed, 'the most important thing in a man isn't his looks but his brain . . .'

The young ladies all sighed and looked at the floor . . . They too clearly agreed that the most important thing in a man wasn't his looks but his brain. At this point I took a sidelong glance at myself in the mirror to check how attractive I was. What I saw was a shaggy head of hair, a shaggy beard, moustache, eyebrows, hair on my cheeks, hairs under my eyes – a perfect thicket with a substantial nose sticking out of it like a forester's watch-tower. A fine-looking chap, I must say!

'But of course, *Nicolas*, it is your spiritual qualities that will win the day,' sighed Nadenka's *maman*, as if confirming some secret thought of her own.

Nadenka was sitting there suffering visibly on my behalf, but at the same time it clearly gave her the greatest satisfaction to know that opposite her was a man who was deeply in love with her. After they had finished with men, the young ladies got on to love. Then after a long conversation about love one of them stood up and left. The others immediately set about tearing her to pieces. They all agreed she was stupid, unbearable, a sight, and that one of her shoulder-blades stuck out.

Then at last, thank God, a maid appeared sent by my *maman* to call me for lunch. Now I could leave this objectionable company and go and get on with my thesis. So I stood up and bowed. But Varenka's *maman*, Varenka herself, and all the variegated young ladies surrounded me and declared I had no right at all to leave as I had firmly promised the previous day to have lunch and go out to the woods with them to pick mushrooms. So I bowed and sat down . . . Hatred seethed within my breast – another minute of this and I felt I would not be answerable for myself, there would be an explosion. But a sense of delicacy and my fear of offending against social decorum always make me defer to the ladies. So I deferred.

We sat down for lunch. The ex-officer, whose jaws had seized up because of the wound in his head, ate as if he had a bit between his teeth. I rolled my bread into balls, thought about the dog-tax, and knowing my tendency to be quick-tempered, tried not to say anything. Nadenka looked at me compassionately. There was cold soup, tongue with boiled peas, roast chicken and stewed fruit. I didn't feel like eating, but did so out of a sense of delicacy. After lunch, as I stood alone on the verandah smoking, Mashenka's *maman* came up to me, squeezed my hand and said in a breathless voice:

'Don't despair, *Nicolas* . . . Ah, what a loving nature she has, what a loving nature!'

So we went to the woods to pick mushrooms . . . Varenka hung on my arm and clung to my side. It was inexpressible torment, but I put up with it.

We entered the wood.

'Tell me, *monsieur Nicolas*,' sighed Nadenka, 'why is your face so sad? Why don't you speak?'

What an odd girl – what was there to speak to her about? What did we have in common?

'Please do say something,' she insisted.

I tried to think of some popular topic which she might be capable of understanding. So after much thought I said: 'The felling of forests is causing enormous havoc in Russia . . .'

'Oh, *Nicolas*,' Varenka sighed, and her nose began to flush. '*Nicolas*, I see you're avoiding a heart-to-heart conversation . . . It's as if you wanted to punish me with your silence. Your emotion is unrequited and you want to suffer in silence, alone . . . It's awful, *Nicolas!*' she exclaimed, suddenly grabbing me by the hand, and I could see her nose beginning to go puffy. 'But what would you say if the girl whom you love were to offer you Eternal Friendship?'

I mumbled something incoherent because I hadn't the faintest idea what to say to her . . . For goodness' sake – in the first place I wasn't in love with anyone, in the second place what on earth did I want with Eternal Friendship? And thirdly – I'm an extremely quick-tempered person. Mashenka (or Varenka) hid her face in her hands and said in an undertone, as if to herself:

'He does not answer . . . He obviously wants me to make a sacrifice. But how can I love him if I still love another! And yet . . . I'll think about it . . . Yes, I shall think about it . . . I shall summon up all the spiritual resources at my command and – perhaps, even at the cost of my own happiness, deliver this man from his suffering!'

It was all double Dutch to me. Some kind of mumbo-jumbo. We went on a bit further and started picking mushrooms. We said nothing. There were signs of inner conflict on Nadenka's face. I heard some dogs barking: that reminded me of my thesis and I sighed deeply. I saw the ex-officer between the tree-trunks. The poor fellow was limping painfully on both sides: he had his wounded hip on the right side and one of the variegated young ladies clinging to him on the left. His face expressed submission to Fate.

After the mushroom-picking we went back to the datcha for tea, then played croquet and listened to one of the variegated damsels singing a ballad: 'Sweet is my love, so sweet, so sweet!' Every time she sang 'sweet' her mouth curled right up to her ear.

'*Charmant!*' the other young ladies moaned in chorus. '*Charmant!*'

Darkness fell. The revolting moon was creeping up from behind the shrubbery. The air was still, with an unpleasant smell of fresh hay. I picked up my hat with the intention of going home.

'I have something to tell you,' Mashenka whispered to me significantly. 'Don't go.'

I had a nasty foreboding, but waited out of a sense of delicacy. Mashenka took my arm and led me off somewhere down an avenue of trees. Her whole being now expressed an inner conflict. She was pale, she breathed heavily and seemed intent on pulling my right arm off. What was the matter with the girl?

'I want to tell you,' she murmured. 'No, I can't . . . No, no.'

She wanted to say something, but kept hesitating. Then I saw from the expression on her face that she had made up her mind. With her eyes flashing and her nose all puffy she grabbed me by the hand and gasped: '*Nicolas*, I am yours! I cannot love you, but I promise to be faithful.'

She pressed herself up against my chest, then suddenly sprang back.

'Someone's coming,' she whispered. 'Farewell . . . I shall be in the summer-house tomorrow at eleven o'clock . . . Farewell – darling!'

And off she went. Completely at a loss, with my heart palpitating terribly, I made my way homeward. There 'The Past and Future of the Dog-Tax' awaited me, but I couldn't do any work. I was furious. I would even go so far as to say I was fearsome in my wrath. Damn it, I will not permit people to treat me like a little boy! I'm quick-tempered, and woe betide anyone who plays games with me! When the maid came in to call me to supper I yelled at her: 'Get out!' Such quick-temperedness bodes ill.

Next morning we had typical summer holiday weather, i.e. temperature below freezing point, a cold, biting wind, rain, mud and the smell of mothballs caused by my *maman* dragging all her winter coats out of the chest. An absolutely foul morning. It was, to be precise, the 7th of August 1887, when there was to be an eclipse of the sun. I must point out that every one of us can do enormously important work during an eclipse even if we are not astronomers. For instance, each of us can: 1) measure the diameter of the sun and the moon, 2) sketch the sun's corona, 3) measure the temperature, 4) observe the behaviour of animals and plants at the moment of total eclipse, 5) note down his own personal impressions, etc. This was a matter of such importance that for the time being I decided to set aside 'The Past and Future of the Dog-Tax' and observe the eclipse instead. We all got up very early. I had allocated the tasks to be performed as follows: I myself was to measure the diameter of the sun and moon, the wounded officer was to sketch the corona, and everything else was the responsibility of Mashenka and the variegated young ladies. So there we all were, waiting for it to begin.

'Why do eclipses happen?' Mashenka enquired.

I replied: 'An eclipse of the sun occurs when the moon, passing through the plane of the ecliptic, assumes a position upon the line joining the centres of the sun and the earth.'

'What does ecliptic mean?'

I explained. Mashenka listened attentively, then she asked: 'When you look through the smoked glass can you see the line joining the centres of the sun and the earth?'

I explained that this line is imaginary.

'But if it's imaginary,' said Varenka, completely bewildered, 'how can the moon assume a position on it?'

I did not answer. I could feel my spleen beginning to swell at the naivety of such a question.

'All that's rubbish,' said Varenka's *maman*. 'No one can possibly foretell the future, and anyway you've never been in the sky, so how can you know what's going to happen to the moon and the sun? It's all make-believe.'

But soon a black spot began to move across the sun. The result was general consternation. Cows, sheep and horses bolted all over the fields with their tails in the air and bellowed in terror. Dogs howled. Bedbugs, thinking it was night again, crept out of their crannies and began biting anyone who was asleep. A local cleric, who was bringing home a load of cucumbers from his allotment, panicked, jumped off his cart and hid under a bridge, while his horse pulled the cart into someone else's yard where the cucumbers were devoured by pigs. An excise officer, who had been spending the night at a certain lady's datcha, ran out among the crowd in just his underwear, shouting wildly: 'Every man for himself!'

Many of the female occupants of the datchas, even some of the young and pretty ones, were woken by the noise and dashed out with no shoes on. And all sorts of other things occurred which I hesitate to recount.

'Ooh, I am scared!' squealed the variegated young ladies. 'Oh, isn't it awful!'

'*Mesdames*, please carry out your observations!' I shouted. 'Time is precious!'

I myself was making haste to measure the diameter . . . Remembering about the corona I looked for the ex-officer. He was standing doing nothing.

'What are you standing there for?' I shouted. 'What about the corona?'

He shrugged his shoulders and glanced down helplessly. Variegated damsels were clinging to both of the poor fellow's arms, pressing up against him in terror and preventing him from working. I took my pencil and noted the time precisely to the second: that was important. I noted down the geographical location of the observation point: that too was important. I was about to measure the diameter when Mashenka caught my arm and said: 'Don't forget: this morning at eleven!'

I freed my arm and knowing that every second counted, attempted to continue my observations, but Varenka seized my arm convulsively and pressed herself to my side. Everything – my pencil, my dark glasses and my drawings – fell on to the grass. For crying out loud! Whenever was this girl going to realise that I'm quick-tempered and once roused I go berserk and cannot answer for my actions?

I couldn't wait to continue – but the eclipse was already over!

'Look at me!' she whispered tenderly.

Oh, this was the absolute limit! It's perfectly obvious that anyone who tries a man's patience like that has got it coming to them. If I murder someone, don't blame me! Dammit, I will not allow myself to be made a fool of, and by God, when my hackles are up, I wouldn't advise anyone to come within a mile of me! I'm capable of anything!

One of the damsels, presumably seeing by my face that I was furious and obviously intending to mollify me, said: '*I* did as you told me, Nikolay Andreyevich. I observed the mammals. Just before the eclipse I saw a grey dog chasing a cat. Then it wagged its tail for a long time afterwards.'

So the eclipse came to nothing. I went home. But as it was raining I didn't go out on to the balcony to work. The wounded officer had risked coming out on to his and even got as far as writing 'I was born in . . .' when I saw one of the variegated damsels dragging him off to her datcha. I couldn't work because I was still livid and could feel my heart thumping. Nor did I go to the summer-house. Maybe that wasn't polite, but it's perfectly obvious I couldn't be expected to go in the rain, could I? At twelve o'clock I got a letter from Mashenka written as if we were the most intimate of friends, full of reproaches, and asking me to come to the summer-house . . . At one o'clock I received a second letter, at two yet another . . . I would have to go. But first I would have to consider what to say to her. I would act in an honourable manner. Firstly, I would tell her she was wrong in imagining that I loved her. Yet one cannot really say a thing like that to a woman. To say to a woman 'I do not love you' is as tactless as saying to a writer: 'You don't know how to write'. The best thing would be to explain to Varenka my views on marriage. So I put on my warm overcoat, took my umbrella and made my way to the summer-house. Knowing how quick-tempered I am, I was afraid of what I might come out with. I would try to restrain myself.

She was there in the summer-house waiting for me. Nadenka's face was pale and tear-stained. When she saw me she gave a shriek of joy and flung her arms round my neck, saying: 'Oh, at last! You're trying my patience so badly. I didn't sleep all night . . . I was thinking and thinking. And I feel if I got to know you better I would . . . would come to love you.'

I sat down and began to expound my views on marriage. To avoid going too deeply into the subject and in order to be as concise as possible, I put things briefly into their historical perspective. I spoke about marriage among the Hindus and Egyptians, then came on to more recent times with a few of Schopenhauer's ideas. Mashenka listened attentively, but suddenly she felt obliged to interrupt me with a curious *non sequitur*.

'*Nicolas*, give me a kiss!'

I was so embarrassed I didn't know what to say to her. She repeated her demand. So there was nothing else for it – I got up and put my lips to her elongated face, experiencing the same sensation I had as a child when I was made to kiss my dead grandmother's face at her funeral. Not satisfied with the kiss I had given her, Varenka leapt to her feet and impetuously flung her arms around me. At that moment Mashenka's *maman* appeared at the summer-house door . . . She gave us a startled glance and saying to someone behind her: 'Shhhh!', vanished like Mephistopheles down a stage trapdoor.

I went back home feeling furious and embarrassed, only to find Varenka's *maman* there embracing my *maman* with tears in her eyes. My *maman* was saying tearfully: 'My dream has come true!'

And then – well, would you believe it? – Nadenka's *maman* came up to me, put her arms around me and said:

'May God bless you both! Take good care of her . . . Never forget the sacrifice she is making . . .'

So now I'm about to be married. As I write these lines the best man is looming over me telling me to hurry up. These people just don't know who they're dealing with! I am extremely quick-tempered and I can't answer for my actions! Dammit, you'd better watch out! Leading a quick-tempered, violent man to the altar – so far as I'm concerned it's as rash as sticking your hand into a frenzied tiger's cage. You'd better watch out, I tell you!

* * *

So here I am married. Everybody congratulates me and Varenka keeps pressing up to me and saying: 'Oh, to think that now you are mine, mine! Tell me you love me! Tell me, darling!'

And her nose goes all puffy.

I learned from the best man that the wounded officer had escaped Hymen's clutches by a cunning ruse. He produced for his variegated young lady a medical certificate to prove that as a result of the wound in his temple he was *non compos mentis* and therefore legally barred from getting married. Brilliant! I could have got a certificate too. One of my uncles drank like a fish, another was extremely absent-minded (he once put a lady's muff on his head instead of his fur hat) and my aunt was always playing the grand piano and sticking her tongue out at men in the street. Then there's my extreme quick-temperedness – that's another very dubious symptom. But why is it that good ideas always come too late? Why, why?

The Reed-Pipe

Stifled by the cloying air of the fir plantation and all covered in spiders' webs and fir-needles, Meliton Shishkin, the bailiff from the Dementyevs' farm, was slowly working his way to the edge of the wood, his shot-gun in his hand. His dog Lady, a cross between a mongrel and a setter, extremely thin and heavy with young, was trailing along behind her master with her wet tail between her legs, and doing her best not to get her nose pricked. It was a dull, overcast morning. Great splashes of water fell from the mist-shrouded trees and the bracken, and the damp wood exuded a pungent odour of decay.

Ahead, where the plantation came to an end, stood silver birches, and between their trunks and branches the misty horizon could be seen. Beyond the birches someone was playing on a shepherd's rustic pipe. They were playing no more than five or six notes, drawing them out lazily and making no effort to combine them into a tune, yet in the high-pitched wail of the pipe there was something both sombre and singularly mournful.

When the plantation began to thin out and the firs mingled with young birch-trees, Meliton saw a herd. Cows, sheep and hobbled horses were wandering among the bushes and snuffing the grass in the wood, crackling branches underfoot. At the wood's edge, leaning against a dripping birch-tree, stood an old shepherd, gaunt, bareheaded and wearing a coarse, tattered smock. He was staring at the ground, thinking about something, and evidently playing the pipe quite mechanically.

'Morning, gaffer! God save you!' Meliton greeted him in a thin, husky little voice that was completely out of keeping with his enormous stature and fat, fleshy face. 'You've got the knack of that whistle! Whose herd is that you're minding?'

'The Artamonovs',' replied the old man grudgingly, and put the pipe away inside the front of his smock.

'So this must be their wood, too?' asked Meliton, looking around him. 'Well I never, so it is . . . I was nearly lost, I reckon. Scratched my face to pieces on those firs.'

He sat down on the damp earth and began to roll a cigarette from a scrap of newspaper.

Like his thin little voice, everything about this man was on a small scale – his smile, his beady eyes, his buttons and the little cap perched precariously on his greasy, shaven head – and seemed at variance with his height, his broadness, and his fleshy face. When he spoke and smiled, his smooth, pudgy face, and his whole appearance, seemed somehow womanish, timid and submissive.

'God help us, what weather!' he said with a roll of the head. 'They haven't got the oats in yet and this wretched rain looks as if it's hired itself out for the season.'

The shepherd glanced at the drizzling sky, the wood, and the bailiff's sodden clothes, pondered, and said nothing.

'It's been like this all summer . . .' sighed Meliton. 'Bad for the peasants, and no joy for the masters either.'

The shepherd glanced at the sky again, pondered, and said deliberately, as though chewing over every word:

'It's all heading one way . . . No good'll come of it.'

'What are things like here?' asked Meliton, lighting his cigarette. 'Seen any grouse coveys in the Artamonovs' scrub?'

The shepherd did not answer at once. Again he glanced at the sky and to left and right, pondered, and blinked . . . Evidently he attached no small importance to his words, and to lend them more weight endeavoured to deliver them slowly and with a certain solemnity. His face bore all the angularity and gravity of age, and because his nose had a deep, saddle-shaped bridge to it and his nostrils curled slightly upwards, its expression seemed sly and quizzical.

'No, I can't say as I have,' he answered. 'Our huntsman Yeryomka said he put up a covey on Elijah's Day, by Pustoshye, but I dare say he was lying. There aren't the birds about.'

'No, brother, there aren't . . . It's the same everywhere! When you come down to it, the hunting's paltry these days, a waste of time. There's no game at all, and what there is, isn't worth soiling your hands for – it's not even full-grown! Such tiny stuff, you feel quite sorry for it.'

Meliton gave a contemptuous laugh.

'Yes, the way the world's going these days is downright daft! The birds don't know what they're doing, they sit on their eggs late and some of them, I swear, aren't off the nest by St Peter's Day!'

'It's all heading one way,' said the shepherd, raising his head. 'Past year there weren't much game about, this year there's even less, and mark my words, in another five there'll be none at all. As I see it, soon there won't be birds of any kind about, let alone game-birds.'

'Yes,' agreed Meliton after a moment's thought. 'You're right.'

The shepherd chuckled bitterly and shook his head.

'It beats me!' he said. 'Where've they all gone to? Twenty odd years back, I remember, there were geese here, cranes, duck and black grouse – it was teeming with them! The gents would go out hunting and all you'd hear was "Bang-bang! Bang-bang!" There was no end to the woodcock, snipe and curlew, and as for teal and the little pipers, they were as common as starlings, or sparrows say – any number there were! And where've they all gone to? You don't even see a bird of prey these days. Eagles, falcons, the big eagle owls – they've all gone . . . There's less of every beast about. Nowadays, brother, you're lucky if you see a wolf or a fox, let alone a bear or a mink. And in the old days there were even elk! Forty years I've been giving an eye to the ways of God's world, year in, year out, and as I look at it, everything's heading one way.'

'One way?'

'To the bad, my boy. To ruination, I reckon . . . The days of God's world are numbered.'

The old man put on his cap and began to stare at the sky.

'It's a sad thing!' he sighed after a short silence. 'Dear God but it's sad! Of course, it's the will of God, it wasn't us made the world, but even so, brother, it's sad. If a single tree withers or, say, one of your cows dies, you feel sorry, don't you, so what will it be like, friend, to see the whole world go to wrack and ruin? There's such goodness in it all, Lord Jesus Christ! The sun, the sky, the forests, the rivers, the animals – they've all been created, fashioned, fitted to each other, haven't they? Each has been allotted its task and knows its rightful place. And all this must come to naught!'

A melancholy smile flickered across the shepherd's face and his eyelids trembled.

'You say the earth is heading for ruin . . .' said Meliton, thinking. 'Perhaps you're right, the end of the world is nigh, but you can't judge just from the birds. You can hardly take the birds as an indication.'

'It's not just the birds,' said the shepherd. 'It's the beasts too, the cattle, the bees, the fish . . . If you don't believe me, ask the old men. They'll all tell you the fish aren't a bit like they used to be. Every year there are less and less of them – in the seas, in the lakes, in the rivers. Here in the Peschanka, I remember, you used to catch pike a good two foot long, and there were burbot, ide and bream, all decent-size fish too, but now you're grateful if you catch a jack-pike or a perch six inches long. You don't see a proper ruffe even. It's worse and worse with every year that passes, and in a little while there won't be any fish at all. Then take the rivers . . . *They're* all drying up!'

'That's true, they are.'

'To be sure they are. Each year they get shallower and shallower, and there are none of the good deep pools there used to be, brother. You see those bushes yonder?' asked the old man, pointing to one side. 'There's an old stream-bed behind them, called "the backwater". In my father's time, that's where the Peschanka flowed, but now look where the devil's led it! She keeps changing course and you see – she'll change it so much, in the end she'll dry up. Back of Kurgasovo there used to be ponds and marshes, but where are they now? And what's become of all the streams, eh? Here in this wood there used to be a running stream, and it was so full that the peasants would set their creels in it and catch pike, and the wild duck used to winter by it; but now there's no water in it worthy the name even at the spring flood. Yes, my boy, everywhere you look things are bad. Everywhere!'

There was silence. Meliton stared before him in a reverie. He was trying to think of a single area of nature that had not yet been touched by the all-consuming disaster. Flecks of light glided over the mist and the slanting bands of rain, as though over opalescent glass, but immediately melted away: the rising sun was trying to break through the clouds and catch a glimpse of the earth.

'It's the same with the forests . . .' muttered Meliton.

'Same with them . . .' echoed the shepherd. 'They're all being felled, they keep catching fire, they dry up, and there's no new growth in their place. What does grow is straightway cut down again, it comes up one day and the next day people have cut it down – and so it'll go on, until nothing's left. I've been minding the village's herd, friend, since we got our freedom, before then I was a shepherd of the master's, and always in this same spot, and I can't remember a single summer day when I haven't been here. And all the time I give an eye to God's works. I've had time to watch them well, brother, in my life, and the way I look at it now, all things that grow are on the wane. Be it rye, or vegetables, or flowers of any sort, it's all heading one way.'

'People are better, though,' observed the bailiff.

'How, better?'

'They're cleverer.'

'Cleverer they may be, lad, true enough, but what's the good of that? What fine use is cleverness to people on the verge of ruin? You don't need brains to perish. What's a hunter want brains for, if there's no game to shoot anyway? What I think is, God's made folk cleverer, but He's taken away their strength, that's what. Folks have become feeble, exceeding feeble. Now I know I'm not worth a groat, I'm the lowliest peasant in the whole village, but all the same, I've got strength, lad. You think: I'm in my sixties, but I mind the herd fair weather and foul, and I do nightwatching for a couple of kopecks, and I don't fall asleep or feel the cold, but if you was to put my son, who's cleverer than me, in my place, why, next day he'd be asking for a rise, or going to the doctor. Ye-s . . . I eat nothing but bread – "give us this day our daily bread", it says – and my father ate nothing but bread, and my grandfather before him, but the peasants these days, they've got to have tea and vodka and white loaves, they've got to sleep from dusk till dawn, go to doctors, and be pampered in every way. And why? Because they've grown feeble, they haven't the strength to stick things out. They don't want to fall asleep, but their eyes start aching and that's that.'

'It's true,' Meliton agreed. 'The peasant's good for nothing these days.'

'Might as well admit it, we get worser every year. And take the gentry now – they've grown feebler than the peasants even. Gents these days have learnt everything, they know things they'd be better off not knowing – and what good does it do? They make you sorry to look on 'em . . . Skinny, weedy, like some Frenchie or Magyar, there's no presence to them, no dignity – they're only gents in name. Poor creatures, they've no place in the world, no work to do, you can't make out what they do want. Either they sit around with a rod catching fish, or they're flat on their backs reading books, or they're hanging about with the peasants trying to put ideas in their heads; and those as are starving take jobs as clerks. So they idle their time away and never think of getting down to a proper job of work. Half the gents in the old days were generals, but nowadays they're just – dross!'

'They're badly off these days,' Meliton said.

'And the reason is, God's taken their strength away. You can't go against God.'

Meliton stared fixedly before him again. After thinking a while, he sighed the way staid, sober-minded people do, wagged his head, and said:

'And you know why all this is? Because we sin so much, we've forgotten God . . . so now the time's come for it all to end. You can't expect the world to last for ever anyway, can you? Enough's enough.'

The shepherd sighed and, as if to cut short a conversation that he found disagreeable, he moved away from the birch and began counting the cattle over silently.

'Hey-hey, halloo!' he shouted. 'Hey-hey! Damn you, where d'you think you're all going? What the devil's made them go into the firs? Halloa-loa-loa!'

He scowled and went over to the bushes to gather the herd together. Meliton rose and ambled quietly along the edge of the wood. As he walked, he stared at the ground beneath his feet: he was still trying to think of at least something that had not yet been touched by death. Again bright flecks crept over the slanting bands of rain; they danced into the tops of the trees, and melted away in their wet foliage. Lady discovered a hedgehog under a bush and tried to attract her master's attention to it by howling and barking.

'Have an eclipse recently, did you?' the shepherd called out from behind the bushes.

'We did!' replied Meliton.

'Thought as much, people everywhere are complaining there was one. So there's disorder in the heavens too, brother! And no wonder . . . Hey-hey! Hup!'

When he had driven the herd back out of the wood, the shepherd leant against a birch, looked up at the sky, calmly took his pipe out of his smock and started to play. As before, he played mechanically, producing no more than five or six notes; he might have been handling the pipe for the first time in his life, the sounds issued so uncertainly, haphazardly and tunelessly; but for Meliton, who was still thinking of the downfall of the world, his playing seemed to contain something desperately mournful and harrowing, which he would rather not have heard. The highest, shrillest notes, which trembled, then broke off abruptly, seemed to be sobbing inconsolably, as though the pipe were sick, or frightened; whilst the lowest reminded him for some reason of the mist itself, the forbidding trees and the grey sky. The music seemed to go with the weather, the old man, and what he had been talking about.

Meliton felt an urge to complain. He went over to the old man and, gazing at his sad, quizzical face and at the reed-pipe, mumbled:

'And life's got harder, too, old friend. Life's barely livable, what with the bad harvests, the poverty . . . the cattle sickness all the time, illness . . . We're at the end of our tether.'

The bailiff's pudgy face flushed crimson and took on a woeful, womanish expression. He twiddled his fingers in the air as though groping for words to convey his indeterminate feelings, and continued:

'I've got eight children and a wife to support, my mother's still alive . . . and all I get is ten roubles a month without board. The poverty's made my wife a proper shrew . . . and I'm always hitting the bottle. Really I'm a steady, sober-minded sort of chap, I've had an education. I ought to be sitting in the quiet of my home, but all day I spend wandering about with my gun, like a stray dog, because I can't abide it, I loathe my own home!'

Realising that his tongue was babbling something totally different from what he had intended to tell the old man, the bailiff gave up and said with bitterness:

'If the world's going to perish, then the sooner the better! There's no point in hanging about and making people suffer for nothing . . .'

The old man took the pipe away from his lips and, screwing up one eye, looked down its small mouthpiece. His face was sad, and covered with large splashes like tears. He smiled and said:

'It's a pity though, brother! Oh Lord the pity of it! The earth, the forest, the sky . . . animals – they've all been created and fashioned, haven't they, there's a sense running through it all. And it's all to come to naught. But it's the people I feel sorriest for.'

A heavy squall of rain rustled through the wood towards where they were standing. Meliton looked in the direction of the sound, did up all the buttons of his coat, and said:

'I'm off to the village. Cheerio, gaffer. What's your name?'

'Poor Luke.'

'Well, goodbye, Luke! Thanks for the conversation. Lady – *ici*!'

Meliton left the shepherd, sauntered along the edge of the wood and then down to a meadow, which gradually turned into marsh. The water squelched beneath his boots, and the russet-headed sedge, whose stems were still green and lush, bowed earthwards as though afraid of being trodden on. Beyond the marsh, on the banks of the Peschanka of which the old man had spoken, stood a line of willows, and beyond the willows the squire's threshing-barn showed blue through the mist. One could sense the proximity of that cheerless time which nothing can avert, when the fields become dark and the earth is muddy and chill; when the weeping willow seems to be sadder than ever and the tears trickle down her trunk; when only the cranes can flee from the all-pervading disaster and even they, as though afraid of offending morose nature by declaring their happiness, fill the skies with mournful, melancholy song.

Meliton wandered towards the river and could hear the sounds of the pipe slowly dying away behind him. He still felt the urge to complain. Sadly he looked to right and left, and felt unbearably sorry for the sky, the earth, the sun, the forest, and his dog Lady; and when the pipe's top note suddenly pierced the air and hung there trembling, like the voice of a person weeping, he felt full of bitterness and resentment at the disorder manifest in nature.

The top note trembled, broke off, and the pipe fell silent.

The Kiss

On the 20th of May, at 8 p.m., all six batteries of the N. Reserve Artillery Brigade stopped for the night at the village of Mestechki on their way to summer camp. At the very height of the bustle and confusion, when some of the officers were busy round the guns and others had assembled by the church wall in the village square to be given their billeting instructions, a man appeared from behind the church wearing civilian clothes and riding a strange horse. The horse was a small light bay, with a beautiful neck and a short tail, and instead of moving straight, it advanced in a sideways fashion, taking small dancing steps as if it were being lashed about the legs. The rider went up to the officers, raised his hat and said:

'His Excellency Lieutenant-General von Rabbek, the lord of the manor, requests the pleasure of your company for tea, gentlemen, as soon as possible . . .'

The horse bobbed its head, danced, and backed sideways; the rider doffed his hat again, and a moment later he and his strange horse had disappeared behind the church.

'That's all we needed!' grumbled some of the officers as they dispersed to their billets. 'Sleep's what we want, not an invitation to tea from this von Rabbek! "Tea"! We know what that means.'

Still fresh in the memory of the officers of all six batteries was an incident during manoeuvres the previous year, when they and the officers of a Cossack regiment had received exactly the same kind of invitation to tea from an ex-army Count-cum-landowner. The cordial and hospitable Count had treated them with great kindness, had plied them with food and drink, and would not let them return to their billets in the village, but insisted they stay the night. All that was fine, of course, what more could one ask for, but unfortunately the old soldier's delight in having young company had gone too far. He had stayed up until daybreak recounting to the officers episodes from his glorious past, conducting them round the rooms, showing them valuable pictures, old engravings and rare weapons, and reading them the originals of letters from high-ranking people, while the weary and exhausted officers looked on and listened, longed for their beds and yawned carefully on the quiet; when their host did finally release them, it was too late to go to bed.

Was this von Rabbek going to be just such another? Whether he was or not, the officers had no choice in the matter. Having cleaned and spruced themselves up, they set off in a group to find the manor-house. In the square by the church they were told that his Excellency's could be approached either by the lower route – by going down behind the church to the river, walking along the bank as far as the garden, and then taking any of the paths to the house – or by the upper route, straight from the church along a road which half a verst from the village brought you to his Excellency's granaries. The officers opted for the upper route.

'Who is he, this von Rabbek?' they debated on the way. 'Isn't he the one who commanded the N. Cavalry Division at Plevna?'

'No, that wasn't von Rabbek, that was just Rabbe and without the "von".'

'What a glorious evening!'

At the first of the granaries the road divided: one branch went straight on and disappeared into the evening haze, while the right-hand branch led to the manor-house. The officers turned right and lowered their voices . . . The road was lined on both sides by stone granaries with red roofs: grim, heavy buildings very much like a provincial barracks. Ahead shone the windows of the manor-house.

'A good omen, gentlemen!' said one of the officers. 'Our setter's leading the way. He must sense there'll be game!'

The officer leading the way, Lieutenant Lobytko, a tall, thick-set man, but completely beardless (though over twenty-five, for some reason no sign of vegetation had yet appeared on his satisfied round face), who was famous in the brigade for his ability to sense the presence of women at a distance, turned round and said:

'Yes, there'll be women here. My instinct tells me so.'

The officers were greeted on the threshold by von Rabbek himself, a fine-looking old man of about sixty, dressed in civilian clothes. As he shook hands with his guests, he told them how happy and delighted he was, but begged the officers most earnestly, on bended knee, to excuse him: unfortunately he could not invite them to stay the night, as his two sisters and their children, his brothers and his neighbours, were visiting him, and he did not have a single spare room left.

The General shook everyone by the hand, made his apologies and smiled, but it was clear from his face that he was nothing like so pleased to see his guests as last year's Count, and had invited the officers only from a sense of social obligation. And as they walked up the carpeted staircase listening to him, the officers themselves felt that they had been invited to this house only because it would have been awkward not to invite them, and the sight of the footmen hurrying to light the lamps downstairs by the entrance and upstairs in the anteroom gave them the impression that their arrival had brought with it extra worry and inconvenience. How could the presence of nineteen unknown officers be welcome in a place where two sisters and their children, the brothers and the neighbours, had probably gathered for some family event or celebration?

Upstairs, at the entrance to the ball-room, the visitors were greeted by a tall, upright old lady with a long face and dark eyebrows, who looked very much like the Empress Eugénie. With a welcoming, regal smile, she told the visitors how happy and delighted she was to see them, and how sorry that on this occasion she and her husband were denied the possibility of inviting the officers to stay the night. From her beautiful, regal smile, which vanished instantly whenever she had to turn away from the visitors for something, it was clear that she had seen a great many officers in her time, that there were other things on her mind now, and that if she had invited these officers to her house and was making apologies to them, this was only from a sense that her upbringing and social position obliged her to do so.

The visitors were shown into a large dining-room, where about a dozen men and women, young and old, were sitting round one end of a long table drinking tea. Behind their chairs stood a dark group of men, wreathed in thin cigar smoke, among whom a lanky young man with ginger sideburns was saying something loudly in English, slurring his r's. Beyond this group was an open door leading to a light room furnished in pale blue.

'Gentlemen, there are so many of you, I can't possibly introduce you all!' said the General in a loud voice, trying to sound very jovial. 'Please make your own introductions!'

The officers made their bows as best they could – some looking very serious and even stern, others giving forced smiles, and all of them feeling extremely ill at ease – and sat down to drink tea.

More ill at ease than anyone was Staff-Captain Ryabovich, a short, round-shouldered officer in spectacles and with whiskers like a lynx's. While some of his colleagues were looking serious and others giving forced smiles, his face, his lynx-like whiskers and his spectacles seemed to be saying: 'I'm the shyest, drabbest and most retiring officer in the whole brigade!' Initially, when they went into the dining-room and then sat down to tea, he was quite unable to focus his attention on any one face or object. The faces and dresses, the cut-glass brandy decanters, the steam off the glasses of tea, the moulded cornices: all these merged into one huge overall impression that filled Ryabovich with anxiety and made him want to hide his head. Like a reader giving his first performance in public, he saw everything in front of him, but what he saw somehow failed to register properly (physiologists refer to this condition, when a person sees but fails to comprehend what he is seeing, as 'mental blindness'). A little later on, when he felt more at ease, Ryabovich began to see normally and to look around. Being a timid and unsociable person, what struck him most about his new acquaintances was the quality completely lacking in himself: their unusual boldness. Von Rabbek, his wife, two elderly ladies, a young girl in a lilac dress and the young man with ginger sideburns, who turned out to be Rabbek's youngest son, positioned themselves very craftily among the officers, as if they had rehearsed it beforehand, and at once launched into a fierce argument in which the visitors could not help but be involved. The young girl in lilac argued fiercely that the artillery had a much easier life than the cavalry or infantry, while Rabbek and the elderly ladies maintained the opposite. A crossfire conversation developed. Ryabovich looked at the young girl in lilac, who was arguing so fiercely about something that must be quite alien and of no conceivable interest to her, and watched the artificial smiles that came and went on her face.

Von Rabbek and his family skilfully drew the officers into the argument, while at the same time keeping a close watch on their glasses and mouths, finding out whether they all had enough tea and were enjoying their food, and why one of them had not tried the tea-biscuits or another was not drinking brandy. And the more Ryabovich watched and listened, the more this artificial but superbly disciplined family appealed to him.

After tea, the officers went into the ball-room. Lieutenant Lobytko's intuition had not deceived him: the room was full of girls and young ladies. The setter himself was already standing next to a very young little blonde in a black dress and, striking a gallant pose as if leaning on an invisible sabre, was smiling and frisking his shoulders coquettishly. He was probably telling her some very tedious piece of nonsense, as the blonde was looking condescendingly into his satisfied face and saying in a bored voice: 'Really?' And had the setter had any intelligence, he would have realised from the indifferent tone of that 'Really?' that he was hardly being told to 'fetch!'

The grand piano resounded; the notes of a melancholy waltz floated through the wide open windows of the ball-room, and for some reason everyone suddenly remembered that it was spring outside now, a May evening. Everyone sensed that the air was fragrant with roses, lilac and young poplar leaves. Under the effect of the music, the brandy he had drunk was beginning to work on Ryabovich, and as he listened to the music, he glanced over to the window, smiled and started following the movements of the women; and soon it seemed to him that the scent of roses, poplar and lilac was coming not from the garden but from the women's faces and dresses.

Rabbek's son invited a scraggy-looking female to dance and waltzed twice round the room with her. Gliding across the parquet, Lobytko flew up to the young girl in lilac and whisked her off across the ball-room. The dancing began . . . Ryabovich stood by the door among the non-dancers and looked on. In the whole of his life he had never once danced, nor had he ever put his arm round the waist of a respectable woman. To see a man take a strange girl by the waist in front of everyone and invite her to put her hand on his shoulder appealed to him enormously, but to imagine himself in that man's position was quite beyond him. There was a time when he envied the confidence and go of his comrades and suffered mental anguish; the awareness that he was timid, round-shouldered and drab, that he had lynx-like whiskers and no hips, hurt him profoundly, but with the passing of the years he had become inured to this, so that now, as he looked at his comrades dancing or conversing loudly, he no longer experienced envy, only a feeling of wistful admiration.

When the quadrille started, young von Rabbek came over to the non-dancers and asked two of the officers if they would like to play billiards. The officers accepted, and followed him out of the room. Having nothing better to do and wanting to take at least some part in the general activity, Ryabovich trailed after them. From the ball-room they went into a drawing-room, then along a narrow glass corridor, and thence into a room where the figures of three sleepy footmen jumped up quickly from the sofas at their appearance. After a whole series of other rooms, young Rabbek and the officers finally entered a small room containing the billiard-table. The game began.

Ryabovich, who had never played anything but cards, stood by the table and looked on impassively as the players, with jackets unbuttoned and cues in their hands, strode about, made puns and shouted out incomprehensible words. The players were unaware of him, and only occasionally one or other of them, after elbowing him or accidentally butting him with a cue, would turn round and say in French: '*Pardon!*' Even before the first game was over, he began to feel bored and had the impression he was in the way and not wanted . . . He felt drawn back to the ball-room and went out.

On his way back a small adventure befell him. He realised about half-way that he was not going in the right direction. He distinctly recalled the three sleepy footman figures whom he ought to pass on his return, but he had gone through five or six rooms and these three figures seemed to have vanished into thin air. Realising his mistake, he retraced his steps a short distance, turned right and found himself in a semi-dark study which he had not seen on his way to the billiard-room; after standing there for half a minute, he hesitantly opened the first door that caught his eye and entered a room which was in total darkness. Through a chink in the door straight ahead a bright light was shining; from beyond the door came the muffled sounds of a sad muzurka. Here too, as in the ball-room, the windows were wide open and there was a scent of poplar, lilac and roses . . .

Ryabovich paused to collect his thoughts . . . Just at that moment there came the unexpected sound of hurrying footsteps and the rustle of a dress, a woman's voice whispered breathlessly 'At last!' and two soft, fragrant, unmistakably feminine arms twined themselves round his neck; a warm cheek pressed itself to his and simultaneously there came the sound of a kiss. But at once the giver of the kiss uttered a little shriek and, so it seemed to Ryabovich, recoiled from him in horror. He too very nearly screamed, and rushed towards the bright light coming from the door . . .

When he returned to the ball-room, his heart was thumping, and his hands were trembling so noticeably that he hastily hid them behind his back. At first, tormented by a feeling of shame and fear that the whole room knew he had just been embraced and kissed by a woman, he made himself small and darted anxious glances all around him, but once he was sure they were dancing and chatting away in the ball-room as imperturbably as ever, he gave himself up entirely to a new sensation, one that he had never experienced in his life before. Something strange was happening to him . . . His neck, which had just been embraced by soft fragrant arms, seemed to have been bathed with oil; at the spot on his cheek by his left moustache where the unknown woman had kissed him, there was a slight, pleasantly cold tingling, such as you get from peppermints, and the more he rubbed the spot, the more pronounced this tingling became; whilst the whole of him, from top to toe, was filled with a new, peculiar feeling that grew and grew . . . He felt he wanted to dance, talk, run into the garden, laugh out loud . . . He forgot completely that he was drab and round-shouldered, and had lynx-like whiskers and a 'nondescript' appearance (as it had once been described in a female conversation that he had overheard). When Rabbek's wife walked past, he smiled at her so broadly and warmly that she stopped and gave him an inquiring look.

'I like your house enormously!' he said, adjusting his spectacles.

The General's wife smiled and told him that the house had originally belonged to her father, then she asked whether his parents were still alive, how long he had been in the army, why he looked so thin, etc. . . . Having received answers to her questions, she moved on, while Ryabovich began to smile even more warmly after his conversation with her, and to think that he was surrounded by the most splendid people . . .

At supper, he ate mechanically everything he was offered, drank, and deaf to the world, tried to explain his recent adventure to himself . . . The adventure had a mysterious, romantic quality to it, but its explanation was not hard to find. No doubt one of the girls or young ladies had arranged to meet someone in the dark room, had been waiting for a long time, and in her state of nervous excitement had mistaken Ryabovich for her hero; especially as Ryabovich, on his way through the dark room, had paused to collect his thoughts, in other words had given the impression of someone who was also waiting . . . Thus Ryabovich explained to himself the kiss he had received.

'But who was she?' he thought, looking round the female faces. 'She must be young, because you don't find old ladies making assignations. And she must be educated, because of her rustling dress, her perfume, her voice . . .'

His eye came to rest on the young girl in lilac, and he liked the look of her very much; she had beautiful arms and shoulders, an intelligent face and an attractive voice. Looking at her, Ryabovich wanted *her* to be the unknown woman, and her alone . . . But she began laughing in an artificial kind of way and wrinkled up her long nose, which struck him as old-looking. Then he turned his attention to the little blonde in the black dress. She was younger, simpler and more sincere, had a charming forehead, and drank very prettily from her wine-glass. Now Ryabovich wanted her to be the one. But he soon found her features lifeless, and transferred his gaze to her neighbour . . .

'It's difficult to decide,' he thought dreamily. 'If you took the lilac one's arms and shoulders, added the little blonde's forehead, and the eyes of the one sitting on Lobytko's left, then . . .'

He put them together in his mind and obtained an image of the girl who had kissed him, the image that he had searched for but been quite unable to find at the supper table . . .

After supper the visitors, feeling tipsy and replete, began to thank their hosts and take their leave. The hosts started apologising again for not inviting them to stay the night.

'Delighted to have met you, gentlemen!' said the General, and this time sincerely (probably because people are much more friendly and sincere seeing visitors off than greeting them). 'Delighted! You must pay us another visit on your return journey! Informally! Which way are you going? Along the top? No, take the lower route through the garden – it's quicker from here.'

The officers went out into the garden. After all the noise and bright lights the garden seemed very dark and quiet. They walked in silence until they reached the gate. They were half-drunk, in a cheerful mood, and contented, but the silence and darkness made them pause for a minute to reflect. Probably each of them had the same thought as occurred to Ryabovich: would there ever be a time when they too would be like Rabbek and have a large house, a family and garden, when they too would be in a position to be kind to people, if only insincerely, and to make them drunk, replete and contented?

Once through the gate, they all suddenly began talking and laughing loudly for no reason. They were now walking down a footpath which descended to the river, where it ran along the water's edge, skirting round bushes growing on the bank, inlets, and willow trees overhanging the water. The near bank and path were scarcely visible, while the far bank was completely plunged in darkness. Stars were reflected here and there in the dark water; they trembled and dissolved, and only from this could one guess that the river was flowing swiftly. The air was still. From the far bank came the plaintive cry of drowsy snipe, while in one of the bushes on the near bank, paying no attention at all to the crowd of officers, a nightingale was in full song. The officers stood by the bush and shook it gently, but the nightingale just went on singing.

'How about that?' they exclaimed approvingly. 'We're standing right by him and the little rascal doesn't give a damn!'

At the end of their walk the footpath began to climb, joining the road near the church wall. Tired by the uphill walk, the officers sat down here for a smoke. A dim red light appeared on the far side of the river, and they spent a long time idly debating whether it was a bonfire, a lighted window, or something else . . . Ryabovich also looked at the light and fancied that it was smiling and winking at him, as if it knew about the kiss.

On reaching the billet, Ryabovich quickly undressed and lay down. He was sharing a hut with Lobytko and Lieutenant Merzlyakov, a quiet, taciturn young fellow who was regarded by his associates as an educated officer and who spent all his spare time reading *The European Herald*, which he carried with him wherever he went. Lobytko undressed, paced up and down for a long time with the look of a man who is not satisfied, and sent the batman out for beer. Merzlyakov lay down, stood a candle by his bed, and buried himself in *The European Herald*.

'But who was she?' thought Ryabovich, looking at the smoke-blackened ceiling.

His neck still seemed to be bathed with oil and he could feel the cold tingle, like that of peppermints, next to his mouth. In his imagination he glimpsed the arms and shoulders of the girl in lilac, the forehead and candid gaze of the little blonde in black, waists, dresses and brooches. He tried to fix his attention on these images, but they jumped about, dissolved, kept flickering. As these images were fading away completely on the wide black ground that everyone sees when they close their eyes, he began to hear hurrying footsteps, a rustling dress, the sound of a kiss – and a powerful irrational joy took possession of him. He was giving himself up to this joy when he heard the batman come back and report that no beer was to be had. Lobytko became terribly indignant at this, and started pacing up and down again.

'The man's an idiot!' he said, stopping in front of Ryabovich, then in front of Merzlyakov. 'Anyone who can't find beer needs his head examining! Well, doesn't he? The man's a rogue!'

'Of course you won't find beer here,' said Merzlyakov, without looking up from *The European Herald*.

'Oh? You think not?' Lobytko persisted. 'Good Lord, you could drop me on the moon and I'd soon find you beer and women! I'll go out and find some now . . . Call me a scoundrel if I come back empty-handed!'

He spent a long time dressing and pulling on his large boots, then silently finished his cigarette and went out.

'Rabbek, Grabbek, Labbek,' he muttered, pausing in the outer passage. 'I don't feel like going on my own, damn it! Fancy a walk, eh, Ryabovich?'

Receiving no reply, he came back, slowly undressed and lay down. Merzlyakov sighed, pushed *The European Herald* to one side and put out the candle.

'Ye–s. . .' murmured Lobytko, lighting a cigarette in the darkness.

Ryabovich pulled the bedding over his head, curled up in a ball, and tried to gather the fleeting images together in his mind and make them into one. But nothing came of it. Soon he fell asleep, and his last thought was that someone had been kind to him and made him happy, that something unusual, absurd, but extremely good and full of joy, had taken place in his life. This thought did not leave him even while he slept.

When he awoke, he no longer felt the oil on his neck or the chill of peppermint next to his lips, but the same joy welled up inside him as on the previous day. With a feeling of exultation he looked at the window-frames gilded by the rising sun and listened to the sounds of activity coming from the street. A noisy conversation was taking place right by the windows. Ryabovich's battery commander, Lebedetsky, had just caught up the brigade and was talking at the top of his voice – not being in the habit of talking softly – to his sergeant-major.

'Anything else?' shouted the commander.

'At yesterday's re-shoeing Boy's foot was injured, your honour. The vet put on clay and vinegar. He's being led separately now. Also, craftsman Artemyev got drunk yesterday, your honour, and the Lieutenant ordered him to be put on the limber of the reserve gun-carriage.'

The sergeant-major went on to report that Karpov had forgotten the new cords for the trumpets, and the tent-poles, and that yesterday evening the officers had been the guests of General von Rabbek. In the course of the conversation Lebedetsky's ginger-bearded face showed up at the window. He peered shortsightedly at the officers' sleepy faces and said good-morning.

'Everything in order?' he asked.

'The left wheeler's rubbed her withers sore on her new collar,' Lobytko answered, yawning.

The commander sighed, thought for a moment, then bellowed:

'I think I'll go on and visit Alexandra Yevgrafovna. Must look her up. Cheerio then. I'll catch you up this evening.'

A quarter of an hour later the brigade moved off. As they were going along the road past the estate granaries, Ryabovich looked over to his right at the house. The blinds were down in the windows. They must all still be asleep indoors. She was asleep too: the girl who had kissed Ryabovich the evening before. He tried to imagine her sleeping. The wide open bedroom window with green branches peeping in, the early morning freshness, the scent of poplar, lilac and roses, her bed, a chair with the rustling dress of yesterday draped over it, her slippers, her little watch on the bedside table – all this he pictured clearly and distinctly to himself; but those things that were really vital and individual to her – her features and her sweet, drowsy smile – slipped through his imagination like quicksilver between the fingers. When they had covered half a verst, he glanced back: the yellow church, the house, the river and the garden were bathed in light; the river with its bright green banks looked very beautiful, reflecting the blue sky, and here and there gleaming silver in the sunlight. Ryabovich took a last look at Mestechki and felt as sad as if he were parting with something very near and dear to him.

As for the sights that lay before him on the journey, they were all only too dull and familiar . . . To right and to left fields of young rye and buckwheat with rooks hopping about; ahead of him – dust and the backs of heads, behind him – the same dust and faces . . . Out in front march four men with sabres: the vanguard. Behind them in a crowd come the singers, and behind the singers the trumpeters on horseback. The vanguard and the singers, like torch-bearers in a funeral procession, forget every so often about the regulation distance and open up a huge gap . . . Ryabovich is with the first gun of the fifth battery. He can see all four batteries ahead of him. To a layman the long, lumbering column of a brigade on the move appears to be a complicated and confusing muddle; it does not make sense for one gun to have so many people round it and to be drawn by so many horses entangled in strange harness, as if it really were that heavy and terrifying. But to Ryabovich it all makes sense and is therefore extremely boring. He has known for ages why a sturdy bombardier rides alongside the officer at the head of each battery and why he is given a special name; behind this bombardier's back he can see the drivers of the first and then the middle trace; Ryabovich knows that the horses on the left, on which the drivers ride, have one name, and those on the right another – and it is all very boring. Behind the driver come the two wheel-horses. On one of them rides a driver with yesterday's dust still on his back and a very clumsy, funny-looking piece of wood on his right leg; Ryabovich knows the purpose of this piece of wood and does not find it funny at all. Every single driver brandishes his whip mechanically and from time to time gives a shout. The gun itself is ugly. Sacks of oats covered by a tarpaulin lie on the limber, while the actual gun has tea-pots, soldiers' packs and haversacks hanging all over it, and gives the appearance of a small harmless creature which for some unknown reason has been surrounded by human beings and horses. On its leeward side, swinging their arms, march the six members of the guncrew. Behind the gun begins another set of leaders, drivers and wheelers, behind which another gun is being pulled, as ugly and unimpressive as the first. The second is followed by a third and a fourth; the fourth has an officer to it, and so on. The brigade has six batteries in all, and each battery has four guns. The column stretches for half a verst. Bringing up the rear is the baggage-train, and walking thoughtfully beside it, drooping his long-eared head, marches a highly sympathetic character: the donkey Magar, brought back from Turkey by one of the battery commanders.

Ryabovich stared with indifference in front and behind, at the backs of heads and the faces; at any other time he would have become drowsy, but now he was totally immersed in his pleasant new thoughts. At first, when the brigade had only just moved off, he tried to convince himself that the incident with the kiss could be of interest only as a mysterious little adventure, that basically it was trivial and to give it serious thought was absurd, to say the least; but he soon cast logic aside and abandoned himself to dreams . . . First he imagined himself in Rabbek's drawing-room, next to a young girl who was like the girl in lilac and the little blonde in black; then he closed his eyes and saw himself with another girl, a total stranger whose features were very shadowy, imagined himself talking to her, caressing her, leaning on her shoulder, pictured war and separation, then reunion, supper with his wife, children . . .

'Brakes!' the command rang out every time they went downhill.

He too shouted 'Brakes!' and was afraid lest his shout should interrupt his dreams and bring him back to reality . . .

As they were going past some large estate, Ryabovich glanced across the fencing into the grounds. His eye was met by a long avenue straight as a ruler, strewn with yellow sand and planted with young birch-trees . . . With the avidity of a man lost in daydreams he pictured small feminine feet walking on the yellow sand, and quite unexpectedly a clear impression arose in his imagination of the girl who had kissed him and whose image he had succeeded in conjuring up at supper the day before. This image fixed itself in his brain and did not leave him.

At midday a shout rang out in the rear by the baggage-train:

'Atten-tion! Eyes left! Stand by, officers!'

The Brigade General drove past in a barouche drawn by a pair of white horses. He stopped by the second battery and shouted something which no one could understand. Several officers, including Ryabovich, galloped up to him.

'How goes it then?' the General asked, blinking his red eyes. 'Any sick?'

After receiving answers to his questions, the General, a skinny little man, chewed his lips thoughtfully, then turned to one of the officers and said:

'The wheel-horse driver on your third gun has taken off his knee-guard and hung it on the limber. Punish the rascal.'

He looked up at Ryabovich and went on:

'Your breechings look too slack . . .'

After making several other tedious observations, the General looked at Lobytko and grinned.

'And you're looking very down in the mouth today, Lieutenant Lobytko,' he said. 'Missing Lopukhova, are you? Eh? Gentlemen, he's pining for Lopukhova!'

Lopukhova was a very stout and very tall lady, well past forty. The General, who was partial to substantial females of whatever age, suspected a similar predilection in his officers. The officers smiled respectfully. The General, pleased with his bitingly witty remark, guffawed, touched his coachman on the back and saluted. The barouche rolled on its way . . .

'Everything I'm dreaming about now and which seems so impossible and unreal, is in fact very commonplace,' thought Ryabovich, watching the clouds of dust race after the General's barouche. 'It's all very ordinary and is experienced by everyone . . . That General, for instance, fell in love once and now he's married and has children. Captain Vakhter also has a wife and is loved, even though the back of his neck is so red and ugly, and he has no hips either . . . Salmanov has coarse features and there's too much Tartar in him, but he had an affair and it ended in marriage . . . I'm just like everyone else and sooner or later I shall have the same experiences as everyone else . . .'

And the thought of being an ordinary person and leading an ordinary life cheered him and encouraged him. He pictured *her* and his happiness boldly now, as he had wished, and let nothing stand in the way of his imagination . . .

When the brigade reached its destination that evening and the officers were resting in their tents, Ryabovich, Merzlyakov and Lobytko were sitting round a box having supper. Merzlyakov ate unhurriedly, chewing slowly and reading his copy of *The European Herald*, which he held on his knees. Lobytko talked incessantly and kept topping up his glass with beer, while Ryabovich, dazed from dreaming all day long, drank and said nothing. After three glasses the beer went to his head, he relaxed, and felt an irresistible urge to tell his comrades about his new experience.

'A strange thing happened to me at those Rabbeks . . .' he began, trying to make his voice sound detached and ironical. 'It was like this: I went along to the billiard-room . . .'

He started to relate the incident of the kiss in great detail and a minute later fell silent . . . In that minute he had told it all and was quite amazed to find that the story had taken such a short time. He had thought he could go on talking about the kiss all night. After listening to him, Lobytko, who was a great liar and therefore never believed anyone, eyed him sceptically and sniggered. Merzlyakov raised his eyebrows and said calmly, without looking up from *The European Herald*:

'Very odd! Throws herself on your neck without warning . . . Must have been some kind of a case.'

'Yes, I suppose so . . .' Ryabovich agreed.

'A similar thing happened to me once,' said Lobytko, looking wide eyed. 'I was travelling last year to Kovno . . . I'd bought a second-class ticket . . . The carriage was packed tight, there wasn't a hope of getting any sleep, so I gave the guard half a rouble and he took me and my luggage along to a sleeping compartment . . . I lay down and pulled the blanket over me . . . It was dark, you understand. Suddenly I feel someone touch me on the shoulder and breathe in my face. I made a movement like this with my hand and felt someone's elbow . . . I open my eyes and – would you believe it? – a woman! Black eyes, lips the colour of fresh salmon, nostrils flaring with passion, breasts like buffers –'

'One moment,' Merzlyakov interrupted calmly, 'I understand the bit about the breasts, but how could you see her lips if it was dark?'

Lobytko began trying to wriggle out of it and laughing at Merzlyakov's lack of imagination. This was too much for Ryabovich. He got up from the box, lay down on his bed and vowed never to confide in anyone again.

Camp routine set in . . . The days flowed past, one very much like the next. All this long time Ryabovich felt, thought and behaved like a man in love. Every morning, when the batman handed him his water for washing, he would pour the cold water over his head and remember on each occasion that there was something warm and precious in his life.

In the evenings, when his comrades began talking about love and women, he would listen in, move up closer, and assume the kind of expression that appears on soldiers' faces when they are listening to a tale of a battle in which they themselves took part. And on evenings when the officers had too much to drink and carried out Don Juan-like raids on the 'suburb' with Lobytko the setter at their head, Ryabovich was always sad after taking part, felt deeply guilty and inwardly begged *her* forgiveness . . . In hours of idleness or during sleepless nights, when he felt a desire to recall his childhood, his father and mother, in fact everything near and dear to him, he never failed to think of Mestechki too, the strange horse, Rabbek, Rabbek's wife who looked like the Empress Eugénie, the dark room, the bright chink in the door . . .

On the 31st of August he set off from camp on the return journey, not with the whole brigade, but with two batteries. All the way he was excited and preoccupied with his dreams, as if returning to his birthplace. He longed passionately to see the strange horse again, the church, the artificial Rabbek family, the dark room; that 'inner voice' which so often deceives lovers whispered to him for some reason that he was bound to see her . . . And questions tormented him. How would he greet her? What would he talk to her about? Would she have forgotten about the kiss? If the worst came to the worst, he thought, and their paths did not even cross, it would be pleasant for him simply to walk through the dark room and remember . . .

Towards evening the familiar church and white granaries appeared on the horizon. Ryabovich's heartbeat quickened . . . He did not hear anything the officer riding beside him said, was oblivious to everything, and fastened his eyes avidly on the river gleaming in the distance, the roof of the big house and the dovecote around which doves were wheeling, catching the light of the setting sun.

When they reached the church and were receiving their billeting instructions, he expected every second to see the rider appear from behind the church wall and invite the officers to tea . . . but the billeting orders were over, the officers had dismounted and wandered off into the village, and still there was no rider . . .

'Rabbek will soon be told by the peasants that we've arrived and will send for us,' Ryabovich thought as he went into the hut, and could not understand why his companion was lighting a candle and the batmen were hastening to put the samovars on . . .

A deep anxiety came over him. He lay down, then got up and looked out of the window. Was the rider coming? No, there was no rider. He lay down again, got up half an hour later, and, unable to endure his state of anxiety any longer, went out into the street and strode along to the church. By the church wall in the square it was dark and deserted . . . Three soldiers were standing in silence next to one another right at the top of the slope. They gave a start when they saw Ryabovich and saluted. He saluted back and began to descend the familiar footpath.

On the far bank the whole sky was bathed in crimson: the moon was rising; two peasant women were talking loudly to each other as they moved across a vegetable plot picking cabbage leaves; beyond the vegetable plots a dark group of peasant huts could be seen . . . But on the near bank it was all just as it had been in May: the footpath, the bushes, the willow trees overhanging the water . . . only there was no intrepid nightingale singing, and no scent of poplar and young grass.

Ryabovich reached the gate and looked into the garden. It was dark and quiet there . . . He could make out nothing but the white trunks of the nearest birch trees and a small strip of pathway; everything else merged into one black mass. Ryabovich listened and looked, straining every nerve, but when he had stood there for about a quarter of an hour without seeing a light or hearing a sound, he began to wander back . . .

He went down to the river. Ahead he could make out the whiteness of the General's bathing-house and the white forms of some sheets hanging over the rail of a little bridge . . . He went up onto the bridge, stood there a while and for no good reason felt one of the sheets. It was rough and cold. He glanced down at the water . . . The river was flowing swiftly, gurgling very faintly round the supports of the bathing-house. The red moon was reflected close by the left bank; little waves ran through the reflection, stretching it out, breaking it into pieces and apparently intent on carrying it away . . .

'How absurd! How absurd!' thought Ryabovich, as he gazed at the flowing water. 'How stupid it all is!'

Now that he was not expecting anything, he could see the incident of the kiss, his impatience, his vague hopes and disappointment, in a clear light. It no longer seemed strange that he had waited in vain for the General's rider and that he would never see the girl who had accidentally kissed him instead of someone else; on the contrary, it would have been strange if he had seen her . . .

The water was flowing he knew not where or why. It had flowed just like this in May; from the small river it had poured in the month of May into a big one, from the big river into the sea, then had become vapour and turned into rain, and maybe what Ryabovich was looking at now was that very same water . . . Why? For what reason?

And the whole world, the whole of life, struck Ryabovich as an unintelligible, pointless joke . . . Raising his eyes from the water and looking at the sky, he remembered again how fate in the person of an unknown woman had accidentally been kind to him, he remembered the dreams and images of the summer, and his life struck him as extraordinarily barren, wretched and drab . . .

When he returned to his hut, not one of his fellow officers was to be found. The batman informed him that they had all gone to the house of 'General Fontryabkin', who had sent a rider for them . . . For a brief moment a feeling of joy blazed up in Ryabovich, but he immediately extinguished it, got into bed, and in defiance of his fate, as if wanting to spite it, did not go to the General's.

No Comment 1888

In the fifth century, just as now, every morning the sun rose, and every evening it retired to rest. In the morning, as the first rays kissed the dew, the earth would come to life and the air be filled with sounds of joy, hope and delight, while in the evening the same earth would grow quiet again and be swallowed up in grim darkness. Each day, each night, was like the one before. Occasionally a dark cloud loomed up and thunder growled angrily from it, or a star would doze off and fall from the firmament, or a monk would run by, pale-faced, to tell the brethren that not far from the monastery he had seen a tiger – and that would be all, then once again each day, each night, would be just like the one before.

The monks toiled and prayed, while their Abbot played the organ, composed music and wrote verses in Latin. This wonderful old man had an extraordinary gift. Whenever he played the organ, he did so with such artistry that even the oldest monks, whose hearing had grown dull as they neared the end of their lives, could not restrain their tears when the sounds of the organ reached them from his cell. Whenever he spoke about something, even the most commonplace things, such as the trees, the wild beasts, or the sea, it was impossible to listen to him without a smile or a tear; it seemed that the same chords were sounding in his soul as in the organ. Whereas if he was moved by anger, or by great joy, or if he was talking about something terrible or sublime, a passionate inspiration would take hold of him, his eyes would flash and fill with tears, his face flush and his voice rumble like thunder, and as they listened to him the monks could feel this inspiration taking over their souls; in those magnificent, wonderful moments his power was limitless, and if he had ordered the fathers to throw themselves into the sea, then, to a man, they would all have rushed rapturously to carry out his will.

His music, his voice, and the verses in which he praised God, the heavens and the earth, were for the monks a source of constant joy. As life was so unvaried, there were times when spring and autumn, the flowers and the trees, began to pall on them, their ears tired of the sound of the sea, and the song of the birds became irksome; but the talents of the old Abbot were as vital to them as their daily bread.

Many years passed, and still each day, each night, was just like the one before. Apart from the wild birds and beasts, not a single living soul showed itself near the monastery. The nearest human habitation was far away, and to get to it from the monastery or *vice versa*, meant crossing a hundred versts or so of wilderness on foot. The only people who ventured to cross the wilderness were those who spurned life, had renounced it, and were going to the monastery as though to the grave.

Imagine the monks' astonishment, therefore, when one night a man knocked at their gates who, it transpired, came from the town and was the most ordinary of sinful mortals who love life. Before asking the Abbot's blessing and offering up a prayer, this man called for food and wine. When he was asked how he, a townsman, came to be in the wilderness, he answered with a long sportsman's yarn about how he had gone out hunting, had too much to drink, and lost his way. To the suggestion that he take the monastic vow and save his soul, he replied with a smile and the words: 'I'm no mate of yours.'

After he had eaten and drunk his fill, he looked around at the monks who had been waiting for him, and shaking his head reproachfully, he said:

'What a way to carry on! All you monks bother about is eating and drinking. Is that the way to save your souls? Just think, whilst you're sitting here in peace and quiet, eating, drinking, and dreaming of heavenly bliss, your fellow humans are perishing and going down to hell. Why don't you look at what's going on in the town! Some are dying of hunger there, others have more gold than they know what to do with, and wallow in debauchery till they die like flies stuck to honey. People have no faith or principles! Whose job is it to save them? To preach to them? Surely not mine, when I'm drunk from morning till night? Did God give you faith, a humble spirit and a loving heart just to sit around here within four walls twiddling your thumbs?'

Although the townsman's drunken words were insolent and profane, they had a strange effect upon the Abbot. The old man glanced round at his monks, paled, and said:

'Brothers, what he says is right! Through their folly and their frailty, those poor people are indeed perishing in sin and unbelief, whilst we sit back, as though it had nothing to do with us. Should I not be the one to go and recall them to Christ whom they have forgotten?'

The townsman's words had carried the old man away, and the very next morning he took his staff in his hand, bade the brethren farewell, and set off for the town. And the monks were left without his music, his verses, and his fine speeches.

A month of boredom went by, then another, and still the old man did not return. At last, after the third month, they heard the familiar tapping of his staff. The monks rushed to meet him and showered him with questions, but he, instead of being glad to see them again, broke into bitter tears and would not say a single word. The monks saw he had aged greatly and grown much thinner; his face was strained and full of a deep sorrow, and when he broke into tears he looked like a man who had been mortally offended.

The monks too burst into tears and began begging him to tell them why he was weeping, why he looked so downcast, but he would not say a word and locked himself away in his cell. Seven days he stayed there, would not eat or drink or play the organ, and just wept. When the monks knocked at his door and implored him to come out and share his grief with them, they were met with a profound silence.

At last he came out. Gathering all the monks about him, he began with a tear-stained face and an expression of sorrow and indignation to tell them what had happened to him in the past three months. His voice was calm and his eyes smiled while he described his journey from the monastery to the town. As he went along, he said, the birds had sung to him and the brooks babbled, and tender young hopes had stirred in his soul; as he walked, he felt like a soldier going into battle, confident of victory; and in his reverie he walked along composing hymns and verses and did not notice when his journey was over.

But his voice trembled, his eyes flashed, and his whole being burned with wrath when he started talking of the town and its people. Never in his life had he seen, never durst imagine, what confronted him when he entered the town. Only now, in his old age, had he seen and understood for the first time how mighty was the devil, how beautiful wickedness, and how feeble, cowardly and faint-hearted were human beings. As luck would have it, the first dwelling that he went into was a house of ill fame. Some fifty people with lots of money were eating and drinking immoderate quantities of wine. Intoxicated by the wine, they sang songs and bandied about terrible, disgusting words that no God-fearing person could ever bring himself to utter; completely uninhibited, boisterous and happy, they did not fear God, the devil or death, but said and did exactly as they wished, and went wherever their lusts impelled them. And the wine, as clear as amber and fizzing with gold, must have been unbearably sweet and fragrant, because everyone drinking it smiled blissfully and wanted to drink more. In response to men's smiles it smiled back, and sparkled joyfully when it was drunk, as if it knew what devilish charm lurked in its sweetness.

More and more worked up and weeping with rage, the old man continued to describe what he had seen. On a table among the revellers, he said, stood a half-naked harlot. It would be difficult to imagine or to find in nature anything more lovely and captivating. This foul creature, young, with long hair, dusky skin, dark eyes and full lips, shameless and brazen, flashed her snow-white teeth and smiled as if to say: 'Look at me, how brazen I am and beautiful!' Silk and brocade hung down in graceful folds from her shoulders, but her beauty would not be hid, and like young shoots in the spring earth, eagerly thrust through the folds of her garments. The brazen woman drank wine, sang songs, and gave herself to anyone who wished.

Then the old man, waving his arms in anger, went on to describe the horse-races and bull fights, the theatres, and the artists' workshops where they made paintings and sculptures in clay of naked women. His speech was inspired, beautiful and melodious, as if he were playing on invisible chords, and the monks, rooted to the spot, devoured his every word and could scarcely breathe for excitement . . . When he had finished describing all the devil's charms, the beauty of wickedness and the captivating graces of the vile female body, the old man denounced the devil, turned back to his cell and closed the door behind him . . .

When he came out of his cell next morning, there was not a single monk left in the monastery. They had all run away to the town.

Let Me Sleep

Night-time.

Varka the nursemaid, a girl of about thirteen, rocks the cradle with the baby in and croons very faintly:

Bayu-bayushki-bayú,
I'll sing a song for you . . .

In front of the icon burns a small green lamp; across the entire room, from one corner to another, stretches a cord with baby-clothes and a pair of big black trousers hanging on it. The icon-lamp throws a large patch of green onto the ceiling, and the baby-clothes and trousers cast long shadows on the stove, the cradle, and Varka . . . When the lamp begins to flicker, the green patch and the shadows come to life and are set in motion, as if a wind were blowing them. It is stuffy. The room smells of cabbage soup and bootmaker's wares.

The baby is crying. It grew hoarse and wore itself out crying ages ago, but still it goes on screaming and goodness knows when it will stop. And Varka wants to sleep. Her eyes keep closing, her head droops, her neck aches. She can scarcely move her lips or eyelids, her face feels all parched and wooden, and her head seems to have become no bigger than a pin's.

'*Bayu-bayushki-bayú*,' she croons, 'I'll cook some groats for you . . .'

The cricket chirps in the stove. Behind the door, in the next room, the master and his apprentice Afanasy are snoring gently . . . And these sounds, along with the plaintive squeaking of the cradle and Varka's own soft crooning, all blend into that soothing night music which is so sweet to hear when you yourself are going to bed. But now that music merely irritates and oppresses Varka, because it makes her drowsy, and sleeping's forbidden; please God she doesn't drop off, or master and mistress will thrash her.

The icon-lamp flickers. The green patch and the shadows are set in motion, steal into Varka's half-open, motionless eyes, and form themselves into misty visions in her half-sleeping brain. She sees dark clouds, chasing each other across the sky and screaming like the baby. But now the wind gets up, the clouds vanish, and Varka sees a broad highway swimming in mud; along this highway strings of carts are moving, people trudging with knapsacks on their backs, and vague shadows flitting to and fro; on either side, through the grim, cold mist she can see forests. Suddenly the shadows and the people with the knapsacks all fall down in the wet mud. 'What are you doing?' asks Varka. 'Going to sleep, going to sleep!' they reply. And they fall into a sweet, deep slumber, whilst on the telegraph wires crows and magpies sit, screaming like the baby and trying to wake them.

'*Bayu-bayushki-bayú*, I'll sing a song for you . . .' croons Varka and sees herself now in a dark, stuffy hut.

Yefim Stepanov, her dead father, is tossing and turning on the floor. She cannot see him, but she hears him rolling about on the floor and groaning. He says his 'rupture's burst'. The pain is so great that he cannot utter a single word, only draw in sharp breaths and beat a tattoo with his teeth:

'Bm-bm-bm-bm-bm . . .'

Pelageya, Varka's mother, has run up to the big house to tell them that Yefim is dying. She's been gone ages, it's time she was back. Varka lies awake on the stove, listening to her father's 'bm-bm-bm'. But now she hears someone drive up to the hut. They've sent along the young doctor from town who is staying with them. The doctor comes into the hut; it's too dark to see him, but Varka hears him cough and fumble with the door.

'Let's have some light,' he says.

'Bm-bm-bm . . .' Yefim answers.

Pelageya rushes to the stove and begins looking for the broken pot with the matches. A minute passes in silence. The doctor rummages in his pockets and lights his own match.

'I won't be a minute, sir,' says Pelageya, rushes out of the hut and returns soon after with a candle-end.

Yefim's cheeks are pink and his eyes have a strange steely glint, as if he can see right through the hut and the doctor.

'Well now, what have you been up to?' says the doctor, bending over him. 'Ah! Been like this long, have you?'

'Beg pardon, sir? My hour has come, your honour . . . I'm not for this world . . .'

'Nonsense . . . We'll get you better!'

'That's as you please, your honour, and we're much obliged to you, but we know the way it is . . . When death comes, it comes.'

The doctor is busy for about a quarter of an hour bending over

Yefim; then he gets up and says:

'There's no more I can do – you must go to the hospital and they'll operate on you. And you must go straight away, without fail! It's rather late, they'll all be asleep at the hospital, but never mind, I'll give you a note. Right?'

'But how can he get there, sir?' says Pelageya. 'We haven't a horse.'

'Don't worry, I'll ask them at the house to let you have one.'

The doctor leaves, the candle goes out, the 'bm-bm-bm' begins again . . . Half an hour later someone drives up to the hut. They've sent along a cart to take Yefim to the hospital. He gets ready and goes . . .

But now it's morning, fine and bright. Pelageya is not there: she's walked to the hospital to find out what's happening to Yefim. Somewhere a baby's crying, and Varka can hear someone with her voice singing:

'*Bayu-bayushki-bayú*, I'll sing a song for you . . .'

Pelageya comes back; she crosses herself and whispers:

'They put him to rights last night, but early this morning he gave up the ghost . . . May he rest in everlasting peace . . . They got him too late, they said . . . He should have come before . . .'

Varka goes into the wood and cries there, but all of a sudden someone strikes her so violently on the back of the head that she bangs her forehead against a birch trunk. She raises her eyes and sees her master, the bootmaker, standing in front of her.

'What are you up to,' he says, 'you lousy slut? Sleep while the kid's crying, would you?'

And he gives her ear a painful twist. Varka tosses her head, rocks the cradle and croons her song. The green patch and the shadows from the trousers and baby-clothes sway, wink at her, and soon possess her brain once more. Once more she sees the highway, swimming in mud. The people with knapsacks on their backs and the shadows are sprawled out fast asleep. Looking at them, Varka feels so dreadfully sleepy; how lovely it would be to lie down, but Pelageya, her mother, is walking along beside her, urging her on. They are hurrying to the town together to look for work.

'Give us alms, for the dear Lord's sake!' her mother begs the passers-by. 'Be merciful unto us, good people!'

'Give the baby here!' someone's familiar voice answers. 'Give the baby here!' the same voice repeats, now harsh and angry. 'You asleep, you little wretch?'

Varka jumps up, looks round and realises what's going on: there's no highway, no Pelageya, no passers-by, there's no one but the mistress who's standing in the middle of the little room and has come to feed the baby. While the mistress, fat and broad-shouldered, feeds the baby and tries to soothe it, Varka stands looking at her, waiting for her to finish. Already there's a bluish light outside, and the shadows and green patch on the ceiling are growing noticeably paler. Soon it will be morning.

'Here!' says the mistress, buttoning up her night-dress. 'He's crying. He's had a spell put on him.'

Varka takes the baby, puts it in the cradle and begins rocking again. The green patch and the shadows gradually disappear, so now there is no one to steal into her head and befuddle her brain. But she wants to sleep as badly as before, oh so badly! Varka rests her head on the edge of the cradle and rocks it with her whole body to overcome her sleepiness, but her lids still stick together and her head is heavy.

'Varka, make up the stove!' the master's voice resounds from the other room. Time to get up, then, and start the day's work. Varka leaves the cradle and runs to the shed for firewood. She is glad. Running and moving about are easier than sitting down: you don't feel so sleepy. She brings in the wood, makes up the stove, and begins to feel her shrivelled face smoothing out again and her thoughts clearing.

'Varka, put on the samovar!' bawls the mistress.

Varka splits a piece of wood, but has scarcely had time to light the splinters and poke them into the samovar before there comes a fresh order:

'Varka, clean the master's galoshes!'

She sits down on the floor, cleans the galoshes and thinks it would be nice to poke her head into the big deep galosh and have a quick doze . . . All of a sudden the galosh starts to grow, swells, fills the whole room, Varka drops her brush, but immediately gives a toss of the head, opens her eyes wide and forces herself to stare at things hard, so that they don't start growing and moving about.

'Varka, wash down the outside steps! The customers mustn't see them in that state.'

Varka washes the steps, tidies the rooms, then makes up the other stove and runs round to the shop. There's lots to be done, she doesn't have a moment to herself.

But what she finds hardest of all is standing on one spot at the kitchen table, peeling potatoes. Her head keeps falling towards the table, the potatoes dance before her eyes, the knife slips from her hands, while the mistress, fat and bad-tempered, crowds round her with her sleeves rolled up, talking so loudly that it makes Varka's ears ring. Waiting at table, doing the washing, sewing: these, too, are agonising. There are moments when she simply wants to forget everything, flop down on the floor and sleep.

The day goes by. Watching the windows grow dark, Varka rubs her hardening temples and smiles without herself knowing why. The evening gloom caresses her heavy eyes and promises her a deep sleep soon. In the evening there are visitors.

'Varka, samovar!' bawls the mistress.

The samovar is a small one and has to be heated half a dozen times before the visitors have finished drinking. After the tea, Varka stands on the same spot for an hour on end, looking at the visitors and awaiting orders.

'Varka, run and buy three bottles of beer!'

She darts off and tries to run as fast as possible, to drive her sleepiness away.

'Varka, run and fetch some vodka! Varka, where's the corkscrew? Varka, clean some herrings!'

But now at last the visitors have gone; the lights are put out, the master and mistress go to bed.

'Varka, rock the baby!' echoes the final order.

The cricket chirps in the stove; the green patch on the ceiling and the shadows from the trousers and baby-clothes steal once more into Varka's half-open eyes, wink at her and befuddle her brain.

'*Bayu-bayushki-bayú*,' she croons, 'I'll sing a song for you . . .'

And the baby screams and wears itself out screaming. Varka sees once more the muddy highway, the people with knapsacks, Pelageya, her father Yefim. She understands everything, she recognises everyone, but through her half-sleep there is one thing that she simply cannot grasp: the nature of the force that binds her hand and foot, that oppresses her and makes life a misery. She looks all round the room, searching for this force in order to rid herself of it; but cannot find it. Worn out, she makes one last, supreme effort to concentrate her attention, looks up at the winking green patch, and, as she listens to the sound of the crying, finds it, this enemy that is making life a misery.

It is the baby.

She laughs in astonishment: how could she have failed to notice such a simple little thing before! The green patch, the shadows, and the cricket, also seem to be laughing in astonishment.

The delusion takes possession of Varka. She gets up from her stool, and walks up and down the room. There is a broad smile on her face and her eyes are unblinking. The thought that in a moment she will be rid of the baby that binds her hand and foot, tickles her with delight . . . To kill the baby, then sleep, sleep, sleep . . .

Laughing, winking at the green patch and wagging her finger at it, Varka creeps up to the cradle and bends over the baby. Having smothered it, she lies down quickly on the floor, laughs with joy that now she can sleep, and a minute later is sleeping the sleep of the dead . . .

Notes

We give below the original titles in transliteration of all the stories in this volume, with brief notes on points in some of them that may be of help or interest to English readers.

The texts from which the translations were made are those of *A.P. Chekhov: Complete Collection of the Works and Letters in Thirty Volumes* published by the Gorky Institute of World Literature of the USSR Academy of Sciences (Moscow, 1974–82). These are the revised versions prepared by Chekhov for his *Collected Works* published in 1899–1902.

The system of transliteration used throughout is that of *The Oxford Chekhov*, with the following qualification.

In many of the early stories Chekhov uses proper names that sound comic, carry comic allusions, or are in other ways meaningful. Simply to transliterate such names fails to convey to the English reader an element that is present in the original and sometimes extremely important. To convert a comic Russian name into a comic English one is not satisfactory, either, since the intrusion of an English form into a Russian story is bound to jar. Moreover, in English comic surnames are comparatively rare and immediately stand out, whereas in Russian they are common and there is nothing very unusual about being called Toothless (Bezzubov) or Parsnip (Pasternak). In rendering these names, therefore, we have tried to convey something of the meaning and flavour of the original, to make the names sound plausibly Russian, and not to let them stand out more in English than they do in Chekhov's Russian. Often this involved a complicated juggling act. It inevitably meant that in the comic stories we have departed from the strict system of transliteration.

Anglicised spellings have been preferred for 'britchka', 'datcha', 'icon', 'kopeck' and 'Tartar'. With the exception of verst (two-thirds of a mile), units of measurement have been converted into British standards.

RAPTURE *Radost* (1883)

p.9 'clerical officer of the fourteenth grade'. The bottom rung in the

Table of Ranks instituted for the civil service by Peter the Great.

THE DEATH OF A CIVIL SERVANT *Smert chinovnika* (1883)

p11 *'The Chimes of Normandy'*. Comic opera to music by Planquette.

AN INCIDENT AT LAW *Sluchay iz sudebnoy praktiki* (1883)

FAT AND THIN *Tolsty i tonky* (1883)

p.17 'Herostratos'. Ephesian who set fire to the temple of Diana.
'Ephialtes'. Greek traitor at Thermopylae, 480 B.C.
'I've got my St Stanislas'. The order of St Stanislas, a standard award for government service.

THE DAUGHTER OF ALBION *Doch Albiona* (1883)

p.20 'Wilka Charlesovna Tvice'. Our partial repatriation of the strictly transliterated Uilka Charlzovna Tfays. 'Uilka' is perhaps Gryabov's version of Willa, 'Charłzovna' is the patronymic meaning 'daughter of Charles', and 'Tfays' perhaps Gryabov's attempt at pronouncing Twiss or Thwaites; although the general opinion is that Chekhov coined the surname from 'twice'.

p.21 'Bit different from England, eh?!' Now a set expression, applied scathingly to things Russian.

OYSTERS *Ustritsy* (1884)

A DREADFUL NIGHT *Strashnaya Noch* (1884)

Horror stories, spiritualism and the paranormal were much in vogue in the Moscow of the 1880s. The words 'The end of your life is at hand' (p.26) were addressed to Chekhov himself at a seance by the spirit of Turgenev. This was one of the very first of Chekhov's early works to be translated into English (Fugitive coffins: a weird Russian tale by Anton Petrovitch (*sic*) Tschechoff. Translated from the Russian by Grace Eldredge. *Short Stories: a magazine of select stories*. New York, 1902, July, p. 50–53).

MINDS IN FERMENT (FROM THE ANNALS OF A TOWN) *Brozheniye umov (Iz letopisi odnogo goroda)* (1884)

THE COMPLAINTS BOOK *Zhalobnaya kniga* (1884)

THE CHAMELEON *Khameleon* (1884)

THE HUNTSMAN *Yeger* (1885)

THE MALEFACTOR *Zloumyshlennik* (1885)

p.46 'a spockerel'. The Russian fish known to science as the 'asp' (*Aspius aspius*).

A MAN OF IDEAS *Myslitel* (1885)

p.50 'Or take spelling, for example.' What Yashkin objects to in Russian spelling concerns the redundant letter *yat*, which was abolished in the spelling reform of 1918. We have translated this into a roughly comparable feature of English spelling.

SERGEANT PRISHIBEYEV *Unter Prishibeyev* (1885)

We have not rendered this meaningful name, partly because it appears to be impossible (it manages to convey bruising, intimidating, depressing and actually killing all in one word), and partly because the story is already well known in English by this title.

THE MISFORTUNE *Gore* (1885)

ROMANCE WITH DOUBLE-BASS *Roman s kontrabasom* (1886)

THE WITCH *Vedma* (1886)

GRISHA *Grisha* (1886)

KIDS *Detvora* (1886)

REVENGE *Mest* (1886)

p.88 'vint'. Popular Russian card game of the whist family.

EASTER NIGHT *Svyatoyu nochyu* (1886)

Although Chekhov skilfully implies that the canticles quoted by Ieronim are the work of Nikolay the monk, they are in fact accepted Russian Orthodox canticles (*akafisty*) that he would have known well from his religious upbringing.

p.96 '*ikos*'. The part of the canticle following the first collect-hymn. It sets out the acts performed by the subject of the canticle.

THE LITTLE JOKE *Shutochka* (1886)

THE OBJET D'ART *Proizvedeniye iskusstva* (1886)

p.106 'No. 223 of the *Stock Exchange Gazette*'. This No. contained an instalment of Zola's novel *L'Oeuvre*, which concerns a painter who transfers his affections from his wife to his paintings of the female nude.

THE CHORUS-GIRL *Khoristka* (1886)

DREAMS *Mechty* (1886)

THE ORATOR *Orator* (1886)

p.123 '*aut mortuis nihil bene*'. Nonsense version of *De mortuis aut nihil aut bene* ('Of the dead speak well or not at all').

VANKA *Vanka* (1886)

VEROCHKA *Verochka* (1887)

p.136 'as forty thousand others'. Common humorous expression of the time adapted from Hamlet's phrase 'forty thousand brothers' (Act V, Scene 1).

A DRAMA *Drama* (1887)

p.142 '*The Cause*'. Radical literary periodical published in St Petersburg from 1866 to 1888. Medusina's play is a parody of the 'ideologically committed' drama of Chekhov's day.

TYPHUS *Tif* (1887)

NOTES FROM THE JOURNAL OF A QUICK-TEMPERED MAN *Iz zapisok vspylchivogo cheloveka* (1887)

THE REED-PIPE *Svirel* (1887)

THE KISS *Potseluy* (1887)

p.171 'Plevna'. Town in northern Bulgaria (now Pleven) besieged by the Russians in the Russo-Turkish war of 1877–1878.

NO COMMENT *Bez zaglaviya* (1888)

LET ME SLEEP *Spat khochetsya* (1888)

The story has become famous in English under Constance Garnett's title *Sleepy*. This is neither very accurate, however, nor does its whimsical tone do justice to the spirit of the story. Katherine Mansfield's *The Child-Who-Was-Tired*, published in her collection *In a German Pension* (1911), is a creative imitation of Chekhov's story, which she appears to have read first in a German translation.

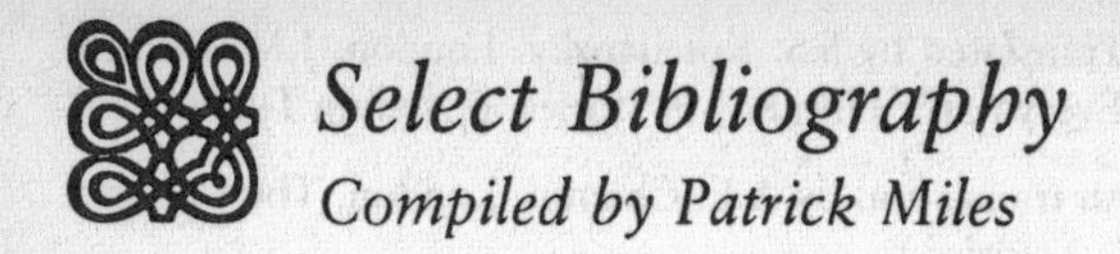

Select Bibliography

Compiled by Patrick Miles

To date at least 264 of Chekhov's early works have been translated into English. The following is a list in chronological order of anthologies containing more than one story. In brackets is given the number of early stories the anthology contains, with the titles of those that also feature in the present volume. Only six anthologies are currently in print.

The Black Monk, and other stories. Translated from the Russian by R.E.C. Long. London, Duckworth & Co., 1903. (7 stories, including *Let Me Sleep*).

The Kiss, and other stories. Translated from the Russian by R.E.C. Long. London, Duckworth & Co., 1908. (10 stories, including *The Kiss, Verochka, The Reed-Pipe, Oysters, The Misfortune*.)

Stories of Russian Life. Translated from the Russian by Marian Fell. London, Duckworth & Co., 1915. (20 stories, including *Easter Night, The Malefactor, Vanka, Dreams, The Death of a Civil Servant, Kids, Fat and Thin, No Comment*.)

Russian Silhouettes; more stories of Russian life. Translated from the Russian by Marian Fell. London, Duckworth & Co., 1915. (19 stories, including *Grisha, Rapture, The Chorus-Girl, The Orator*.)

The Steppe, and other stories. Translated by Adeline Lister Kaye. London, W. Heinemann, 1915. (4 stories, including *Vanka*.)

The Bet and other stories. Translated by S. Koteliansky and J.M. Murry. Dublin, Maunsel & Co., Ltd., 1915. (9 stories.)

The Tales of Tchehov. Translated by Constance Garnett. London, Chatto & Windus, 1916–22. 13 volumes. (147 stories, including all but *An Incident at Law, A Dreadful Night, The Complaints Book, A Man of Ideas, Sergeant Prishibeyev, Romance with Double-Bass, Revenge*.)

Nine Humorous Tales. Translated by Isaac Goldberg and Henry T. Schnittkind. Boston, The Stratford Company, 1918. (9 stories, including *The Objet d'Art, Revenge*.)

The Grasshopper and other stories. Translated with introduction by A.E. Chamot. London, S. Paul & Co., Ltd., 1926. (6 stories, including *A Dreadful Night*.)

Plays and stories. Translated by S.S. Koteliansky. London, J.M. Dent & Sons, Ltd., 1937. (Everyman's Library.) (4 stories, including *Typhus*).

Short stories. English translation by A.E. Chamot. London, The Commodore Press, 1946? (10 stories.)

The Portable Chekhov. Edited, and with an introduction by Avrahm Yarmolinsky. New York, The Viking Press, 1947. (14 stories, including *Vanka, The Chameleon, Sergeant Prishibeyev, The Malefactor, Dreams, The Kiss*.)

The Woman in the Case, and other stories. Translated by April FitzLyon and Kyril Zinovieff and with an introduction by Andrew G. Colin. London, Spearman-Calder, 1953. (21 stories, including *Romance with Double-Bass*.)

Short novels and stories. Translated by Ivy Litvinov. Moscow, Foreign Languages Publishing House, 1954. (6 stories, including *The Death of a Civil Servant, The Chameleon, The Misfortune, Vanka*.)

The Unknown Chekhov; stories and other writings hitherto untranslated. Translated with an introduction by Avrahm Yarmolinsky. New York, Noonday Press, 1954. (14 stories.)

St. Peter's Day, and other tales. Translated with an introduction by Frances H. Jones. New York, Capricorn Books, 1959. (22 stories.)

Selected Stories. Newly Translated by Ann Dunnigan. With a Foreword by Ernest J. Simmons. New York, New American Library, 1960. (A Signet Classic.) (15 stories, including *The Kiss*.)

Early Stories. Translated by Nora Gottlieb. London, Bodley Head, 1960. (14 stories, including *Sergeant Prishibeyev*.)

Selected Stories. Translated with an introduction by Jessie Coulson. London, Oxford University Press, 1963. (3 stories.)

The Image of Chekhov. Forty stories. Translated by Robert Payne. New York, Knopf, 1963. (24 stories, including *Rapture, The Death of a Civil Servant, The Huntsman, The Malefactor, Sergeant Prishibeyev, Vanka, Typhus, Let Me Sleep*.)

Late-blooming flowers and other stories. Translated by I.C. Chertok and Jean Gardner. New York, McGraw-Hill, 1964. (3 stories, including *The Little Joke, Verochka*.)

Lady with Lapdog, and other stories. Translated with an Introduction by David Magarshack. Harmondsworth, Penguin, 1964. (Penguin Classics.) (3 stories, including *The Misfortune*.)

The Thief, and other tales. Translated by Ursula Smith. New York, Vantage Press, 1964. (19 stories.)

Shadows and Light. Translated by Miriam Morton. New York, Doubleday, 1968. (8 stories, including *The Malefactor, Vanka, Oysters*.)

The Sinner from Toledo, and other stories. Translated by Arnold Hinchliffe. Rutherford, Fairleigh Dickinson University Press, 1972. (17 stories, including *The Witch, Romance with Double-bass, The Little Joke, No Comment.*)

The Short Stories of Anton Chekhov. Translated by Helen Muchnic. Avon (Connecticut), Cardavon Press, 1973. (7 stories, including *The Malefactor, Let Me Sleep, Dreams, Vanka*.)

Short Stories. Translated and with an introduction by Elizaveta Fen. London, Folio Society, 1974. (5 stories, including *Romance with Double-Bass, Let Me Sleep*.)

Chuckle with Chekhov. A Selection of Comic Stories. Chosen and translated from the Russian by Harvey Pitcher in collaboration with James Forsyth. Cromer, Swallow House Books, 1975. (19 stories, including *Romance with Double-Bass, An Incident at Law, A Man of Ideas, Revenge, The Objet d'Art, A Dreadful Night, Notes from the Journal of a Quick-Tempered Man, A Drama, No Comment, The Complaints Book.* Harvey Pitcher wishes to thank James Forsyth for his kindness in agreeing to allow these ten translations to be used as working drafts in preparing the present volume.)

The remarkable novel by the internationally acclaimed author of THE WHITE HOTEL.

ARARAT

D M THOMAS

Leaping from 19th century Russia to the Cold War world of today, and from the comic to the nightmarish to the sublime, ARARAT is a brilliant fantasia on the theme of poetic improvisation – and of the soul's tormented quest for pastoral, symbolised by the twin peaks of Ararat, the magic mountain of Armenia . . .

As dazzlingly constructed and intense in imaginative power as its astonishing predecessor THE WHITE HOTEL, ARARAT offers further proof of D. M. Thomas's prodigious talent.

'A deep and serious exploration of the poetic impulse and its relation to the historical world . . . Confirms Thomas's creative fluency and force, indeed his status as one of our best contemporary writers.'
Malcolm Bradbury, *Vogue*

'Fascinating and impressive . . . Boldly creative . . . THE WHITE HOTEL added a new dimension to contemporary British fiction. ARARAT proves that it was no fluke.'
The Sunday Times

'D. M. Thomas has written a brilliant and extraordinary work . . . His protagonists . . . are towering figures into whose lives we are irresistibly drawn.'
The Daily Telegraph

'His most interesting and arresting text to date . . . A tour de force.'
The Guardian

'D. M. Thomas has a powerful gift for invention . . . *Ararat* has a subliminal power that drives its themes into your head.'
The Financial Times

FICTION 0 349 13387 5 £1.95